THE TURTLE MOVES!

THE TURTLE MOVES!

Discworld™'s Story

UNAUTHORIZED

UNAUTHORED BY

Lawrence Watt-Evans

BenBella Books, Inc.

Dallas, Texas

Copyright © 2008 by Lawrence Watt-Evans

Terry Pratchett™, Discworld™, Wee Free Men™, and Nac Mac Feegle™ are trademarks of Terry Pratchett.

All rights reserved. No part of this book may be used or reproduced in any manner whatsoever without written permission except in the case of brief quotations embodied in critical articles or reviews.

BenBella Books, Inc.
6440 N. Central Expressway, Suite 503
Dallas, TX 75206
Send feedback to feedback@benbellabooks.com
www.benbellabooks.com

Printed in the United States of America
10 9 8 7 6 5 4 3 2 1

Library of Congress Cataloging-in-Publication Data

Watt-Evans, Lawrence, 1954–
The turtle moves! : Discworld's story (unauthorized) / unauthored by Lawrence Watt-Evans.
p. cm.
Includes bibliographical references.
ISBN 1-933771-46-1
1. Pratchett, Terry—Criticism and interpretation. 2. Pratchett, Terry. Discworld series. 3. Discworld (Imaginary place) I. Title.

PR6066.R34Z97 2008
823'.914—dc22

2008009671

Proofreading by Emily Chauviere and Adrienne Lang
Cover design by Laura Watkins
Cover illustration by J. P. Targete
Design and composition by John Reinhardt Book Design
Printed by Bang Printing

Distributed by Independent Publishers Group
To order call (800) 888-4741
www.ipgbook.com

For special sales, contact Robyn White at Robyn@benbellabooks.com

For Terry Pratchett.
Of course.

Contents

PART ONE
Introductions

PART TWO
Comments

PART THREE
The Stories

PART FOUR
More Comments

PART FIVE
The Series

PART SIX
Yet More Comments

PART SEVEN
References

PART ONE
Introductions

INTRODUCTION

Why I'm Writing This

IT'S TOTALLY RIDICULOUS, you know. Discworld, I mean. The whole thing.

The idea of a flat world carried through space by four elephants standing on the back of a gigantic turtle is absurd to begin with, but sure, I suppose you could get away with using it in one novel. Maybe two. Three if you stretched. But dozens of best-selling novels and an assortment of spin-offs?

It's ridiculous, I tell you!

I mean, really, how does Terry Pratchett™[1] sell millions of books with such a silly premise? Most of us fantasy writers struggle to get by with our carefully thought-out worlds of quests and heroes and Dark Lords and so on, getting maybe a couple of trilogies out of a world, and he throws together this completely absurd hodge-podge and merrily turns out *scores* of books! Good ones, too.

Just because the Discworld books are wonderfully written and hysterically funny and humane and insightful and all that, that doesn't mean he should be able to do this! I mean, *I* haven't managed to do it—how did he?

Well, that's the question, innit?

I decided that the only thing to do, when confronted with such an obvious absurdity, was to go through the entire series carefully, and figure out just exactly what he's doing.

You may be asking, if I think the whole thing is ridiculous, why I would want to waste my time on such a project. Well, you did see that bit above about him selling millions of books, right? If he can do it, and I can figure out how he did it, then maybe *I* can do it, too!

[1] Yes, his name is now a trademark. So's Discworld, and a few other names that will come up in this book. Not a joke.

Oh, I know, you probably think I could try finding a completely original way of writing my own series of brilliant, insightful, and funny fantasy novels, the way Mr. Pratchett did, instead of copying someone else, right? After all, who'd want a cheap imitation when the real thing's available? But it's not like that's *easy*; I wouldn't have the first idea where to begin.

Ideally, I'd like to find some nice, simple secret, some single ingredient that I could swipe, without everyone realizing I'd stolen it—but what would it be? A bizarre setting, perhaps? Would that be enough?

I could invent a square world instead of a disc. Or an elephant carrying four turtles—but that's hardly got the same sort of appeal; the poor turtles would be forever slipping off, which would make for a very bumpy sort of world.

Or I could go some other route entirely, perhaps with, oh, a hexagonal world carried through space by six gigantic pterodactyls....

But I know that would be dismissed as derivative. Never mind that Pratchett hasn't got a single cosmic pterodactyl anywhere in sight, you can just bet that some troublemaker would say I used pterodactyls as a play on "Terry Dactyls," or some such, and come up with some incredibly strained way to make "Dactyl" a pun on "Pratchett."[2]

No, a bizarre setting obviously isn't enough. All that would do is get me labeled a copycat. Critics love to say fantasy is derivative.

Oh, I suppose it's not quite as bad as the old days, back when you couldn't write fantasy, funny or otherwise, without being accused of imitating J.R.R. Tolkien or Robert E. Howard. Back then, if your hero had a sword and knew how to use it, you were obviously imitating Conan of Cimmeria, and if he didn't, you were clearly aping Tolkien's hobbits.[3,4]

---

[2] If you can make such a pun work, please don't tell me. I don't want to know.

[3] I know this firsthand. People who read my first novel said I was imitating Howard. People who didn't read it said I was imitating Tolkien.

[4] For those of you not already aware of it, and wondering what's with the footnotes, allow me to explain. The Discworld novels are notorious for having plenty of footnotes, and even footnotes to footnotes. Footnotes are not particularly common in novels of any sort, including humorous fantasy, so this is a quirk, an oddity, a trademark—perhaps even a gimmick.

It's also where Mr. Pratchett puts some of his best jokes. If I'm going to claim to be his peer, then doesn't it behoove me to use lots of footnotes as well? I won't be the first to do this, by any means; for example, John Moore included humorous footnotes referring to Mr. Pratchett's known predilection for them in his novel *Bad Prince Charlie*.

Rest assured, I won't go as overboard as Jasper Fforde does with the footnoterphone in his Thursday Next novels, but I will put good stuff in some of these footnotes. Don't ignore them.

Oh, and if I cite a book here you've never heard of—for example, if you never heard of John Moore or Jasper Fforde—I probably won't footnote it, but you might find it useful to check the bibliography at the back of the book, where I've listed most of the books I mention. I won't always list *all* of the books in a series, or by a particular author, but there should be enough to get you started.

Nowadays, as long as you stay away from schoolboy wizards and don't go trying to be funny, you can write fantasy without being accused of imitating anyone.

And lots of people do just that. The shelves are full of fantasy novels about quests and heroes and magic. And then here's Mr. Pratchett, writing fantasy novels about *people*.

That's what he does, you know. He writes about people. Not great and noble heroes, who can be uncomfortable to have around for too long, nor about grand adventures, which get tiresome, but about people who act like human beings.[5] That's part of what's kept him going so long—people don't get tired of reading about people as quickly as they get tired of reading about stereotypes.

But that can't be enough. Other writers do that. Shucks, *I* try to do that. There's got to be more.

So I sat down to figure out what it was.

And if I was going to do all that research anyway, hey, why not write it up as a book and make a little money off it?

So that's what I'm doing.

Of course, having decided that, I had to decide what *kind* of book I was going to write. I didn't want to get all scholarly—that would take too much effort, given that I'm not actually a scholar, and besides, publishers like those best when they're written by professors, and I'm not one.[6] Besides, while they're a high-status sort of thing to do, scholarly books generally don't make very much money.

You know what makes money? Scandal. Exposés. So I thought about writing a vicious exposé about poor Mr. Pratchett, pointing out everything that's wrong with the Discworld novels[7]—how they're horrible sinful evil books that corrupt the youth of the world—and explaining what a rotten person he is, but alas, I can't do that, because in fact there *isn't* anything very wrong with them, other than the fact that *I* didn't write them, I've seen no evidence that they've ever corrupted anyone, and Mr. Pratchett is, by all accounts, a very nice man, though he did

---

[5] Often, even when they technically *aren't* human beings.

[6] My father was, though—a professor of organic chemistry. Which is one reason I'm not one. It didn't look like a job I'd enjoy. He loved it, though; no accounting for tastes.

[7] I know he's written lots of stuff besides Discworld, but I'm not going to say anything about any of it in this book. I'm going to stick with Discworld because that's quite enough to tackle without worrying about Johnny Maxwell or the Bromeliad or the rest.

look a bit annoyed at me once when I interrupted his conversation to get him to sign a book.[8]

I could lie, of course. I could just make up all sorts of terrible things—after all, I'm a professional fiction writer, I tell lies for a living—but then I might run afoul of all those nasty laws about libel. Lawyers can be so very awkward about these things. And I have an aversion to lawyers, in any case. It's probably an allergy or something.

So a sensational tell-all book was out; I had to resign myself to not writing a bestseller.

The next possibility was to write an obsessive trivia book, giving away all the endings and explaining all the jokes and generally trying to ruin everyone's fun.

Unfortunately, even *that* won't really work, because other people have already gone to great lengths to explain most of the jokes and references,[9] and to cite the sources of various things, and it just wouldn't be *fair* of me to duplicate their work. Or to steal it.[10] Instead I'll point you at the magnificent resource various obsessive Pratchett fans have assembled online at www.Lspace.org, in particular the part labeled "Annotations," and you can go read up on all the references and jokes yourself and save me the trouble and embarrassment of stealing them, getting accused of plagiarism, and having my life ruined. (I told you I have an aversion to lawyers, right?)

---

[8] That was at the World Science Fiction Convention in Chicago in September 2000. I don't really blame him, since I *did* interrupt his chat, but I do have an excuse for my rudeness—I hadn't been able to stand in line for his signature because I was signing books at the same time. I'd assumed we'd be seated side-by-side at the same table, so I could squeeze it in then, but *no*, oh no, *that* would have been too convenient, and his line of fans wouldn't fit in the regular autographing area anyway, so they put him in the other room where there was more space, and I dashed over there after I'd finished my own signing, but he'd just left, which is why I resorted to interrupting his conversation when I stumbled across him somewhere else later that day.

I'd like to say he growled and refused and generally acted as if I was rudely intruding, since after all I was, because then I'd have some dirt to report, but *no*, he just looked mildly annoyed and signed the book. Or books, it might have been two of them, though I only seem to have one of them on hand, *Witches Abroad*, and I can't actually make out one word of the inscription.

So I don't have any good anecdotes to report about Terry Pratchett yelling at me or refusing me an autograph or playing the prima donna or otherwise providing me with some juicy counter to all the stories about his generosity and kindness; no, I have to settle for, "Well, he was a trifle irritated with me once. Maybe even irked. And I can't always read his handwriting." Which, let's face it, really doesn't cut it as vicious gossip, does it? So all I have in the way of gossip and disparagement is this oversized footnote.

Drat.

[9] Though, as of this writing, they're still a couple of books behind. They're much more thorough on the earlier books in the series than the more recent ones, too. And none of them are complete, in any case; they don't bother to explain either the really obvious or the impossibly obscure.

[10] And let's face it, it would be dumb to waste a lot of time and effort duplicating it, because who'd believe I *didn't* just steal it all? *I* wouldn't believe it, so why should you?

Really, if you're interested in references and sources, or puzzled by some little detail where you think you're missing a joke, check the website's annotations out. They're pretty amazing. Not 100 percent complete, by any means, but very impressive all the same. That's Lspace.org. If you're a Discworld fan but you don't have your own computer and Internet access, it's definitely worth a trip to the library or borrowing someone else's machine for a while.

It occurred to me that maybe I could take all that trivia, and use it to write quizzes instead of just listing it all, but *that's* been done, too, by the esteemed and admirable David Langford, under such titles as *The Unseen University Challenge*[11] and *The Wyrdest Link*.[12]

So with dense scholarly analysis, juicy scandal, detailed annotations, quiz books, and outright lies eliminated, what does that leave me?

A popular guide! I decided to go ahead and write a sort of reader's guide to the whole thing, and see if I couldn't find *some* way to keep you readers entertained by telling you things you could probably figure out for yourself if you read all of the Discworld books cover to cover, tracked down all the obscure stories, and so on, obsessively taking notes and looking stuff up.

It's not likely to sell as well as an exposé, but what can you do?[13]

And really, getting serious for a moment,[14] I won't generally spoil the jokes or give away the endings unless it's absolutely necessary for some point I'm making.[15] That wouldn't be fair to you, after you were kind enough to buy my book.[16]

Of course, in order to fill up the pages, I'll have to present my own theories about What Mr. Pratchett Is Really Up To, and how the series develops as it goes along, and all that, and I might even get some of it right and say something entertaining along the way, but it's all just to

---

[11] Gollancz, 1996.

[12] Gollancz, 2002.

[13] Well, you could read all the Discworld books cover to cover, and track down all the obscure stories, obsessively taking notes and looking stuff up. But I've done that *for* you, you see. That's why you're paying for this book, so you don't have to go have all that fun yourself.

[14] Which I'll do fairly often later on; it's mostly just these introductions and most of the footnotes that are deliberately silly.

[15] Or I just forget. Unlike *some* people, I'm merely human.

[16] And thank you for buying it. Sincerely.
On the other hand, if you're reading this in the bookstore or library and haven't bought a copy yet, get out your wallet and cough up the bucks, already.

get the word-count up to a reasonable level, it's not as if I actually know what I'm talking about. I just felt I had to do *something* in response to Discworld's success.[17]

But then there's the question of why you would want to read such a thing, because I can't expect you to buy my book if you don't have any reason to read it, and if you don't buy it, I don't make any money off it, and that would rather defeat the whole purpose.

This is really two questions, though, because there are two kinds of people out there who might be reading this: Discworld readers, and everyone else. So let me address the two groups independently.

[17] And, success aside, in response to the fact that I love the series.

INTRODUCTION 2

Why You Should Read This Book If You Haven't Already Read a Bunch of Discworld Stuff, and Maybe Even If You've Never Heard of Discworld

WELL, FIRST OFF, if you've never heard of Discworld at all, odds are you aren't British.[18] This is not a problem; I'm not British, either. Americans, Australians, Canadians, and even Frenchmen[19] can appreciate Mr. Pratchett's work.[20]

In Britain, though, the series is a huge success—not at the level of Harry Potter, but it's a major hit, with every new book making the best-seller lists. Besides the novels, there are Discworld calendars, diaries, maps, CDs, animated TV series, live-action TV, plays, radio adaptations, art books, reference books, cookbooks[21]—there are even fake postage

[18] If you *are* British, which I admit is possible, you probably just haven't been paying attention.

[19] Yes, fine, it's a cheap joke. I have no shame. In fact, Discworld novels have been translated into scads of languages and been successful in most of them.

[20] I should probably mention once again at this juncture that he's written a lot of stuff besides Discworld. This book won't cover any of it. If you're looking for something about Johnny Maxwell or *Strata* or whatever, you're in the wrong book; I'm only doing Discworld. Sorry.

[21] Okay, *one* cookbook. And yes, I know it's not all recipes.

stamps based on it, and people who collect these stamps. It's a phenomenon, it is.

So here's a chance to see what all the fuss is about. You can read my book and have a pretty good idea what's going on much more quickly than if you took the time to read all those dozens of books Mr. Pratchett wrote! You can also get some idea of where you might want to start reading, because one of the most annoying features of the series is that the best place to start, as even Mr. Pratchett himself will tell you, really isn't at the beginning—it took a couple of books before the author really got a handle on the material.

And he still hasn't fallen into a rut. The series keeps mutating and evolving.[22] If you *did* try to read a Discworld novel and didn't care for it, well, maybe looking through my commentary will give you an idea of one that might be more to your liking.

Or, hey, maybe it'll convince you to give up entirely, for all I know.

At the very least, it may clear up some misconceptions. In fact, let me tackle a couple right now:

No, it's not all parodies of fantasy novels by other authors. You don't need to have read any fantasy to appreciate Discworld. Lots of Discworld fans don't read any other fantasy; in fact, Mr. Pratchett says *he* doesn't read other people's fantasy anymore.[23] He's more likely to include references to fairy tales, movies, and real-world events than to fantasy novels.

No, it's not just a bunch of silly jokes and cheap farce—not after the first couple of books, anyway. There's a lot more than humor here, and what humor there is, is mostly character-based, not cheap puns and pratfalls, nor mere absurdity. Don't let the giant turtle mislead you.

No, it's not impenetrably British. Yes, Terry Pratchett is English, and that does show sometimes, but it's not the basis of most of the humor, or essential for understanding what's going on. This isn't Monty Python or Benny Hill.[24]

So what *is* it? Well, that's why you need to read this book....

---

[22] My choice of terminology here is considered, and will seem more significant once you've read farther.

[23] This was in response to a question at a bookstore event in Rockville, Maryland, in October 2006. Someone who admitted to not having read any of Mr. Pratchett's work but said he was sufficiently impressed by the evening's presentation that he intended to start, asked what other fantasy authors Mr. Pratchett recommended.

Being a fantasy writer myself, standing unobserved at the back of the crowd, I had this momentary wild hope that he would say, "Well, there's Lawrence Watt-Evans, of course...."

Didn't happen, alas. Instead, after some hesitation, Mr. Pratchett admitted that he no longer reads fantasy, though he then said that you can't go wrong with the classics: J.R.R. Tolkien, Ursula K. Le Guin, and Fritz Leiber, Jr.

[24] Thank heavens for that!

INTRODUCTION 3

Why Discworld Fans Should Read This Book

DO I REALLY NEED to explain this? Really?

I do?

Okay, fine.

Well, first, there's the possibility that I'll provide some insight into the stories that you hadn't thought of, explain some gag you didn't get, illuminate a detail you hadn't noticed. Even if you're a complete obsessive, I might get lucky and stumble on something you missed. It could happen. Even a blind pig finds a truffle sometimes.[25]

Then there's the convenience of having all the stories described here in chronological order, so you can check half-remembered things without having to go through three dozen volumes that, if you're like me, are scattered around wherever you last put them down. If you want to remind yourself whether Sam Vimes first met Lady Sybil in *Guards! Guards!* or *Men at Arms*,[26] you can just look at the appropriate chapters here instead of flipping through the two novels—it's almost a sort of condensed *Reader's Digest* version you can use as reference. *The Discworld Companion* (assuming you have a copy; there's no U.S. edition, and not everyone's willing to spring for international postage)[27]

[25] That's such a nice old saying. We'll just ignore the fact that pigs hunt truffles by smell, won't we? Sure we will. You're *all* kind, understanding, generous people. You wouldn't have bought this book if you weren't! You did buy it, right? If not, give this copy back and go get your own immediately.

[26] Okay, maybe not a realistic example, since obviously it was *Guards! Guards!*, but you get the idea.

[27] A word to the wise American: It's cheaper to ship from Canada than from the U.K., and most British books are available in Canada. I wish I'd picked up on that a little sooner.

can tell you who Lady Sybil *is*,[28] but it doesn't mention which book she first appeared in.

And if there's a book or story you missed, you can read my comments on it here and decide just how important finding it really is to you.[29]

You can feel superior if I missed something you spotted, something that I'd obviously have mentioned if I thought of it. Feeling superior to a published author is always good fun, and I've probably provided dozens of opportunities. It's harmless, too—I'll never know. And if I did, I wouldn't mind.

Well—not much, anyway. I mean, if I didn't mind at *all*, that would take some of the fun out of it for you, and I wouldn't be entirely human. Last I checked, I was human, or at least so my wife assures me. I already mentioned that once in a footnote.

What's more, you can wallow in nostalgia as you read through all this stuff—"I remember *that*," you'll say, as you're reminded of some particularly lovely bit of story from a Discworld novel you haven't looked at in years. "Wasn't that a great scene? I wish we'd see more of that character. Did he ever explain that?" It's almost as much fun, and probably more socially acceptable, than gloating at how much more you know about this stuff than I do.

But that's all just minor stuff. You know the *real* reason you want this book.

It's because Terry Pratchett only writes one or two books a year, and that's not enough for a real addict. You need a Discworld fix. This isn't the real thing, of course, it's just a sort of low-grade methadone equivalent, but it's better than *nothing*, and there are all these empty months to fill. You've got a habit to feed, and a book like this can take the edge off until *Unseen Academicals* (or whatever's next by the time you read this) hits the stores.

Well, I'm happy to do what I can to ease the hunger.

I mean, really, all that nonsense in the first introduction aside, why do you think I *wrote* this book? I'm hooked, too.

So, now that that's clear, let's get started. For new readers, this will be easing you in; for established fans, it'll be a review. We'll start at the beginning, with the basics, by telling you something about the Discworld series itself—not the world, but the books.

---

[28] If you're bright enough to look under her married name. If you aren't (and don't remember her maiden name to find the cross-reference), and just try looking under "Lady" or "Sybil," you're screwed.

[29] I would not put much effort into finding "Theatre of Cruelty," if I were you. For one thing, it's on L-space at www.Lspace.org.

PART TWO
Comments

1

The Nature of the Series

THE DISCWORLD SERIES IS, as of this writing, a collection of thirty-one novels aimed at a general audience, four "young adult" novels, one illustrated story, five short stories, three stories interspersed with science essays, and assorted oddities and spin-offs,[30] all written in whole or in part by Terry Pratchett over the past twenty-five plus years. Annoyingly, most of the oddities and spin-offs do not have American editions; fortunately, all the novels and four of the short stories do, though not all from the same publisher.

The series began in 1983 with the novel *The Colour of Magic* (sometimes rendered in American editions as *The Color of Magic*), and is still going. As of this writing, late in 2007, the most recent book is *Making Money* (see Chapter 46). Before that, the last actual adult novel was *Thud!*, but that was followed by a children's picture book entitled *Where's My Cow?* (see Chapter 44), and a "young adult" novel entitled *Wintersmith* (see Chapter 45). Another "young adult" book, *I Shall Wear Midnight*, has been announced as forthcoming.

Now, you may well ask, "What sort of a series could possibly justify this motley assortment of books and stories?"

Go on, ask; I'll wait.

Okay, I can't tell whether you asked or not, but I'll give you the benefit of the doubt and assume that you did, so I'll try to answer. It's a very *varied* series. Calling it a series at all is perhaps misleading. It apparently wasn't originally intended to be a series as such; the second volume, *The*

[30] Maps, diaries, calendars, a cookbook, and so on. More about these much later.

Light Fantastic, ends quite satisfactorily, with everything resolved. In many ways, it isn't what people think of when you say "series." There's no one hero having adventures, no ongoing protagonist, not even a continuing ensemble in every book. There's not a single character who appears in every story (though two do come fairly close). This is not a case where each book picks up where the previous one left off. There's no nemesis, no great foe to be defeated. There's no continuing plot, no planned end. The only obvious unifying feature is that all the stories take place on Discworld,[31] a gigantic rotating disc carried on the backs of four elephants, who are in turn standing on the back of a cosmic turtle named Great A'tuin as she (or perhaps he) swims through space.

Here's the current list of all the Discworld stories—I'm not listing spin-offs, supplements, or references, only actual stories—to date, in order of publication, which is usually, but not always, the internal chronology as well. Novels are in italics, short stories are in quotes, and other items are annotated.

The Colour of Magic
The Light Fantastic
Equal Rites
Mort
Sourcery
Wyrd Sisters
Pyramids
Guards! Guards!
Eric (originally an illustrated novel with art by Josh Kirby, somewhat shorter than the novel norm; now available in text-only form)
Moving Pictures
Reaper Man
Witches Abroad
Small Gods
"Troll Bridge"
Lords and Ladies
Men at Arms
"Theatre of Cruelty"
Soul Music
Interesting Times
Maskerade

---

[31] My spelling checker keeps trying to tell me I mean "discord," not "Discworld." That seems appropriate, somehow.

Feet of Clay
Hogfather
Jingo
The Last Continent
"The Sea and Little Fishes"
Carpe Jugulum
The Science of Discworld (a long story interwoven with related essays on real-world science—not really what the title implies. The story is by Terry Pratchett, while the science is by Ian Stewart and Jack Cohen.)
The Fifth Elephant
The Truth
Thief of Time
The Last Hero (lavishly illustrated by Paul Kidby, probably not actually a novel by word-count; the illustrations include many informative diagrams, as well as characters and scenes.)
The Amazing Maurice and His Educated Rodents
The Science of Discworld II: The Globe (again, a long story by Pratchett interwoven with science essays by Stewart and Cohen)
Night Watch
"Death and What Comes Next"
The Wee Free Men
Monstrous Regiment
A Hat Full of Sky
Going Postal
"A Collegiate Casting-Out of Devilish Devices"
The Science of Discworld III: Darwin's Watch (once more, story interspersed with science, co-written by Pratchett, Stewart, and Cohen)
Thud!
Where's My Cow? (A spin-off from *Thud!*, this is a children's book illustrated by Melvyn Grant, based on [but not identical to] the one that Sam Vimes reads to his son. It's not much of a story, but it has a certain charm.)
Wintersmith
Making Money

Those are all the stories to date. I am not going to attempt to catalog all the spin-offs, but a good browse at Amazon.co.uk will help you find most of them. If you want to find the short stories all in one place, the first four were collected in a volume called *Once More* with Footnotes*, along

* Figuring out how to present that title was something of a challenge. The "with footnotes" part is supposed to be, well, a footnote, but when I tried treating it as one, it just looked stupid. So I went for this explanation instead.

with assorted other interesting writings by Mr. Pratchett, most of them not directly related to the Discworld. That book was available from NESFA Press; I'm told it's now sold out, but you may be able to find a used copy, if you're lucky. Two of the stories, "Theatre of Cruelty" and "Death and What Comes Next," are also available for free on Lspace.org.

There are some less-obvious unifying features as well, but I'll get to those later.

This is why the series is called "Discworld," rather than being referred to by the name of a character or some magical gadget or prophecy or whatever. Really kind of self-explanatory, when you think about it. Disc, world. . . .

So what is the series *about*?

Well, it's not about the elephants or the turtle. This has been the cause of some confusion among would-be readers. In all the stories to date, the elephants and turtle have never yet had a line of dialogue, or intervened in human affairs. In several stories, they're never mentioned at all, even in passing.

Nor is it about the actual physics of a disc-shaped planet. Oh, much of the absurd mechanics has been worked out, and every so often some amusing geophysical detail will pop up,[32] but it's not what the series is *about*.

It's about people, and it's about stories. I don't just mean it's *composed* of stories, like every other series; I mean it's *about* stories. And it's about people in general, not just the specific individuals having adventures.

You'll notice I'm being vague and unhelpful. I'm sorry about that. It's because this is not an easy series to describe. I mean, you can point to *The Lord of the Rings* and say, "It's about some hobbits, men, and elves who are trying to defeat a Dark Lord." Which doesn't convey the feel of the series, but it's reasonably accurate. You can point to Anne McCaffrey's *Dragonriders of Pern* and say that it's about people who ride telepathic flying dragons on a planet called Pern. You can point to Batman and say it's about a guy who dresses up like a giant bat to fight crime.

But Discworld is about people. And stories.

Some people will say that it's a series of humorous fantasies. That's basically true, but it's misleading, because often, especially in the later

[32] Often in a footnote.

volumes, the humor is secondary, and in a few cases the fantasy elements are so understated they almost don't need to be there at all.

Some people will tell you it's all a parody of more traditional fantasy stories. That's just wrong. It *started out* as a parody of fantasy stories, but it's been a long time since that was an accurate description.

Some people will tell you it's satirical, using a fantasy setting to exaggerate and mock the foibles of our own world. That's usually true, and closer to the point, but still not really a satisfactory summary.

Part of the difficulty in describing it is because it's changed; it's evolved as it's grown, and the latest entries really don't bear a very strong resemblance to the earliest. Another part is that it isn't really one series, it's several; they overlap and interlock. They're all set on the Disc, but they're distinct series, all the same.

Yes, it's time to admit that when people (including me) talk about "the Discworld series," as if there were only one, that's misleading.

Besides the multiple series contained within the overall framework, it wasn't originally meant to be a series at all, and still isn't a normal one.

For one thing, it got better as it went along. In many other fantasy series, the stories start off well, but then decline in quality as the author runs out of ideas and starts rehashing the same old material, or resorts to retrofitting things that shouldn't be there. That hasn't happened with Discworld.[33]

Generally speaking, with most series, it is best, in the words of Lewis Carroll, to begin at the beginning, and go till you come to the end, then stop. The Discworld series, however, is an exception to this rule. Many readers agree that the first two volumes are unrepresentative of the series as a whole, and are *not* the best place to start.[34] Some readers only follow certain series within the greater whole. It's entirely possible to love some of the Discworld series, and hate others.

So when I say that it's really multiple series, I mean just that. It's several separate series that happen to be set against a common background and written by the same author, and where characters from one may turn up in another, but they *really aren't the same*, any more than all the CSI TV shows are the same series.

There is room for debate as to just how many series there are within the whole of the Discworld corpus. I make it eight. That the number

---

[33] Yet.

[34] Most people start with them anyway, though. I'll discuss where one *should* start in Part Six.

eight has great mystic significance in the Discworld has *nothing at all* to do with this. Nothing. Really. I wouldn't jigger things around just to make it come out to eight, would I?

Well, actually, I might have, but I didn't have to, because it came out to eight anyway when I first made up my list. It's even possible that Mr. Pratchett did this on purpose, but I very much doubt it.

I could be off. I've seen other people come up with as few as three series, but I think that's silly. Six or seven, one could make a case. Some people argue that several novels are singletons, not part of any sub-series, and one might make a case for that, too. Certainly I had difficulty deciding where to slot in a couple of the books.

And then there's the fact that every so often Mr. Pratchett will add a *new* series. Moist von Lipwig[35] appears to have only very recently become a series, or at least to have taken over an existing one.

I'll have something to say about each series, but some stories may be discussed in more than one place. It gets complicated because the series-within-series don't always stay in their neat little boxes; characters and settings and plot devices from one will turn up in another, sometimes far in the background, sometimes right up front. There are stories that seem to be in two series simultaneously, or mostly in one with pieces from another. It's messy. It's rather like the real world in that regard, where stories may be partly about Hollywood and partly about Washington and partly about Wall Street.

At any rate, here are the eight series I see:

1. Rincewind and the Wizards of Unseen University
2. The Witches of Lancre
3. The Watch
4. Death in the Family
5. Ankh-Morpork and Moist von Lipwig: Beyond the Century of the Fruitbat
6. Gods and Philosophers
7. The Education of Tiffany Aching
8. The Amazing Maurice

[35] This is a character's name. Yes, it's ridiculous. I told you right on the first page of this book that Discworld was ridiculous. See Chapter 42, *Going Postal*, and Chapter 47, *Making Money*, for more details about Moist von Lipwig.

Each one[36] will have its own chapter toward the back of this book, starting with Chapter 52. As I said, many people would argue with how I've divided these up, but they can darn well write their own books.

The alert and informed reader will notice that there's only one story about the Amazing Maurice—*The Amazing Maurice and His Educated Rodents*, a "young adult" novel which doesn't seem to fit anywhere else. It gets to be the eighth series all by itself. If you really insist on disagreeing with some of my other classifications, then you can call this series "one-offs," or "singletons," or something along those lines, and move other titles into it. If you *insist* on being difficult.

Since there's only one story in the Amazing Maurice series, which gets discussed in Chapter 34, there's no chapter about that series as a whole.

How important it is to read each series in order varies. It's a good idea to read The Watch, The Witches, and Tiffany Aching in order, but most of the others work fine regardless of which you read when.

It's very difficult to read the Amazing Maurice series out of order; I'd be interested in hearing from anyone who's managed it.

What's in all these stories I've neatly divided up for you? I'm glad you asked! Because I was going to tell you anyway, and this way you can't complain about it. We'll start out with an overview of Discworld itself, and then proceed to a chronological, story-by-story account of the whole thing.

And along the way I'll propound my Theory.

When I started writing this book, I didn't actually have a theory; I was planning to just sort of chat about the series and hope I could fill up enough pages. As I researched and re-read, though, I contracted a thesis, and it hasn't cleared up yet, so I intend to explain it here and see whether it's catching.

I said above that the only *obvious* unifying factor of the series as a whole was that all the stories are set on the Disc. There are other unifying factors as well—the use of puns and references to our own reality as sources of humor, the consistent humanity and morality of the series, the Englishness of it, and so on.

After reading through a couple of dozen Discworld novels in quick succession, I came to the conclusion that another unifying factor is that the entire series is about stories. I don't mean it *is* stories; obviously, every fiction series is made up of stories. No, the Discworld stories are all

[36] Well...seven of them will.

about stories, as well as *being* stories themselves. Sometimes it's obvious, as in *Witches Abroad*, and sometimes it's subtle, but it's always there.

In fact, *The Science of Discworld* trilogy even explains *why* the whole series is about stories—because stories are what people *do*, the way we understand the world. Stories make us human.

Another recurring element—and I use the term "element" deliberately, because Mr. Pratchett presents these as actual elements essential to the existence of Discworld—is belief. According to *The Science of Discworld*, two of the elements[37] Discworld has that our world explicitly lacks are narrativium, the stuff of stories, and deitium, the stuff of the gods, and the gods draw their sustenance from belief. Long before Mr. Pratchett gave narrativium a name, he had explained repeatedly that reality is very thin in Discworld, and that it's story, belief, and magic that make up that lack and allow the whole thing to exist. Discworld runs on stories and belief, and that's really what the whole series is about.

That, and evolution.

Mr. Pratchett is a great believer in evolution. Not only is that the major subject matter of the three *Science* volumes, but it's been a recurring feature of the series all along. I think that, too, will become plain as I discuss the stories.

On, then, to the good stuff.

---

[37] There's also chelonium, the stuff that star turtles like Great A'tuin are made of, and assorted others, but they're less important.

2

The Disc Itself

OUR FIRST LOOK AT DISCWORLD came in 1983, with the publication of *The Colour of Magic*. That book opened with a prologue describing the Disc, introducing us to the cosmic tortoise Great A'tuin, and the four giant elephants who stand upon A'tuin's back: Berilia, Tubul, Great T'phon, and Jerakeen.

We'll get back to them in a moment, but first a word about prologues to fantasy novels.

I've been writing fantasy for about thirty years now, and reading it for much longer. I've taught workshops for would-be fantasy writers, and judged contests. I've seen a *lot* of fantasy, good and bad, and I long ago came to a conclusion: Fantasy prologues are pretty much always a bad idea.

Fantasy novels often have them *anyway*, of course, introducing the reader to some of the characters and establishing a lot of the background details that are too boring to waste actual story time on. I've certainly written a few of them myself. When you've just *got* to explain the prophecy your hero is going to fulfill though none of the characters are going to mention it for thirty or forty chapters, or you *really* want the reader to know where the magic sword is hidden so he can appreciate the suspense as our heroes finally get close to it, you just explain it all in a prologue. It seems so simple. Classier than footnotes,[38] and preferable to stopping the action later to say, "By the way, there's this ancient story our heroes haven't heard yet..."

[38] Not that there's anything *wrong* with footnotes!

But generally, they're clunky. A good prologue is a rare thing. Mostly, not to put too fine a point on it, they suck.

And the prologue to the *Colour of Magic* . . . well, it's troublesome. One might almost suspect it of being a deliberate parody of a prologue. One *might*, if one were suspicious that way. One might suppose that Mr. Pratchett had himself noticed that fantasy-novel prologues tend to be less a good storytelling device and more a way of showing off all the spiffy world-building the author has done. Yes, one might.

Or one might remember that Mr. Pratchett was a young and inexperienced writer at the time, who might not have realized yet that prologues are usually a bad idea.

But let us move on to look at what the Prologue tells us. It introduces us to five characters by name, but they aren't the heroes of the story, nor the villains. They aren't even human. They have no dialogue, and do not participate directly in the story. They are, as you might say, in an unusually literal sense, the supporting cast.

They have cool names, though. Good fantasy names. Berilia, Tubul, Jerakeen—lovely fantasy-world names.

Great T'phon, though—is there a *Lesser* T'phon somewhere? If not, how come he gets a "Great" while the other three do not? Great A'tuin, sure, the turtle's the base on which everything stands, so putting a "Great" in there seems perfectly reasonable, but why does T'phon get one, while Jerakeen, Tubul, and Berilia do not?

Either T'phon's got a better PR guy, or there really *is* a Lesser T'phon somewhere. Or there was once—many, many volumes later we are told that there had once been a fifth elephant. Maybe that was Lesser T'phon. Maybe he was the runt of the litter, which is how he lost his footing and fell off.

Or not. Maybe "Great T'phon" just sounded cool.

But that's another thing—who named these guys? How does anyone *know* their names?

I suppose it's magic. Or the gods told someone.

At any rate, we are introduced to the Discworld in a surprisingly literal fashion, not by meeting our protagonists or our villains, but by meeting the five beings upon whose backs the entire world rests.

Typical of Mr. Pratchett, that, being cleverly literal. He's good at that sort of thing, and that's on display right from the start, what with the awe-inspiring descriptions of the turtle and the elephants who, one has a suspicion, were really intended in the original myths to be metaphysical concepts, or perhaps metaphors of some sort, rather than literal animals with meteor scars and hydrogen frost. One doesn't expect to see words like "meteor" and "hydrogen" in a description of a giant turtle with a world on its back.

Which is rather the point. Our Mr. Pratchett is playing the science-fictional game of "What if it were real?" here. He's taken a bit of Hindu mythology and shoved it into outer space as if it were a solid, physical world in the cosmos that we now know is out there.

Hindu myth? Why, yes—the idea that the world is supported on the backs of four gigantic elephants is from Hindu mythology. Earthquakes happen when the elephants shift their weight.

Another Hindu myth says that the world rests on the back of a gigantic tortoise. (Actually, that idea appears in several cultures, whereas the elephants are specifically from Hindu myth.) Mr. Pratchett has resolved the apparent contradiction by suggesting that both are true—the elephants are standing on the tortoise, while the world rests upon their backs. He has then sent this curious construct hurtling through interstellar space as we now understand it (which I suspect was not what the authors of the Hindu scriptures had in mind), and has given some thought to what such creatures might look like after a few millennia drifting—or rather, *swimming*[39]—through hard vacuum.

Though of course he ignores details like what the elephants eat, what they breathe, and why they don't just shrug their shoulders and rid themselves of that awkward Disc, and so on. I suppose that's all just to be put down to magic. Discworld, as we're told from the first, has an intense magical field.

And it's not as if the Hindu mythmakers worried about such details, either.

One might wonder, though, why an Englishman with no particular ties to India should choose to model his fantasy world after Hindu myth.

Well, why not? Fantasy novelists have been borrowing various other mythologies for their settings for years. C.S. Lewis had happily borrowed the creatures of classical mythology for his invented land of Narnia, even while building his story around Christian themes. He had

[39] Just what is Great A'tuin swimming through, anyway? You can't get much traction on hard vacuum. Ether? There's no good evidence it exists in Discworld's vicinity any more than it does here. The Disc's magical field? But that travels along with it. Interstellar hydrogen? Not enough of it.

I think we must assume that those continent-sized flippers are shoving spacetime itself. That's just the sort of thing you'd expect of the Discworld.

It's probably because of quantum.

made it a flat world, and in *The Voyage of the* Dawn Treader he sent his heroes sailing out to its edge.

J.R.R. Tolkien's Middle Earth does not appear to be on a spherical planet; the western lands whither the elves go are not just the Americas. Like almost all of Tolkien's work, this was built up in emulation of a variety of European myths.

Fritz Leiber's Nehwon existed in a gigantic bubble—the inside of a sphere, rather than the outside.

Other fantasy authors have cheerfully swiped the worlds of Norse myth,[40] or Russian folklore,[41] or a China that never was,[42] or the settings of Irish or Finnish or Arabian myth, as well as any number of variations on medieval Europe. Mr. Pratchett simply borrowed the most amusing cosmology that he happened upon. He was writing absurd fantasy, so he wanted an absurd setting for it.

He was, in fact, letting the reader know right from the start what he intended to do all down the line—take everything that one normally found in fantasy, and push it just a little farther than usual, in order to show its fundamental absurdity.

So he presented us with a world based on a real myth, but considered both logically and cosmologically—as we go along through the series we'll get detailed explanations of how the eight seasons work, for example, even though it's never actually relevant to the story. Here in this first two-page prologue, he manages to jam in not only a description of Great A'tuin and its burden, but a brief account of the space program the kingdom of Krull has created to study the nature of their world, complete with puns on astronomical theories from *our* world—another theme that will continue throughout the series, the humorous and often punning references to commonalities between Discworld and our own less-magical planet. (These bizarre resemblances do get explained, after a fashion, in *The Science of Discworld*—see Chapter 29. And see also Chapter 62.)

This description of the Disc is all given as an explanation of how a Krullian astronomer happened to have a telescope pointed toward Ankh-Morpork, the oldest city in the world, and therefore became the first person on the Disc to see the smoke of that city's burning. That fact, that this particular person was the first to see it, turns out to have

[40] E.g., Poul Anderson, or Fletcher Pratt and L. Sprague de Camp.

[41] E.g., C.J. Cherryh.

[42] E.g., Barry Hughart.

absolutely nothing to do with the story we're about to be told; it's merely an excuse for a prologue describing the Disc.

One might, as I said, suspect the author of parody.

And in *The Colour of Magic*, once past the prologue, one would undoubtedly be right. That first book was quite plainly a parody of the genre of heroic fantasy (including science fantasy) as it existed circa 1980. As the series progressed, though, it moved away from parody, through satire, to become something else entirely.

So that opening description of Discworld set up the essentials, which do not change, but we gradually learned more and more about the structure and nature of this strange world as the series went on.

As far as geography goes, Discworld has three continents, but the inhabitants would probably say there are at least four. The largest doesn't seem to have a name; it includes the Hublands at the center of the Disc, but extends almost to the Rim. A body of water called the Circle Sea intrudes into it at one point, and the area rimwards of the Circle Sea is called Klatch, which is sometimes referred to as a separate continent; this is very roughly parallel to our world's distinguishing Europe and Asia, even though, by any sensible definition, they're obviously two sides of one continent.

The other continents are the Counterweight Continent, home to the Agatean Empire, and EcksEcksEcksEcks, or XXXX, or FourEcks, initially so called because its true name is unknown elsewhere.[43]

For reasons that don't actually hold up under close scrutiny, Mr. Pratchett set it up so that lands at the center of the Disc are colder than lands at the edge. Klatch and EcksEcksEcksEcks are mostly hot desert, while the more central lands are cold, with snowy winters. The central area is also mountainous, culminating in a central spire that acts more or less as the axis on which the Disc rotates; this miles-high spire is called Cori Celesti, and is the abode of the gods.

The rim is almost entirely covered with water, and a gigantic waterfall is perpetually spilling from all sides. We get some lovely descriptions of this now and then in the course of the stories, but no explanation of where all that water comes from and why the Disc hasn't long since run dry. It's presumably magic.

If you want a more detailed rendering of all this geography, the best thing to do is to get hold of a copy of the official Discworld Mapp, by

---

[43] And because there's an Australian beer called XXXX. See www.xxxx.com.au/.

Terry Pratchett and Stephen Briggs, published by Corgi in 1996 and still in print in Britain. It's not absolutely complete,[44] but it's close. There are also some lovely depictions of what the whole thing would look like in the various art books and animated adaptations.

The Disc is orbited by a small sun and a moon; the orbital mechanics of these subsidiary bodies are nonsensical and I'm not going to waste everyone's time trying to explain them. Gravity as we understand it is clearly not the primary force at work here.

In fact, the physics of the Discworld is different from our own in several ways. There are at least two crucial elements in its make-up, narrativium and deitium, that don't exist in our universe, but those are just the beginning. Really, it *can't* have the same physics we do, or it wouldn't be possible—a flat disc several thousand miles in diameter would not be stable, could not retain a breathable atmosphere, and wouldn't generally have gravity pointing the right direction. And we won't even think about the turtle or the elephants.

Not to mention slood.[45]

Discworld has an intense magical field which affects practically everything—unlike our own world, which has *no* magic. This field distorts probability, makes wizardry and witchcraft possible, gives belief real power, allows anthropomorphic personifications to exist—no, *requires* anthropomorphic personifications to exist—and generally complicates life for the Disc's inhabitants.

Perhaps this field's strangest effects are on light. Light travels much more slowly than it does in what we consider "normal" space, and behaves more like a liquid than it has any right to. This is described in detail many times in the early volumes. Oddly, several volumes in, it seems to be deemed unworthy of further attention, and ceases to have any noticeable effect on the stories, though it's still getting the occasional mention as late as *Thief of Time*.

The spectrum on the Disc contains an eighth color in addition to the customary seven: octarine, the color of magic. That also starts out as an important feature of the setting, but becomes less significant over time.

Furthermore, reality itself is very thin on the Disc, so that things (and Things) from other dimensions and alternate realities tend to leak in on

---

[44] It doesn't seem to show the Chalk Hills, where the Tiffany Aching stories are set, for one thing. That the map was drawn before those were written is no excuse.

[45] A joke I hope to remember to explain later.

occasion. As Mr. Pratchett put it in a recent interview, Discworld is far out at the absurd end of the bell curve, right at the edge where if it were any more absurd, it couldn't exist at all.

Many fantasy authors go to great lengths to work out the internal logistics necessary to give their invented worlds the appearance of independent existence and substantial reality; Mr. Pratchett did not go that route. In fact, he seems to have kicked over the signposts and burned the maps to *avoid* that route. Heraldic mottos are in dog Latin, while exotic names are mostly French, Latin, German, Arabic, Welsh, or bad pastiches of those languages; there's no pretense of any linguistic sense to any of it. The economy of Ankh-Morpork makes very little sense. In the course of the series, an ostensibly late-Medieval/early-Renaissance society somehow transforms into more or less a nineteenth-century setting, developing motion pictures, rock music, tabloid newspapers, an analogue of computer networks, and assorted other outrageous anachronisms along the way. This is all explained away as the Disc's magical field interacting with ideas leaking through from other realities.

This is all possible because the Disc is *not* a world, but merely a setting for storytelling, and Mr. Pratchett generally hasn't bothered to pretend otherwise. More than one character in the course of the series is described as wanting the world to make sense, and encountering difficulties because it simply doesn't. It's out at the end of the bell curve, well past where things stop making sense.

The really amazing thing is how well it all hangs together, and how often it *does* seem to make sense.

Rather less amazing, given how extensive the series has become and how little advance planning went into setting it up, is how many things have altered over time. I'll try to point some of these out as we work through the story-by-story descriptions. The basics are constant; the details change.

So let's get on with the stories, and see how it goes.

PART THREE
The Stories

3

The Colour of Magic (1983)

IT'S FAIRLY CLEAR THAT MR. PRATCHETT'S intent in this first Discworld book wasn't to launch a twenty-plus-year series of brilliant satirical novels, but to poke some good-natured fun at the popular fantasy of the day. A great many things here are not as they were in most of the later books in the series. He did, however, set out some of the basic geography, cosmology, theology, and so on, as described in the previous chapter.

The first Discworld novel set out to parody fantasy novels by sending a naïve tourist to visit various settings in various portions of a world much like the worlds of certain fantasy novels, only more so. It manages, in the process, to parody the behavior of tourists just as much as it parodies commercial fantasy.

It is, like all the Discworld stories, about stories and belief. In this case, it's about the genre of fantasy as it existed in the early 1980s, and about certain fantasy stories in particular. The commentary is not anything very sophisticated, but just parody gently mocking those assorted well-known works.

It's also about the stories our tourist has heard, and his belief in those stories, and in his own safety.

Unlike most of the later volumes in the series, *The Colour of Magic* has chapters—or I suppose one could consider them to be four separate novellas making up the novel, since each one is more or less a separate story. Each of the four stories parodies a certain sort of fantasy that was popular in the late 1970s and early 1980s.

The first novella, also entitled "The Colour of Magic," mocks the genre of Sword & Sorcery[46] in general, with its impossibly squalid and violent cities, its sword-wielding homicidal heroes, its wizards who somehow rarely seem to use their powerful magic very effectively, its corrupt rulers, its taverns and thieves and assassins and intrigue, its maidens and monsters.

More specifically, the two scoundrels we meet before the story really begins, Bravd and the Weasel, are clearly a parody of Fritz Leiber's Fafhrd and the Grey Mouser, and the city of Ankh-Morpork, while incorporating elements of several cities both real and fictional,[47] seems to owe something to the city of Lankhmar, which served as Fafhrd and the Mouser's home.

Rincewind the Wizard: The Series

This series is defined by the presence of Rincewind and his fellow wizards of Unseen University in leading roles. It consists of:

The Colour of Magic..Chapter 3
The Light Fantastic..Chapter 4
Sourcery..Chapter 7
Eric...Chapter 11
Interesting Times..Chapter 21
The Last Continent...Chapter 26
The Last Hero...Chapter 33
"A Collegiate Casting-Out of Devilish Devices"
(Rincewind isn't mentioned, but I choose to
assume he was present)..................................Chapter 42
All three volumes of *The Science of Discworld*.....Chapters 29, 35, 43

The series as a whole is considered in Chapter 52.

---

[46] "Sword & Sorcery," typified by Robert E. Howard's stories about Conan of Cimmeria or Kull of Atlantis, was the dominant form of fantasy adventure for a few years in the middle of the twentieth century. It generally involved sword-wielding "heroes" of questionable virtue battling sinister magic—evil wizards, supernatural monsters, curses on tombs, that sort of thing. It fell out of favor when J.R.R. Tolkien's The Lord of the Rings caught on, and most particularly when publishers realized they could make lots of money publishing cheap imitations of Tolkien, replacing the barbarian thief of sword and sorcery with the farm-boy with a destiny, and promoting the evil wizard to the status of Dark Lord.

[47] Mostly the most sordid and foul-smelling elements. Some people have argued that Ankh-Morpork is merely a fantasy version of London, but Mr. Pratchett has denied this, saying that while it's got bits of London in it, it's got bits of *lots* of cities, and isn't based on any particular one.

Fafhrd and the Grey Mouser were the protagonists of a series of adventures extending from 1939 ("Two Sought Adventure," published in *Unknown*)[48] to 1988 (*The Knight and Knave of Swords*). The characters were the invention of Fritz Leiber, Jr., and his friend Harry Fischer; the poetically inclined northern barbarian Fafhrd was based on Leiber himself, and the witty little thief, the Grey Mouser, was based on Fischer. They were originally created in a series of letters the two exchanged, and then became the protagonists of stories the two wrote. Fischer dropped out early on, before any of the stories were actually published, and Leiber wrote almost the entire series by himself.

This pair of protagonists were notable at the time for being less than entirely heroic; these were no larger-than-life white knights, but a couple of good-hearted rogues.

Pratchett's parody gives us a couple of murderous cutthroats, instead, but manages to capture some of the essence of the characters all the same.

Their part in the story is fairly small, though; they serve mostly to introduce us to the young and rather sorry wizard Rincewind, who will be our guide for the remainder of the book. Rincewind is not based on any specific character from elsewhere, so far as I can see, but is rather a mockery of the standard fantasy heroes. He's a wizard who knows no magic, a hero who's a greedy coward, an adventurer who mostly wants to stay quietly at home.

And Rincewind winds up, at the insistence of the Patrician[49] who rules

---

[48] *Unknown* (or sometimes *Unknown Worlds*) was an American pulp magazine, published from 1939 until the wartime paper shortages killed it in 1943, edited by John W. Campbell, Jr. "Pulps" were called that because they were printed on the lowest available grade of wood-pulp paper, produced as cheaply as possible—even comic books and newspapers generally used better paper, comic books because the color printing would smear on pulp paper, newspapers because they used smaller type and had to hold up to being folded and handled more. Pulp magazines were cheap, disposable entertainment for the masses in the pre-television era, and most of what they published was forgettable crap. Modern readers often misunderstand this, since the only pulp stories anyone remembers are the exceptionally good ones, giving many people the mistaken idea that the typical pulp magazine was good fun.

The typical pulp magazine was tedious junk, on a par with the worst of present-day television, or very-low-end romance novels and TV spin-offs. *Unknown* was not typical at all, and in its brief existence it published a lot of those exceptionally good stories that people remember, mixed in with some of the tedious junk. Its particular niche was fantasy, but it aimed at a somewhat more sophisticated audience than most.

[49] The Patrician is not named here, and is described as having several chins; later on, the Patrician will be a thin man named Havelock Vetinari. Some readers have assumed that this means this is his predecessor in *The Colour of Magic*, but the author has said otherwise in interviews. This is most probably Lord Vetinari, Mr. Pratchett says, he's just badly described.

Ankh-Morpork operates on a "One man, one vote" system. The Patrician is the one man, and has the one vote.

the city, acting as native guide and bodyguard to an Agatean[50] tourist named Twoflower, the first tourist in Ankh-Morpork's history, who has heard all the stories about heroes and adventure in Ankh-Morpork and the surrounding lands, and has come to see the place for himself. He's brought a not-very-good phrasebook, a large quantity of gold, the Discworld equivalent of a camera,[51] and a magical trunk known hereafter as the Luggage.[52]

Twoflower has *heard* the stories, but he obviously hasn't really understood them. He's quite sure that *he* won't be harmed, no matter how dangerous the place may be, because after all, he's just a tourist, not an adventurer.

That adventurers can be people who just happened to be in the wrong place at the wrong time, and that the famous ones are the minority who didn't die, has never occurred to him. He looks on Ankh-Morpork as a big theater putting on a show for his entertainment, and doesn't for a minute see himself as a participant; he's just an observer. He wants to see the tavern brawls, the barbarian heroes, the Whore Pits,[53] and so on, and is completely oblivious to any possible danger in this.

And he *does* get to see tavern brawls, barbarian heroes, and Whore Pits. Amazingly, thanks to Rincewind, he also survives intact, though he's responsible (quite unintentionally) for setting a large part of Ankh-Morpork ablaze.[54] The two of them escape the city (and Bravd and the Weasel) and venture elsewhere.

---

[50] At this point in Discworld's development, the Agatean Empire is merely a very distant, mysterious, fabulously wealthy, dangerously advanced, and powerful civilization on the far side of the Disc. Later in the series it'll become the Discworld's analogue of Imperial China, with a slight admixture of other Asian cultures, but I don't see that here. Twoflower is an insurance salesman back home, and insurance salesmen in shorts and aloha shirts do not immediately bring ancient China to my mind. Really, in this first story he comes across as more like an American than anything else. Quite a bit more.

[51] The iconograph doesn't have any of this stuff with lenses and chemicals that our film cameras have, nor the pixilated electronics of a digital camera; instead, it's a box containing a tiny imp who paints pictures of whatever the box is pointed at. Apparently the wizards of Ankh-Morpork found this easy to duplicate; in *The Colour of Magic* no one in Ankh-Morpork has ever seen one before, but a few volumes later they're commonplace.

[52] The Luggage rates a chapter all to itself in Part Six, Chapter 60. It's more a character than a prop, and reappears in every Rincewind story hereafter.

[53] Yes, Ankh-Morpork had Whore Pits at this point. They're never described in any detail, and fade out of the series rather quickly, though it's eventually mentioned in passing that certain concerned individuals have had the Whore Pits renamed the Street of Negotiable Affection. The old name does appear for one last time on the map in the front of *Night Watch*, which depicts the city's streets at least a decade before *The Colour of Magic*, so it wasn't forgotten, merely thought better of.

[54] As I said a couple of footnotes back, he's an insurance salesman. When he tries to explain this to the fine people of Ankh-Morpork, he inadvertently introduces the concepts of arson for profit, and insurance fraud.

Oh, dear, now I've spoiled a joke, haven't I? Bad author! What was I thinking?

Well, really, it was a rather obvious one, wasn't it? But I'll try to behave myself better in the future. And if you *want* an explanation of some of the rather labored puns in *The Colour of Magic*, I'll once again direct you to check out Lspace.org on the World Wide Web.

The second section (or chapter, or novella) of *The Colour of Magic*, "The Sending of Eight," gives us haunted forests and mysterious ancient crypts and destinies guided by the whims of gods—dark fantasy, in the mode of *Weird Tales*,[55] with some distinctly Lovecraftian[56] touches, but adapted to the Discworld.

We now learn that, like many fantasy characters, these characters are caught up in a game played by the gods, notably Fate and the Lady, the latter clearly being Lady Luck, though her name is never mentioned, since it's bad luck to address her by name.

The Lady, being who she is, cheats.

While the idea of names or words one mustn't say aloud for fear of attracting the attention of hostile supernatural powers is an old and familiar one—for example, in Lovecraft's stories, speaking the name of Hastur the Unspeakable aloud is "a punishable blasphemy"—Mr. Pratchett carries this a step farther into absurdity in this story with the unspeakable *number*, the one between seven and nine. This is the Number of Bel-Shamharoth, also known as the Sender of Eight and the Soul Eater, an abominable god much like the Great Old Ones that H.P. Lovecraft originated. (Many other authors have imitated Lovecraft's creations since then.)

Rincewind attempts to rescue Twoflower from the Temple of Bel-Shamharoth; Twoflower, the determined innocent tourist, does not make this easy.

We also see a good bit of Hrun the Barbarian, who makes his living robbing ancient temples, battling monsters, and so on, and who is clearly based on Robert E. Howard's Conan the Barbarian. We're defi-

---

[55] *Weird Tales* was a pulp magazine back in the first half of the twentieth century; it lasted much longer than *Unknown* (see footnote 48). Like *Unknown*, *Weird Tales* was not a typical pulp, and published a lot of good stories (and as well as a lot of crap). Its particular niche was fantasy, adventure, and horror, and unlike Unknown, it was perfectly willing to wallow in the lurid and sensational. It's best remembered today as the major outlet for the work of three authors: Robert E. Howard, H.P. Lovecraft, and Clark Ashton Smith. Howard was the creator of Conan of Cimmeria, the prototypical barbarian hero; Lovecraft is best remembered as the creator of the Cthulhu Mythos; and Smith authored about a hundred mordant and gloriously-overwritten short stories about wizards, demons, and the like. The three of them traded ideas back and forth freely, so that Conan might occasionally find himself battling one of Cthulhu's kin. A great deal of modern fantasy, at least that portion that's not aping Tolkien, emulates Howard, Lovecraft, and Smith.

Weird Tales has been revived several times, and the latest incarnation is still in operation today, but the current version is not much like the original.

[56] H.P. Lovecraft's specialty was the tale of someone discovering unspeakable horrors and going mad from the knowledge of their existence. He was fond of "non-Euclidean" architecture, elder gods, long-buried vaults containing hideous secrets, evidence of civilizations older than humanity, eldritch beings from other worlds, and the like.

nitely in *Weird Tales* territory here, even though I don't see much that's specifically taken from Clark Ashton Smith—but on the other hand, there's also the frequent mention of the sound of rolling dice. While that's a reference to the game being played by the gods, it's also a reference to the unfortunate spate of second-rate fantasy novels in the late seventies and early eighties that were a little too obviously based on Dungeons & Dragons and other role-playing games, games where dice rolls determine the outcome of every fight. Readers of the time would often say disparagingly of such obviously game-based novels, "You can hear the dice rolling."

Well, in "The Sending of Eight," the characters can *literally* hear the dice rolling, as the gods play with them.

There are other interesting tidbits here, as well. Rincewind, despite being a wizard, doesn't much like magic, and often wishes the world operated on more sensible principles, but alas. . . .

"It was all very well going on about pure logic and how the universe was ruled by logic and the harmony of numbers, but the plain fact of the matter was that the Disc was manifestly traversing space on the back of a giant turtle and the gods had a habit of going round to atheists' houses and smashing their windows."

In short, where people in our world dream of a world full of magic and wonder, people on the Disc dream of a world that makes sense, and doesn't have all that magic and wonder confusing matters.

As the series progresses, several different characters will have this attitude—most of them wizards, perversely enough—though it will eventually settle most thoroughly not on Rincewind, but on one Ponder Stibbons.

As far as the development of Discworld itself goes, we encounter our first troll as just one of the various menaces Rincewind and Twoflower meet on the road; it dies rather more easily than is entirely in accord with later depictions, and is otherwise not quite what we'll see in subsequent volumes.

Trolls and dryads appear, but no dwarfs. Elves are mentioned that don't appear to be the sort we'll meet in *Lords and Ladies*. A great many things aren't what we'll wind up with. There are various place-names mentioned—Chirm, B'Ituni, Re'durat, and so on—that are remarkable for their failure to reappear in later stories. Generally, throughout the series, names keep turning up over and over even if we never learn much about the places mentioned, but that's not the case in this first volume, where any number of exotic names are thrown about, never to be seen again.

I suppose Chirm *might* be an alternate spelling of the city of Quirm, which does indeed appear many times, but I wouldn't bet on that being deliberate.

Well, moving on, the third part of *The Colour of Magic* is "The Lure of the Wyrm." This is largely a direct parody of Anne McCaffrey's Dragonriders of Pern series, but generalizes nicely to the whole wish-fulfillment sort of setting that some fans[57] disparagingly call "magic pony" fantasy, where powerful magical beasts selflessly serve the whims of their human masters for no very clear reason. In this case, the wish-fulfillment aspect becomes a bit more literal than usual.

In case you aren't familiar with it, in "magic pony" fantasy, the protagonist is always a girl or young woman (often red-haired) who has been abused or mistreated in some fashion, but who mystically bonds with some wonderful, powerful, empathic or telepathic creature, whether horse, dragon, unicorn, wolf, or whatever, because she's just so *special*, and uses this bond to elevate herself to some exalted status. Mercedes Lackey, Jennifer Roberson, and assorted others—pretty much all of them female—have written this sort of thing, with varying degrees of talent and success, but Anne McCaffrey's *Dragonflight* is the classic in the field, in which a kitchen drudge named Lessa of Ruatha bonds with the great golden dragon Ramoth and becomes Weyrlady of Benden, leader of all the dragonriders of Pern.

In "The Lure of the Wyrm," Liessa Wyrmbidder is the rider of the great dragon Laolith, and the Lady of Wyrmberg. I think it's pretty clear what's going on here. Liessa Dragonlady is not quite as likeable as Lessa of Ruatha, but the resemblance is unmistakable.

Hrun says that dragons are extinct,[58] but obviously, these people are riding dragons; plainly, something strange is up.

Here, Twoflower's invincible optimism finally finds useful application; if anyone has wishes looking for fulfillment, he does. It seems Wyrmberg is even closer to the edge of reality than the rest of Discworld, and Twoflower, like Liessa, can use that. Though not always safely or effectively.

---

[57] Including me.

[58] Well, the big ones, anyway, not the little swamp dragons. And we'll have more to say on this subject in *Guards! Guards!*

In the end, Rincewind and Twoflower briefly fall out of their native reality entirely, into another plane[59]—but only briefly, before plummeting back to another part of the Disc, and into the fourth and final novella.

And that last novella, "Close to the Edge," parodies the Yes album covers Roger Dean was famed for in the 1970s.[60]

Okay, well, perhaps not. Though honestly, it does seem to, with all those strange craft falling off the edge of the world and all, and having the same title as one of Yes's early albums.

Really, it's an assortment of more fantasy clichés, but this time without an obvious specific source—heroes doomed to be sacrificed, gods manifesting, and so on. If I had to tie it to a single author, I'd pick John Brunner, author of *The Traveler in Black*, but I suspect Mr. Pratchett would react to that with puzzlement, or maybe, since he doesn't seem to do outrage, minor annoyance.

I'm probably simply displaying my own eccentricity by picking Brunner. Perhaps L. Sprague de Camp would be a better fit, or even Lord Dunsany. The L-space annotations suggest some Jack Vance influence, and I can see that, too. It's not so much a single author as an entire style of fantasy—the witty, mildly cynical, sometimes lyrical sort that has been around since the nineteenth century, while usually being outsold by the sword-and-sorcery or magic-pony or pseudo-Tolkien stuff.[61]

At any rate, "Close to the Edge" concludes *The Colour of Magic* without actually ending the story. Rincewind and Twoflower are thrust through a series of further adventures, and then finally escape the last menace by replacing the crew of a spaceship and falling off the edge of the world.

One thing about setting a story on a flat world—there's a great temptation to sooner or later send someone falling off the edge. The problem with that is, where do you go from there?

Having already once saved Rincewind and Twoflower by miraculous-

---

[59] Specifically, a jet airliner.
Yes, fine, it's a dreadful pun. I didn't invent it, Mr. Pratchett did. Take it up with him.

[60] If you don't know what I'm talking about, don't tell me, it'll just make me feel old. Go look through the Yes albums in a used record shop, especially *Fragile*, *Close to the Edge*, and *Yessongs*, if you can find them with the original album covers and inserts.

[61] One of the curious features of *The Colour of Magic* is that it parodies most of the major fantasy subgenres of the day while ignoring the biggest, baddest of them all—Middle Earth and its imitators. Perhaps Mr. Pratchett felt that that had already been done.

ly translating them to another plane, apparently Mr. Pratchett felt no need to do so again. The result is a rather unsatisfying ending. Yes, they escaped the people who were trying to kill them, but now the *universe* is trying to kill them.

Fortunately, the story really *didn't* end there. The three-year wait for the conclusion, though, must have seemed interminable.

You, lucky reader, can just go on to the next book—or, since you're here, the next chapter.

Before you do, though, I should perhaps mention that the British network Sky One, prompted by the success of their video adaptation of *Hogfather*, began filming their version of *The Colour of Magic* in July of 2007, starring David Jason as Rincewind. The production aired in Britain for Easter of 2008, but as of this writing has not reached the U.S.

4

The Light Fantastic (1986)

THIS SECOND BOOK IN THE SERIES picks up exactly where *The Colour of Magic* left off, with Rincewind and Twoflower plummeting through space. Like *The Colour of Magic*, it's still parodying various elements of fantasy fiction.

This is where the Standard Model Discworld Novel first appears, with no chapters, just one continuous book-length narrative. Rather than mocking specific works in separate stories as *The Colour of Magic* did, it pretty much throws everything in together.

This one parodies scheming wizards, druids, New Agers, Conan the Barbarian and his ilk, red-headed warrior women, trolls, mysterious little shops, and doomsday cults, and wraps up the various loose ends from the first book, providing Twoflower and Rincewind with a reasonably happy ending, in which they avoid being devoured by unspeakable creatures from the Dungeon Dimensions.[62]

Twoflower gives the Luggage to Rincewind at the end, so that it will continue to appear in the series whenever Rincewind does, without the need for Twoflower's rather annoying presence.

This book also introduces the Librarian, who will go on to appear in almost every story hereafter.

In an early scene, the *Octavo*, the book containing the eight spells that supposedly created the Discworld in the first place,[63] sends a burst of magic shooting upward, and it transforms the head Librarian of Unseen

[62] At least for the moment.

[63] Well, it's *supposed* to contain them; at this point in the story one of the spells has escaped and is residing in Rincewind's head.

University[64] into an orangutan. He remains an orangutan for the rest of the series (excluding a period of illness in *The Last Continent*), and is one of the most frequently-seen characters, matched only by Death.

Another important introduction is Cohen the Barbarian. In *The Colour of Magic*, we saw one parody of Robert E. Howard's Conan in the form of Hrun the Barbarian; here we meet another, rather more original one. Genghiz Cohen (whose first name won't be mentioned until *Interesting Times*) is the barbarian hero's barbarian hero, a man whose exploits are legendary throughout the Disc, a man who can triumph over any foe, and who has been doing so for a long time—after all, it takes awhile to have all those adventures, and for word of them to get around. As the greatest, most famous barbarian hero in the history of Discworld, he's been doing it for a *really* long time.

And that's why we need a second barbarian hero, instead of just bringing back Hrun. Cohen is, when we meet him, eighty-seven years old and still adventuring, because after all, what else does he know how to do?

This is an obvious but rarely-considered consequence of heroes too tough to ever be beaten—since they don't die, and in fact *specialize* in not dying, they're going to get old. Examining such necessary but never-mentioned consequences of something is an excellent source of humor, and one that Mr. Pratchett makes extensive use of throughout the series.

In *The Light Fantastic*, we also visit Death's home for the first time and meet Ysabell, Death's adopted daughter, as well as Famine, War, and Pestilence, who happen to be visiting. Death's friends call him "Mort" here, a detail that will be quietly ignored forever after.

While I won't identify the parties involved, since I don't want to spoil

---

[64] Unseen University is the center of wizardry on the Discworld. The name is a parody of the Invisible College, a loose federation of seventeenth-century scientists that became the Royal Society. In its earliest mentions, Unseen University had no fixed location; a few books later it's solidly in Ankh-Morpork, on Sator Square, where it has remained ever since.

"Sator Square," by the way, is a pun—the Sator Square is an ancient charm, a five-by-five grid of letters:

SATOR
AREPO
TENET
OPERA
ROTAS

It reads the same in every direction, and is ambiguous Latin that might be translated as "The sower Arepo works to hold the wheels." It dates back to at least the first century A.D.; its exact origins and significance are obscure, but it has long been thought to have magical power, so it's an appropriate name for a plaza next to a college of wizards.

Discworld is full of this sort of moderately obscure joke. You don't *need* to get the references like this to appreciate the humor and enjoy the series, but if you *do* get them, they're a nice little extra.

any surprises, I will say that the reason we see Death's home is that one character has died, and another is trying to rescue him anyway.

The idea of retrieving a soul from the house of Death is, of course, an ancient one, found in any number of classic myths, in any number of cultures: Gilgamesh, Orpheus, and so on. Only on Discworld, though, would the rescuer find his friend teaching Death and the other Horsemen of the Apocalypse to play something not entirely unlike bridge. Blending the mythic and the mundane is another reliable humor source that Mr. Pratchett taps frequently.

Although a mountain troll appeared briefly in *The Colour of Magic*, it's here in *The Light Fantastic* that it's first explained that trolls are made of stone, that they eat stone, that their teeth are diamonds because something that hard is needed to chew stone, and that heat is bad for their brains. They aren't *quite* like what we see strolling the streets of Ankh-Morpork a few books later—they aren't noticeably stupid at moderate temperatures, for one thing—but they're definitely getting there.

The creatures from the Dungeon Dimensions appear as well.

All in all, a good many of the lasting details of Discworld are starting to fall into place now, in a way they didn't in the first book. It's still mostly playing off other fantasy stories, commenting on the absurdities of them, but it's also developing its own personality.

So far, other than the humorous elements, it looks rather like an ordinary fantasy series. It started off as one thing—parodying specific fantasy tropes—but then started to become its own new thing in the second volume. Our heroes, who were fairly two-dimensional in the first volume, start to be fleshed out in the second. The normal progression would be for them to start to turn from parodies into real heroes in the third volume.

Mr. Pratchett didn't do that. Sneaky git.

Instead, we're at a fork. The third volume doesn't have Rincewind or Twoflower in it; they aren't even mentioned in passing. Rather, it begins the second of the eight sub-series.

So you, dear Reader, now have a choice. You can go on to Chapter 5, about the third book, *Equal Rites*, or you can instead follow the adventures of Rincewind. If you want to follow Rincewind, then skip ahead to Chapter 6 for his bit part in *Mort*, or to Chapter 7 to read about his more significant role in *Sourcery*.

5

Equal Rites (1987)

YOU WOULD THINK, with a title like that, this book would be mocking either feminism or sexism. That may even be what Mr. Pratchett intended. It isn't, however, what he actually gives us.

It starts off looking very much as if that was what he meant to do, as we see Drum Billet, a powerful wizard, arrive in the town of Bad Ass[65] during an appropriately theatrical thunderstorm, with the intention of passing his wizard's staff on to a child about to be born. The local smith is an eighth son, and has seven boys already. You'll recall that eight is the magically potent number in Discworld, rather than seven, so it's the eighth son of an eighth son, rather than the seventh son of a seventh son, who is marked for magic.

The child is born, the staff handed on—but the baby is a girl.

Oops. Discworld's wizards are all male. Women who take up magic are witches, with a rather different approach to the subject. This child, Eskarina[66] Smith, seems destined to be a problem.

Now, if this were following the pattern of the first two books and parodying common or garden-variety fantasy novels, we'd have lots of funny scenes where little Esk demonstrates the truth of that old femi-

---

[65] Notice that the names are changing style. In the first two books, we got personal names like Hrun, Bravd, Rincewind, and Zlorf, and place-names like Agatea and Ankh-Morpork—pure fantasy names, with no reasonable etymological explanation. Oh, a few more familiar names crept in, right from the start (such as "Hugh"), but most were just collections of phonemes. Now, though, we're getting recognizable words, though admittedly "Drum Billet" would not look particularly at home on a roster of ordinary English names.

And Bad Ass, we will eventually be told, was named for a troublesome donkey.

[66] Okay, there are still *some* fantasy names in there.

nist slogan, "In order to get ahead, a woman has to be twice as good as a man. Fortunately, that isn't difficult." Male wizards would act like complete dickheads, and good old feminine common sense would win the day. That, frankly, was what I expected when I first got a look at the book.

It's not what I got.

I tell you, you can't trust Mr. Pratchett. Just when you think you have him figured out, tagged as another purveyor of easy parody, he switches modes entirely, and without being obvious about it.

What he does here is to present a straightforward account of a young woman trying to find a comfortable place for herself when she's been saddled with talents inappropriate to her station.

That's not to say it isn't funny, because it *is* funny; it just isn't the sort of broad farce the first two books were. The characters are more like people than caricatures, and the humor doesn't derive from mocking the stereotypes of fantasy fiction, nor even the stereotypes of feminist rhetoric, but from mocking the behavior of real people. Eskarina Smith isn't a superwoman, but an ordinary girl with an extraordinary talent. The wizards refusing to accept her aren't exaggerations of fantasy-world wizards, but exaggerations of real-world academics, more concerned with office politics than with magic, and sexist not as a result of deliberate misogyny, but from confusion, tradition, and uncertainty.

And Esk's mentor, the witch who takes the girl under her wing... well, there's no easy way to sum her up, because this is where we're introduced to one of Mr. Pratchett's finest creations, one of the great characters of fantasy fiction, Granny Weatherwax.

Esmerelda Weatherwax is the local witch for the town of Bad Ass, in the kingdom of Lancre, in the Ramtop Mountains. Her formal education is sketchy, but her intelligence and understanding of human nature are formidable.

Witches weren't really mentioned in the first two books, but *Equal Rites* presents us with a great deal of detail on just how they operate on the Discworld, and sets the pattern that witches will follow throughout the rest of the series. Witches can do real magic, but are most effective when they know better than to use it; most of their power comes from seeing things as they are, rather than as how they're assumed to be. Granny Weatherwax is the ultimate expression of this—which is why we eventually learn, in later books, that she's Discworld's top witch. In

Equal Rites, she's a highly respected practitioner of her art, but there's no indication she's *that* extraordinary.

The Witches of Lancre: The Series

This series is defined by the presence of Granny Weatherwax in a leading role, and the absence of Tiffany Aching. The witches also appear in the Tiffany Aching "young adult" series, but I consider that a separate series. This one includes:

Equal Rites .... Chapter 5
Wyrd Sisters .... Chapter 7a
Witches Abroad .... Chapter 14
Lords and Ladies .... Chapter 17
Maskerade .... Chapter 22
"The Sea and Little Fishes" .... Chapter 27
Carpe Jugulum .... Chapter 28

The series as a whole is considered in Chapter 53.

Granny and Esk share the lead in *Equal Rites*. A third character, Simon, a young wizard of exceptional promise who arrives at the Unseen University at about the same time as Esk, is also of major importance in the story, though he doesn't appear until some way into the book.

Rincewind and Twoflower don't appear. Cohen the Barbarian is nowhere to be seen, nor is there any mention of Hrun, Bravd, or the Weasel. This is, in fact, clearly not the same series as the previous two books at all—except that it's still set on Discworld, and features more or less the same Unseen University we saw before.

A quick summary of the plot: Granny attempts to deal with Esk's wizardly abilities by training her to be a witch, but alas, Esk's magic is not witch's magic, it's wizardry. Granny recognizes the inevitable and sets out to deliver Esk to Unseen University, so that she can be trained as a wizard and learn to control her magic before she inadvertently does something truly dreadful with it. They have a few adventures along the way—not the swordfight-and-monster sort of adventures that would be there if this were another straightforward fantasy parody, but the sort of adventures a real girl might get into, such as slipping away from her guardian and falling in with bad company. They meet Simon and other wizards, and then arrive at Unseen University, where Granny's letters asking for Esk's admission haven't even been taken seriously enough to be laughed at.

Granny and Esk do not give in easily, though, and when Simon unintentionally manages to stir up the creatures from the Dungeon Dimensions, Esk employs her wizardly magic and witch's training to save the day, and thereafter is admitted to the University.

If anything in that is a direct parody of any other fantasy novel, it's news to me, and I read a *lot* of fantasy. No, with this book Mr. Pratchett has shifted from parody to something else—satire, perhaps, though it doesn't really seem to be that yet, or perhaps just plain comic fantasy. He's begun the transformation of his Discworld from a collection of silly ideas borrowed from all over to an actual world, with its own consistent (if somewhat ridiculous) society.

It's still about stories, though; it's merely shifted from being about fantasy fiction to being about the stories people actually believe and use to arrange their lives. The wizards of Unseen University never say that female wizards are against nature, against the law, or against tradition, but that they're against the *lore*—that is, that they're not something that's in all the stories about how the world works.

Yes, I know that it's a pun, that in British English "lore" and "law" are far more similar in pronunciation than they are in my own American dialect, but still, why bother with such a pun, and repeat it so often? It's clearly important, and what's important about it is that Discworld is a world that's shaped by stories.

In the first two volumes, there were certainly plenty of stories that affected the characters; Twoflower had become the Disc's first tourist in response to the stories he had heard, Rincewind had heard all the stories about Bel-Shamharoth, Liessa was living out a story, everyone knew stories about Cohen, and on and on, but no one tried to make reality (thin as it is on the Disc) fit the stories, unless you count Twoflower's frequent inability to see when it *didn't* fit.

In *Equal Rites*, though, wizards consider it essential to obey the lore, and abide by the story.

Not that these are necessarily the same wizards we encountered before. Although Unseen University is important in all three volumes up to this point, the only characters from the first two books to appear in this one are the Unseen University's Librarian, whom we saw transformed into an orangutan back in the early pages of *The Light Fantastic*, and Death himself—oh, and the creatures from the Dungeon Dimensions, if those count as characters.

Somewhere between volumes, Unseen University changed management; at the start of *The Light Fantastic* it was run by Galder Weatherwax, Supreme Grand Conjuror of the Order of the Silver Star, Lord Imperial of the Sacred Staff, Eighth Level Ipsissimus, and 304th Chancellor, while in *Equal Rites* the title is Archchancellor and Archimage of the Wizards of the Silver Star.[67] The incumbent in that office is a man named Cutangle, and there are no mentions of all that unpleasantness that preceded his elevation to the post. Despite that, and despite the change in titles, since the Librarian is still there, and in orangutan form, it can't have been *that* long since the messy events described in *The Light Fantastic*.

Admittedly, not all the wizards who were characters in *The Light Fantastic* survived the book, but it still seems a bit odd that we don't see *any* familiar faces among the faculty. It's almost as if Mr. Pratchett were not thinking of this as the next volume in a coherent series at all.

Perverse of him.

At any rate, at the end of *Equal Rites* we have Simon and Esk established at Unseen University, ready to continue their adventures....

And we never see them again. Granny Weatherwax, on the other hand, does return, fairly often.

But not right away. The next book was *Mort*, and the series forked again—or a new series was launched, if you prefer.

For the next news on Granny Weatherwax, skip ahead to Chapter 7a. For *Mort*, and the launch of that third sub-series, read on.

---

[67] The eight orders of wizardry are mentioned several times in the first few books, and are clearly considered important, but they apparently didn't turn out to be as useful in story construction as Mr. Pratchett had expected, as they fade away. By the time Mustrum Ridcully becomes Archchancellor in *Moving Pictures*, there's no mention of them at all, nor any evidence that they ever existed.

In fact, the significance of both the number eight and the color octarine also dwindles away as the series progresses. Those were elements parodying fantasy novel conventions that ceased to be relevant as the series moved away from simple parody and into other areas.

6

Mort (1987)

AT THIS POINT IN THE SERIES, four volumes in, things are settling down to more or less their final form. The geography is fairly consistent, and the underlying attitude is not only firmly established, but stated outright a few pages in:

"He was determined to discover the underlying logic behind the universe. Which was going to be hard, because there wasn't one."

That's reminiscent of Rincewind's attitude in the first two books, but stated more directly and up front here. With this novel, we are definitely no longer in fantasy-parodying mode, but in the far more interesting realm of commenting on human beings—or, as Douglas Adams called it, life, the universe, and everything.

The storyline this time is both fairly simple and completely unlike any fantasy cliché: Death, the anthropomorphic personification we've met in all three previous books, takes a human boy named Mort as an apprentice.[68] After a bit of a rough start, Mort starts to get the hang of the job, though he does screw up one assignment with potentially nasty results, and discovers that his master took an apprentice for much the usual reason *any* master takes an apprentice—to hand off the business and retire. Which is not what anyone else, including Mort, wants; there are, in fact, good reasons for ordinary people to not want Mort to take over.

Death's adopted daughter Ysabell, first encountered in *The Light Fantastic*, is a major character in *Mort*. Death's home was also seen in

[68] The fact that Death himself was called "Mort" in *The Light Fantastic* is conveniently ignored.

The Light Fantastic, and is much the same here, though we get much more detail. We also meet Death's servant, Albert, and Death's horse, Binky, both of whom will be regular cast members hereafter.

Most of Mort's problems revolve around Queen Keli of Sto Lat; for once, Ankh-Morpork isn't a central location.

Death in the Family: The Series

Death appears in almost every story, but he and his family are central to these:

Mort .... Chapter 6
Reaper Man .... Chapter 13
Soul Music .... Chapter 20
Hogfather .... Chapter 24
Thief of Time .... Chapter 32
"Death and What Comes Next" .... Chapter 37

His granddaughter Susan appears to have gradually taken over the series, much as Snuffy Smith gradually took over the comic strip *Barney Google*, or the Fonz took over *Happy Days* from Richie Cunningham. For a discussion of the series as a whole, see Chapter 54.

Despite Mort's bungling, matters get put to rights, of course—one thing the reader can rely on in a Discworld novel is that, while various characters may come to unfortunate ends, the story will conclude with Discworld as a whole carrying on much as it always has. The threatened catastrophe, whatever it may be, will be averted or survived or undone. In this case, Death takes his job back and finds Mort a new position.

Along the way, though, we learn a great deal about the metaphysics of the Discworld. In *The Colour of Magic*, we got to see Fate and the Lady playing games with the characters; here we see that the entire Discworld actually has a pre-ordained history, and that Bad Things Happen if it gets disturbed. This might be considered the first significant appearance of the effects of narrativium, one of the basic elements of the Discworld, the element that pushes events along the paths that make a good story.

Narrativium is *why* those threatened catastrophes are always averted, survived, or undone.

It's not mentioned by name here, and won't be for many volumes yet, but its effects are obvious. History—which is simply the story of everything—has a course laid out, and pushing it off-course, pushing against the narrativium, damages reality.

It could be argued that the first hints of the existence of narrativium were earlier, such as Granny Weatherwax pointing out in *Equal Rites* that million-to-one chances come in nine times out of ten, but it's only in *Mort* that it first becomes a major force.

It could also be argued that this idea of preordained history has something to do with the History Monks, who won't be introduced until *Small Gods* (see Chapter 15) and don't really come into their own until *Thief of Time* (see Chapter 32), but that doesn't seem to fit. No monks show up to help undo the damage Mort causes, so I think we need to put this down to narrativium—the need for a story to play out properly.

Story has been important all along, of course, but here it's made explicit that story is the single most powerful force in the Discworld, that it influences everything that happens. To some extent, everything is predetermined—but not really, because stories allow for twist endings, alternate plots, and so on. It's sometimes possible to derail a train of events, switching it from one story to another.

We also get further into questions about the nature of reality. These were mentioned in passing in the first two books, with such incidents as Rincewind finding himself briefly on a different plane[69] in order to escape death, and in *Equal Rites*, where Simon's studies endangered Discworld's reality, but here we find Death (and sometimes Mort) becoming realer than the ordinary inhabitants of the Disc, with interesting consequences. It's obvious that "real" isn't an absolute in the Discworld, but something measured on a sliding scale—not only is reality thin on the Disc, it's not distributed evenly.[70]

And where *Equal Rites* seemed almost to be deliberately avoiding links to the first two books, staffing Unseen University with unfamiliar faces except for the Librarian, *Mort* ties itself back in. When the action moves to Unseen University *this* time, Rincewind appears in exactly the role he had at the end of *The Light Fantastic*, and is clearly that same familiar character. He plays a small but significant part in the story. The Mended Drum, the tavern we'd seen in *The Colour of Magic*, is mentioned. The

[69] There's that pun again.

[70] Which was implied in "The Lure of the Wyrm" in *The Colour of Magic*.

Patrician is mentioned, and the "One Man, One Vote" system explained, though this Patrician doesn't quite match the description in *The Colour of Magic*.

If you ask me, this must be where the author realized that yes, he was writing a series, and that consistency can be a virtue in such an enterprise. Readers appreciate the little connections; it makes them feel smart, a part of the in-crowd, when they recognize a reference to previous volumes. It gives the whole thing an added touch of reality by demonstrating that these elements exist even when they aren't part of whatever story's being told at the moment.

You know, after four volumes, most series are starting to run out of ideas and momentum. Four books in, Discworld was just getting up to speed.

As Mr. Pratchett said in an interview, "By about book four, I discovered the joy of plot."

At any rate, at this point Discworld has pretty much taken on its standard form, though it's still well short of its eventual mature state, and we have three sub-series going, starring Rincewind, Granny Weatherwax, and... no, not Mort, nor Ysabell, but Death himself. He'll appear briefly in almost every book, but won't play the lead again until *Reaper Man*, discussed in Chapter 13.

First, it's back to Rincewind and the wizards.

7

Sourcery (1988)

AH, RINCEWIND IS BACK, ALONG with all the rest of Unseen University, as we return to a pre-existing series for the first time.

It was already established that the eighth son of an eighth son is a wizard. Generally it ends there, since wizards are supposed to be celibate, but what would the eighth son of an eighth son of an eighth son be?

The answer is a sourcerer. The spelling is deliberate; where wizards use the Disc's existing magical field, sourcerers generate their *own* magic, and lots of it.

Ipslore the Red, a wizard with ambitions unsuited to his position, deliberately sires eight sons in order to create a sourcerer, one who will do his bidding. He has the misfortune of dying while the boy, Coin, is still an infant, but doesn't let that stop him.

In due time, Coin arrives at Unseen University, whereupon a great many university inhabitants—not including most of the wizards—flee for their lives, Rincewind among them. Rincewind falls in with Conina, a daughter of Cohen the Barbarian, and later with Nijel the Destroyer, a book-taught barbarian hero, and Creosote the Younger, Seriph of Al Khali. The Archchancellor's hat, oddly reminiscent of the Hogwarts Sorting Hat,[71] is also involved.

---

[71] "Oddly" because *Harry Potter and the Philosopher's Stone* would not be published until six years after *Sourcery*. I suppose it's possible that J.K. Rowling drew her inspiration from Mr. Pratchett's little yarn, but somehow that seems very unlikely. I imagine it's a case of great minds thinking alike, or some such thing. Obnoxious journalists and clueless readers have pointed out several parallels between bits of Discworld and bits of Harry Potter's world; see Chapter 65.

Frankly, at least to me,[72] this book feels like a step backward. The humanity of *Equal Rites* and *Mort* has been cast aside in favor of pyrotechnics and parody. Several of the characters are surprisingly one-note. Al Khali is a parody of King Shahriyar's capital in the *Thousand Nights and a Night*, combined with Xanadu from Coleridge's "Kubla Khan," and bits of a few other "Oriental" settings. Conina and Nijel are parodies of various sword-and-sorcery heroes. The Four Horsemen of the Apocalypse appear, to little purpose beyond some cheap humor.

Of course, lots of things appear in Discworld books solely for cheap humor, all the way through the series, so I suppose I shouldn't cavil at that, but there doesn't seem much more than that here.

In fact, the author himself agreed: "I went back a bit with *Sourcery*, because I knew the fans wanted more of Rincewind. I didn't particularly enjoy writing *Sourcery*, but it stayed on the bestseller list for three months. And then I said, 'Sod the fans, I'll do what I like.'"[73]

At any rate, it's not one of the highlights of the series, despite all the magic being thrown around. Once again, we have no continuity in the population of Unseen University other than Rincewind and the Librarian, though at least details such as the title of Archchancellor and the description of the Tower of Art are now consistent. Whereas *Equal Rites* ended with the Archchancellor deciding to admit Esk and perhaps other promising females to the University, here Rincewind tells Conina that women are not permitted inside the gates—we've reverted to the earlier model. There's no sign of Esk or Simon.

The Patrician of Ankh-Morpork appears again, albeit briefly, and this is where we first learn that he is the head of the Vetinari family. The name is a pun on Medici—the founders of the Medici family really were physicians, so I suppose one must assume that the Patrician's ancestors really were veterinarians. Much later we'll learn that as a boy Vetinari was called "Dog-Botherer," so the name's resemblance to "veterinarian" is obvious to the people of Ankh-Morpork; it's not just a coincidence of pronunciation.[74]

Lord Vetinari's description is starting to read more like the character as we'll come to know him as in later books; his first appearance, in *The*

---

[72] And who else's opinion matters here?

[73] From a March 2005 interview published in *Science Fiction Weekly* #449.

[74] "Dog-Botherer" is also a play on "God-botherer," a term for an officiously religious person, or British military slang for a chaplain. Mr. Pratchett is never reluctant to layer his puns.

Colour of Magic, was so unlike the later version that many readers have suggested that it was Vetinari's predecessor, Lord Snapcase. However, Mr. Pratchett has explicitly denied this in interviews, instead attributing the dissimilarity to his own inexperience as a writer when he produced *The Colour of Magic*.

One thing about the high levels of magic thrown around in *Sourcery* is that it gives Mr. Pratchett a chance to write lots of descriptions of what amount to special effects—lights and sparks and colors splashing about, things melting, and so on. There's quite a bit of this in the earlier books, and it occurs to me to wonder whether it might have something to do with his old job with the Central Electricity Generating Board; he probably spent some time imagining what could go wrong with power plants, and adapted it into his accounts of magic running loose. Once he left that job to write fiction full-time the descriptions became less common, though of course that might simply have been because he'd been there, done that, and felt no need to further repeat himself.

At the end of *Sourcery*, despite the titanic magicks tossed about, everything is restored to what it should be, or at any rate what it generally was, and Coin is gone—but so is Rincewind, who we last see trapped in the Dungeon Dimensions, pursued by Things.

Naturally, he'll be back in *Eric* (see Chapter 11), but that's not for three books yet. First it's back to Lancre....

7A

Wyrd Sisters (1988)

READERS WERE INTRODUCED to Granny Weatherwax in *Equal Rites*; in *Wyrd Sisters* we are privileged to meet the other two members of her newly formed coven, Nanny Ogg and Magrat Garlick.

And in many ways, this is the novel where everything really comes together. The plot is intricate but entirely sensible, insofar as anything on the Discworld is sensible. The witches are in fine form. The other characters, from King Verence down to our Shawn, are all people, rather than mere parodies. Death and the Librarian put in their customary appearances in grand style. The Patrician, appearing only in a footnote, finally displays the cunning and efficiency that will be his hallmark hereafter. Leonard of Quirm is mentioned for the first time. Nanny Ogg's fearsome cat Greebo appears, along with the infamous song, "The Hedgehog Can Never Be Buggered At All." And there are no obvious inconsistencies with any of what's gone before.

The effects of the still-unnamed narrativium are at the heart of everything, and a second important phenomenon that I call "reality leakage"[75] is apparent.

The story begins with Lancre's King Verence being assassinated by Duke Felmet and his vicious wife. A resemblance to *Macbeth* is obvious and intentional, though the story takes its own direction right from the start. A band of traveling players is involved; when Felmet wants to strengthen his position as king, he hires them to write and perform a

---

[75] Because I like the sound of it. It's not Mr. Pratchett's preferred term, by any means.

play about how a heroic duke supplants a bad king, only to have three evil witches interfere. The troupe's playwright is a dwarf[76] by the name of Hwel.

Narrativium is evident in the way Hwel's play refuses to behave itself; it wants the story to be told *properly*, which is to say, more or less as the *Macbeth* Shakespeare wrote. The story knows what it ought to be.

And reality leakage—well, it seems that in addition to writing plays suspiciously like Shakespeare's, Hwel has these dreams that are unmistakably familiar material from the Marx Brothers, Laurel and Hardy, and Chaplin's Little Tramp, even if he can't quite capture the humor in a way the other players appreciate. He also uses bits of story that the discerning reader will recognize as originating in Gaston Leroux's *Phantom of the Opera*, Oscar Wilde's *The Importance of Being Earnest*, and the like.

We already knew, from Rincewind's brief venture into an alien plane[77] in *The Colour of Magic*, that it was possible for things to move between our world and the Disc. We saw in the account of the Seriph of Al Khali in *Sourcery* that there were some inexplicable similarities in certain stories and poems. Now, in *Wyrd Sisters*, it's made explicit that some residents of the Discworld have somehow tuned in to our reality. They see and hear it in their dreams. The similarities are not mere coincidence, but reality leakage between the two worlds.

This will be developed much further in later novels, but this is where it's solidly established.

There are other hints of things to come, as well. Hwel mentions a human raised among dwarfs—this would presumably be Carrot Ironfoundersson, whom we'll meet in *Guards! Guards!* There is discussion of the nature of kings, which will also be reflected in Carrot's eventual adventures.

Some of Mr. Pratchett's strengths really begin to emerge here. In previous novels, his attempts at the frightening have mostly taken the form of long falls, sharp blades, wild magic, and tentacular horrors such as the Things from the Dungeon Dimensions, none of which are actually scary to the typical reader. Oh, he may have conjured a few chills in *Mort*, but after all, that was all about Death. In *Wyrd Sisters*, on the other

[76] This is the first time a dwarf has appeared in the series, or even been mentioned. Hwel is not really the helmeted, bearded, axe-wielding stereotype we'll see so much later on (mostly in the Watch series). He does mention that he's not at all a typical dwarf.

[77] Last time, I hope.

hand, he manages a couple of genuinely creepy scenes, notably the final fate of the Duchess.

The depth of characterization also takes a quantum leap here. We *care* about these people. Granny Weatherwax and Nanny Ogg and company are wonderful creations. We met Granny before, in *Equal Rites*, but she's much more strongly realized here.

This jump in quality may be why *Wyrd Sisters* was the first of the novels to make the transition to the screen, in six animated half-hour episodes that aired on Britain's Channel 4 in 1996. It was a fairly faithful adaptation, and generally enjoyable, if not brilliant. The cartoon versions of Granny and Nanny don't quite live up to their ancestral text, but I quite liked the animated Magrat. The series was released on DVD, but is no longer widely available.

Alas, we won't see the witches on the page again until *Witches Abroad*, six(!) novels later. You can skip to Chapter 14 for that. The next one chronologically instead begins what I call the "Gods and Philosophers" series. . . .

9

Pyramids (1989)

THERE ARE THOSE WHO SAY that some Discworld books are one-shots, singletons, stand-alones, not part of any of the several sub-series. They will name *Pyramids* and *Small Gods* and *The Truth* as examples.

Naaah.

All of these alleged singletons fall into two categories, so far as I can see—they deal with either religion and philosophy (as in *Pyramids* and *Small Gods*) or with the effects of some new technology or other significant sociological change on Ankh-Morpork (as in *The Truth*). I've therefore labeled them as two series: "Gods and Philosophers," and "Ankh-Morpork: Beyond the Century of the Fruitbat."

The former series is never set primarily in Ankh-Morpork, while the latter is almost entirely in Ankh-Morpork, and on those occasions when the city isn't the actual setting (as in *Moving Pictures*), most of the characters are natives of Ankh-Morpork.

That's reasonable enough; the people of Ankh-Morpork aren't especially interested in religion and philosophy, but they're *very* interested in new technologies that might make them some money.

Pyramids is unrelated to anything that went before, except that it's set on the Discworld—we've seen that happen before, with *Equal Rites*, when a new series was starting. Being one of the "Gods and Philosophers" series, it's mostly set well away from Ankh-Morpork—but not entirely.

One oddity of *Pyramids*, relative to other Discworld novels, is that it's divided into four "books"—not chapters as such, but "The Book of

Going Forth," "The Book of the Dead," "The Book of the New Son,"[78] and "The Book of 101 Things a Boy Can Do."[79] These aren't independent stories making up a larger narrative, like the four sections of *The Colour of Magic*, but just very long chapters.

Our protagonist, Teppic (or Pteppic, or Teppicymon XXVIII), is the son of the god-king of the ancient river kingdom Djelibeybi.[80] When we first meet him, however, Teppic is a student in the Guild of Assassins in Ankh-Morpork, preparing for his final exam.

Gods and Philosophers: The Series

These stories are about the relationships of humans, their gods, and the universe at large, and don't fit into any of the other series:

Pyramids .... Chapter 9
Small Gods .... Chapter 15
The Last Hero .... Chapter 33

It could be argued that *The Thief of Time* (Chapter 32) and "Death and What Comes Next" (Chapter 37) should be included as well, but I classified them as part of the Death series instead. Maybe the two series are merging.

For a discussion of the series as a whole, see Chapter 55.

The scenes at the Assassins' Guild, which take up much of that first book, "The Book of Going Forth," don't really have all that terribly much to do with the main plot, but they do give Mr. Pratchett a chance to shamelessly parody *Tom Brown's School Days*. Teppic's chum Arthur is a character swiped directly from *Tom Brown*, save that where the original was a devout Christian, the Discworld version is a devotee of the

[78] The names of the first two books refer to actual ancient Egyptian texts, but this third appears to be a reference to Gene Wolfe's four-volume "Book of the New Sun."

[79] Do people still buy those books of things that are supposed to keep their kids busy without involving either parental supervision or calls from the police? I wouldn't think they're needed much in these days of video games and cable TV. We acquired a couple when my own children were young, such as *838 Ways to Amuse a Child*, but they've mostly sat unread on a shelf while my daughter found new and interesting ways to restrain My Little Pony with drapery cords and a few bits of string, and my son discovered just how much damage you can do to expensive furniture with nothing but a golf tee.

[80] I assume most of you can't have missed the pun, but some of our American readers may be unaware that Jelly Babies are a popular English candy, something like Gummi Bears, and despite the similar names almost completely unlike jelly beans.

Great Orm,[81] a rather less kindly deity than the Christian one. It makes the bedtime prayer scene rather more entertaining than the one in *Tom Brown*.

This modern education is how Teppic manages to grow up with ideas and attitudes that are rather inappropriate for a pharaoh.

No, I don't mean a willingness to dispose of political obstacles with blades or poison; that's perfectly normal for monarchs in most circumstances, though I admit it doesn't seem the sort of thing one might expect of most current European royalty. I mean an unwillingness to throw himself wholeheartedly into a life of meaningless ritual.

Still, when his father dies, Teppic returns to Djelibeybi to take up the role of god-king, and rather carelessly agrees to entomb his paternal predecessor in the largest pyramid ever built.

The thing is, the Discworld has a very intense magical field, as has been noted many times by now, and that means that pyramids on the Disc really *do* focus cosmic energy, just as some New Age believers claim they do here. Sharpening razor blades is nothing; they do *far* more than that.

Most of Djelibeybi's pyramids harmlessly flare off their excess energy every night, rather like oil refineries flaring off natural gas that's not worth the trouble of recovering, but the big new one Teppic has inadvertently commissioned—well, things don't go quite as planned in that regard.

Djelibeybi, as should have been bloody obvious by now, is a parody of ancient Egypt, complete with sacred crocodiles, animal-headed gods, pyramids, mummification, cat worship, god-kings, and the like. The neighboring land of Ephebe, which Teppic will visit, is a parody of Golden Age Greece, well-stocked with philosophers and replete with references to the Discworld version of the Trojan War—or rather, not so much a parody of the actual ancient Athens as of the popular misconceptions thereof.

Yes, it's definitely parody, and arguably a parody of fantasy, but it's not the sort of "fantasy" one finds shelved with the science fiction at your local bookstore; instead it's the fantasy versions of actual history that's being mocked, what one might call the Hollywood versions of Egypt and Greece—or perhaps the schoolboy version.

And the story winds its way through commentary on tradition, re-

[81] Not Om; that's a different god we'll meet later.

ligion, politics, philosophy, business, family, and camels, among other things, before finally reaching a satisfactory conclusion.

There's a great deal of entertaining nonsense about time and energy, which are grotesquely distorted by the pyramids; once again, I have a suspicion that Mr. Pratchett's work in the power industry contributed something to the descriptions.

All in all, though, this really doesn't do much to change the series as a whole. We don't see the major characters again hereafter, nor do any of the regular Discworld cast appear (except Death, of course). While Ephebe will turn up again, Djelibeybi will never again get more than a brief mention. *Pyramids* is a lovely novel, but it doesn't really *connect* much of anywhere.

Teppic does not return in any later stories—or at any rate, he hasn't reappeared yet—but we see more of gods and philosophers six books later, in *Small Gods*—see Chapter 15. The next to be written, though, launched yet another series, one that's probably the most successful of the bunch. . . .

10

Guards! Guards! (1989)

MANY PEOPLE (which in this case means, as it so often does, "people I agree with, even if it's really just me and everyone else thinks I'm a loon") consider the stories of Ankh-Morpork's City Watch to be the best, on average, of the various Discworld series, and *Guards! Guards!* starts the series off well. Our tale opens (after a brief introductory note about dragons)[82] with Captain Samuel Vimes lying drunk in a gutter, a practice he's clearly well-accustomed to.

Vimes, we learn, is the commanding officer of the Night Watch, which consists of himself, Sergeant Colon, and Corporal Nobby Nobbs, and until very recently included someone named Gaskin, whose death is the excuse for Vimes's latest round of inebriation. These fine—no, skip the adjective—these men are responsible for keeping the peace in Ankh-Morpork.

The book is dedicated to all those faceless guards and watchmen in countless fantasy novels whose basic function is to die pointlessly; this is apparently exactly the sort of watchmen the people of Ankh-Morpork want. This is not what Vimes and company want to *be*, however.

I'll have more to say about that when I discuss the series as a whole in Chapter 56.

At any rate, a new Watchman by the name of Carrot[83] arrives fairly

---

[82] Back in *The Colour of Magic*, Hrun said that large dragons were extinct. This is where we learn that they aren't dead, they just aren't on the Disc anymore—a situation that may not be permanent.

[83] Referred to obliquely in *Wyrd Sisters*, as I mentioned earlier. If you skipped that chapter, shame on you. You don't even have the excuse that you're following a particular sub-series, since *Guards! Guards!* is the first volume in the Watch series.

quickly after Gaskin's death. These four—Vimes, Colon, Nobby, and Carrot—will remain at the heart of the cast in all the subsequent Watch stories.One might wonder how a staff of four can hope to patrol a city the size of Ankh-Morpork, which is described in this book as having a population of about a million.

Well, obviously, they can't. No one expects them to. It's been well established in previous volumes that law enforcement in Ankh-Morpork is largely the responsibility of the Thieves' Guild, which has an elaborate system of quotas and receipts, and which vigorously (often fatally) discourages freelancers. Once the Patrician had this system in place, the traditional City Watch was allowed to wither away to almost nothing.

A feeling that this system, however effective it may be, just isn't *right* is a major reason Captain Vimes is so familiar with finding himself drunk in the gutter.

The Watch: The Series

Samuel Vimes and the Ankh-Morpork City Watch are featured in these stories:

Where's My Cow? is a spin-off from *Thud!*, but isn't a Watch story so much as a gimmick.

At any rate, someone has devised a scheme to take over the city government by conjuring up a dragon, having a handsome young man with a shiny sword dispatch it, and then declaring this fellow to be the rightful heir to the ancient kings of Ankh-Morpork. The mastermind would then become the power behind the throne, guiding the malleable youth.

The plot hits a few snags, however. One is that the Night Watch, under the direction of Vimes, insists on actually investigating what's going on and treating it as a crime. Another is that the dragon, once conjured, turns out to have some ideas of its own.

This idea of acting out a classic story everyone knows, and turning it to one's own ends, is the Discworld's excess of narrativium at work again. The story of the rightful heir returning to save the city from a dragon is so very obviously how things *should* play out that it takes someone exceptional like Vimes to resist its appeal. The story *wants* to happen. Everyone expects it to, and knows how it should go.

And then there's the power of cliché. At one point in the plot, some of our heroes know they're attempting something very unlikely, and they make a concerted effort to make it even *less* likely, because as everyone knows, if it's a million-to-one chance, then it's just *got* to work, because it always does in the stories.

If it's only 999,943 to one, though, it just isn't gonna happen.

Because this is the Discworld, some of this works. Million-to-one shots do come in. There really is a rightful heir to the ancient kings.

But because Mr. Pratchett is a very clever man, things never work out in the obvious fashion. The heir does not slay the dragon; in fact, the dragon isn't slain at all, really. It's dealt with, but not in any of the traditional ways.

What really makes the whole story work, though, is the character of Vimes. This is a man full of rage and despair who sees all too well the sordid realities of his situation, but who refuses to give up. He *knows* he's attempting the impossible, that nobody really wants him to succeed, that even if he *does* succeed it won't really help, but he refuses to quit, because to do so would be untrue to who and what he is.

He is, as we are told, someone who had the misfortune of being born knurd.

"Knurd" is drunk spelled backward, and it's the opposite of drunk. Sobriety is merely the absence of drunkenness; knurd is its *opposite*. Where alcohol can provide a warm glow and pleasant haze that obscures life's little difficulties, being knurd throws them into sharp focus.

Samuel Vimes was born knurd, and needs two drinks just to get to sober.

This has not made for a pleasant life. Commanding the Watch in a city that doesn't want a Watch and only has one because no one has gotten around to eliminating it yet doesn't help. And really *caring* about his job and his city makes it all even worse.

Everyone knows that a hero needs problems to overcome, but Vimes has more than his share.

Fortunately he has the brains and the sheer tenacity to handle most of them. Mere dragons and Patricians do not intimidate him.

Lady Sybil Ramkin does, but that's rather different.

There are some things that crop up in this story that aren't entirely consistent with what's gone before or what's to come. For example, Vimes initially doesn't even remember that Ankh-Morpork ever *had* a king, while in later books he's well aware that one of his own ancestors killed the last of those kings.

Just how long ago the last king reigned also seems to be a variable.

It is established in *Guards! Guards!*, though, that there *was* a king, and there *is* a rightful heir, and that that heir is a handsome and upright young man who was raised as a dwarf, but who has a crown-shaped birthmark, an ancient sword, and the other appropriate indicators of his status.

Even his name is a tremendously obscure indication. After all, why would a couple of respectable dwarfs name their child "Carrot"? Why did Mr. Pratchett name his *character* Carrot? Apparently even he found it unlikely, as it emerges many years later, in *Thud!*, that Carrot's dwarfish name actually translates not as Carrot, but as "Head Banger."

So why is he called Carrot?

Yes, fine, he's ginger-haired, narrow-hipped, and broad-shouldered, and therefore vaguely carrot-shaped, but is that all?

Well, there's this comic opera first performed in 1872, composed by Jacques Offenbach, called *Le Roi Carotte*—"King Carrot." The title role calls for a comic tenor, and is a carrot who becomes a human being and deposes a tyrant.

The resemblance surely isn't a coincidence.

As for other developments, the Librarian appears in *Guards! Guards!*, of course, and is temporarily deputized into the Watch, but even he isn't completely consistent with other books. While he's always objected violently (and with good reason) to being called a monkey, his reaction here is presented as involuntary and uncontrollable, when elsewhere it's been presented as a natural reaction to an unforgivable display of rude stupidity.

On the other hand, this is also where we see the first real explanation of L-space, which became a basic recurring concept in later volumes. L-space is where libraries and the better sort of bookshop exist, you see. They aren't in normal space at all, and they all interconnect.

The explanation is simple. Books represent knowledge. Knowledge is power. Power is energy. Energy, as Einstein told us, equals matter. Matter has mass. Mass warps space.

Therefore, anywhere enough books are gathered together, space is warped, and a connection to L-space forms. A skilled librarian—and the Librarian is *very* skilled—can navigate through L-space from any one library to any other, anywhere in time or space. This will prove very useful in later books.

Guards! Guards! is where a great many things really start to fall together. The whole idea of monarchy was addressed in *Wyrd Sisters*, but here it is again, seen from rather a different angle. The Patrician's methods, heretofore only mentioned in passing, are examined in more detail, though Lord Vetinari's personality has still not reached its final forbidding form. Cut-Me-Own-Throat Dibbler is introduced, as is the troll Detritus. The magical power of books is refined into the concept of L-space.

Certain details from earlier books reappear in new forms. "Inn-sewer-ants," introduced by Twoflower back in *The Colour of Magic*, is back, but in the form of protection money paid to the Thieves' Guild.

We get a look at dwarf society, and that's a bit different. Up until now, the only dwarf who had any time on stage was Hwel, in *Wyrd Sisters*, and the dwarfs in *Guards! Guards!* aren't much like him—but he did say that he wasn't much like his father, or he'd have been a hundred feet underground digging rocks, so it's pretty clear Hwel wasn't a typical dwarf.

But back in *Equal Rites*, we encountered the gypsy-like Zoons, who had trouble with the concept of lying; the Zoons are never seen again, and their literal-minded honesty has now been transferred to the dwarfs.

We won't see the Watch featured again until *Men at Arms*, seven volumes later, as described in Chapter 19; first it's back to tie up some loose ends regarding Rincewind.

11

Eric (1990)

THE ACTUAL TITLE IS *~~FAUST~~ ERIC*. This was originally an illustrated volume, with nifty pictures by Josh Kirby, and is a good deal shorter than the average Discworld novel—in fact, it was originally labeled a Discworld *story*, rather than the usual "a novel of Discworld."

Unlike all the other short stories and illustrated volumes, though, it's an essential part of the series, because this is where we learn how Rincewind escaped from the Dungeon Dimensions, where we left him at the end of *Sourcery*—he was summoned by an amateur demonologist named Eric Thursley.

Eric wasn't *trying* for Rincewind; he wanted a proper demon who would grant him three wishes. He got Rincewind instead.

And to Rincewind's own astonishment, Eric gets his three wishes—mastery of the kingdoms of the world, to meet the most beautiful woman who has ever lived, and to live forever.

(If these sound familiar, well, there's a reason the title has Faust's name crossed out and Eric's substituted.)

Naturally, they didn't work out as expected. They never do, do they? One wonders why anyone tries the whole "three wishes" thing; really, why not try for, oh, *five* wishes? Maybe that would turn out more pleasantly. Three, though, that's always a disaster, and especially getting them from a demon. It's just *asking* for it—to borrow Mr. Pratchett's evocative phrase, it's like standing on a hilltop in a thunderstorm wearing wet copper armor and shouting, "All gods are bastards!"

I mean, all the stories warn you that three wishes will turn out badly, and the Disc *runs* on stories.

As the author points out, if summoning demons was a way to get power, wizards would do it. They don't. This should serve as a warning.

But Eric refuses to be warned, and he and Rincewind (and Eric's parrot) get swept off to the Tezuman Empire, where Eric is indeed recognized as the master of the kingdoms of the world. Had Sir James Frazer's *The Golden Bough* been published in Ankh-Morpork, Eric might have seen the flaw in this particular prize.

When they manage to escape that particular nasty fate, it's off to the ancient war between Tsort and Ephebe that was described in *Pyramids*, the one that's the Discworld equivalent of the Trojan War.[84] Here Eric does indeed meet the woman generally acknowledged to be the most beautiful who has ever lived on the Disc. He failed to specify meeting her while she was still beautiful, however. Or meeting her not in the middle of a bloody great war.

After that it's off to the dawn of time—after all, if you're going to live forever, you have to start at the beginning. If you just started where you were and lived to the end of time, you'd only live for *half* of forever. Eric and Rincewind get to watch the Creator create the Discworld, and find it somewhat less awe-inspiring than one might have hoped—an egg and cress sandwich is involved, and it doesn't even have mayonnaise.

Then they get to sit there and wait for life to evolve.

This is not really something for which either of them can work up much enthusiasm, and they therefore arrange to go elsewhere, courtesy of Eric's skill at demonology. Unfortunately, there's only one place *that* can take them. They go to Hell.

Hell, as it happens, has been looking for them. Astfgl, King of the Demons,[85] was not at all pleased to have Rincewind appear instead of a demon when Eric finally got his summoning to work, and has been pursuing the pair as they collect on Eric's wishes.

Still, they escape in the end, though where to isn't revealed.

I include *Eric* in the Rincewind series because, well, it's about Rincewind. But it's atypical in that almost none of it is set at Unseen University, Rincewind doesn't really appear in the bit that is, and no other

---

[84] More of that reality leakage stuff here, I suppose—at any rate, the Tsortean War very closely resembles the Trojan War as described by Homer, though with the polish knocked off in the usual Pratchett manner.

[85] Colin Smythe, Mr. Pratchett's agent, suggests that "Astfgl" may be pronounced as a very hasty "That's difficult." He has not, however, confirmed with the author that this was intentional; it's merely his personal theory, albeit an appealing one.

wizards really have much to do with the plot. We do get to meet yet another Archchancellor, Ezrolith Churn, who was given the job because it had finally registered on the other senior wizards that, of late, the life expectancy of Archchancellors had really gotten distressingly low. That tended to reduce the job's appeal significantly, since a wizard doesn't become competitive for the post without a very good instinct for survival.

Took them long enough to notice.

I suppose I ought to mention that the Luggage appears, loyally (if angrily) following its master through time, space, and other, less usual dimensions.

At any rate, *Eric* is a short, lightweight book, doing very little to advance the series as a whole other than extracting Rincewind from the dire situation in which he was left at the end of *Sourcery*. It does serve to reduce Rincewind's depth as a character. . . .

That's really rather perverse, you know, but it's true. Generally, the more we see of a character, the more we learn about him, and the more depth and solidity he acquires. Rincewind, however, gets *simpler* as the series progresses. In his earlier appearances he was cowardly and lazy, sometimes clever, but also greedy, and with an odd streak of heroism that cropped up now and then. In *Eric* and his subsequent appearances, though, he's simply cowardly and lazy, with moments of cleverness—his greed has vanished, and the streak of heroism has withered away. Perhaps his stay in the Dungeon Dimensions was responsible, but it makes him a less interesting character, and I'm not the only reader to feel that the Rincewind series is the weakest of the lot.

At a bookstore signing for *Wintersmith*, in October 2006, a reader asked Mr. Pratchett whether we would be seeing more of Rincewind. His answer was that we probably would not, at least not any time soon, because Rincewind is not a terribly interesting character—he is, Mr. Pratchett said, primarily an observer, rather than someone who *does* things.

While this is fairly accurate as far as his appearances in *Eric* and all subsequent stories are concerned, prior to this it wasn't really the case. The Rincewind we saw in *The Colour of Magic* and *The Light Fantastic* wasn't so much an observer as a sidekick—he didn't *just* observe things, he also sometimes made them happen. He tried to talk sense to heroes, and sometimes pulled them out of bad situations.

From *Eric* on, though, he really doesn't do that any more. He's just along for the ride.

Fortunately, Mr. Pratchett does not focus on Rincewind all that often; in fact, we won't see him featured again until *Interesting Times*, nine full volumes later, as seen in Chapter 21. The next book in the series instead begins the series I've named "Ankh-Morpork: Beyond the Century of the Fruitbat," concerned with the effects of new technologies, new magics, and other social changes on the people of the Disc's oldest, largest, and most foul-smelling city.

12

Moving Pictures (1990)

IT WAS ESTABLISHED back in *Equal Rites* that in the Discworld universe, ideas are not just the immaterial concepts we're familiar with; they have actual physical existence. In that earlier volume they were described as subatomic particles sleeting through space, looking for a receptive mind.

In *Wyrd Sisters*, we saw various ideas, many of them cinematic, registering with poor Hwel, who tried to make sense of movies of the likes of Laurel and Hardy in the context of Discworld. They made his life difficult at times, but no worse.

In *Moving Pictures*, certain ideas are a little larger and more aggressive than that. One idea in particular has been carefully imprisoned and guarded by a succession of priests in a place named Holy Wood. Alas, the last priest dies, and the idea escapes and reaches Ankh-Morpork.

As the title makes obvious, the idea is movies, of course—not just a few images of the sort Hwel dreamed, but the entirety of the motion picture industry.

In response to this unleashed idea, The Alchemists' Guild develops a method of transferring images to film, and then projecting them. An alchemist named Silverfish[86] sets out for Holy Wood to make movies, as

[86] I assume this is a reference to Samuel Goldfish, who co-founded the companies that eventually became Paramount Pictures, MGM, and the Samuel Goldwyn Studios. The Goldwyn Company (which after his departure merged with Mayer to become Goldwyn-Mayer, and then with Metro to become Metro-Goldwyn-Mayer or MGM) took its name from Goldfish and his two partners, the Selwyn brothers, and Goldfish liked the name "Goldwyn" so much that he legally changed his own name to match the company.

Note that it clearly wasn't difficult to choose "Goldwyn" as the more commercially viable combination of those two names. "Selfish" just wasn't going to cut it.

the light's better there—or at least, that's the excuse he tells himself.[87] Actually, it's the Things under Holy Wood Hill luring him.

A great many people are lured to Holy Wood, from Ankh-Morpork and elsewhere, including Victor Tugelbend, a student at Unseen University, who serves as our primary viewpoint character and the eventual hero. He and his co-star, Theda Withel,[88] who calls herself Ginger, find themselves caught up in the magic of the movies—which is not at all the same sort of magic Victor studied at Unseen University, but which is potent nonetheless—and they become the Disc's first movie stars.

Ankh-Morpork: Beyond the Century of the Fruitbat

Although some people just consider these to be one-shots, I see them as a series concerned with how the people of Ankh-Morpork and their ruler, Patrician Havelock Vetinari, are dealing with the march of progress:

Moving Pictures .... Chapter 12
"Troll Bridge" .... Chapter 16
The Truth .... Chapter 31
Going Postal .... Chapter 41
Making Money .... Chapter 46

Two important notes: "Troll Bridge" isn't set in Ankh-Morpork and has no specific sociological innovations in it, but I include it here simply because it's on the same general theme of dealing with changing times, and Cohen the Barbarian hasn't got his own series.

Also, Moist von Lipwig, protagonist of *Going Postal*, returns in *Making Money*, and will probably be reappearing again in the future, so either he's a separate series, or he's taking over this series. I say he's taking over this series.

For a consideration of the series as a whole, see Chapter 57.

---

[87] In our own world, the American movie industry started on Long Island, in New York, but moved fairly quickly to southern California because the sunlight was more reliable there. New York has far fewer sunny days than Los Angeles even now, and a hundred years ago L.A. had much less smog.

[88] Whether she's related to one-eyed Withel, a fellow described in *The Colour of Magic* as the second-greatest thief in Ankh-Morpork, who Rincewind lays out cold by punching him while holding a roll of solid gold coins, is never mentioned. The name Theda, of course, is a reference to Theda Bara, the silent film star for whom the term "vamp" was first invented. "Theda" was short for "Theodosia," her real name; it was pure coincidence that it's an anagram of "death."

Among those who have been lured from Ankh-Morpork by the movies is our old friend Cut-Me-Own-Throat Dibbler, sausage-seller extraordinaire, last seen in *Guards! Guards!* He's fallen under Holy Wood's spell more completely than anyone else, and usurps control of Century of the Fruitbat Pictures from poor Silverfish.

And there's Gaspode the Wonder Dog. Holy Wood has given him the power of speech—but he's still an ugly little mutt no one can take seriously; only Victor will listen to him. (Gaspode will be back in later books. Victor, perversely, won't.)

It develops that the real danger here isn't anything inherent in the concept of motion pictures as such; rather, it's that because reality is thin on Discworld to begin with, something that blurs the line between reality and illusion the way movies do can weaken reality to the point that our old friends the Things from the Dungeon Dimensions can use it to cross over from their normal state of nonexistence into Discworld's reality.

They are, of course, stopped, by Victor and Ginger and Gaspode and the Librarian, before they do very much damage.

The idea that Discworld's a little short on reality—"The Discworld is as unreal as it is possible to be while still being just real enough to exist"—is introduced right on the first page, but it's not obvious until much later that this actually *means* anything, and isn't just a throwaway bit. Mr. Pratchett's very good at that, really—telling you something that doesn't look important but turns out to be at the heart of the whole story.

The first two Discworld novels were parodies of fantasy novels; the next several drifted away from parody and into satire. Even when *Guards! Guards!* built its plot around fantasy clichés such as dragons, long-lost royal heirs, and useless guards, it really wasn't so much mocking fantasy novels as using their trappings to satirize the real world. Lady Sybil Ramkin, for example, is a stereotype, but not one from fantasy novels; instead she's a stereotype from England's imperial past.

Moving Pictures is a swing back toward parody—but it's not fantasy novels being parodied, it's Hollywood. Slapped-together scripts, movie stars who were nobody a few days ago, mad producers, a boom town awash in money—it's all there, but translated into Discworld terms.

One thing that strikes me as a bit off, symbolically, is using the figure of an Oscar as the guardian keeping the monsters of Holy Wood in check. It would be *nice* if the Oscars played some part in keeping the worst excesses of Hollywood in check, but it sure doesn't look to me as if that's anything remotely like the real-world situation.

At any rate, the plot here is not especially complicated or coherent; it exists largely as an excuse to incorporate lots of mockery of Hollywood. This novel is jammed full of parodies and punning references—and not all of them Hollywood-related, either. There's a little spoof on the famous opening line of H.G. Wells's *War of the Worlds* thrown in at one point, for example. Reality leakage runs amok, and a great deal of the humor comes from recognizing just which real-world thing is being referenced, whether it's a one-line reference to *The Bride of Frankenstein* or an extended riff on *Blown Away*, the Discworld version of *Gone with the Wind*. This climaxes with an extra-dimensional Thing climbing the Tower of Art at Unseen University while carrying the Librarian—hardly a knee-slapper if looked at on its own terms, but when you realize that the Thing has taken on a larger-than-life version of Ginger's appearance from the movies, so that what you have is a fifty-foot woman climbing the world's tallest building while clutching a screaming ape in one hand....

There's a lot of that sort of thing. Frankly, while it's amusing, it's not what I prefer to see at the heart of a Discworld story. I'd rather see Mr. Pratchett focusing on humanity's foibles rather than demonstrating his cleverness with puns and parodies.

Fortunately, there are good character moments, as well. Dibbler's creative frenzies and Gaspode's observations on canine nature add a good bit to the scenes in Holy Wood. Detritus the troll's romantic efforts have their charm, as well.

Perhaps the best material, though, is what's happening to the wizards of Unseen University. After nine volumes of a constantly shifting cast, with never the same Archchancellor twice, we are now presented with what will hereinafter be the permanent faculty—Mustrum Ridcully as Archchancellor, Windle Poons as the oldest member,[89] and several wizards known only by their titles: the Bursar, the Lecturer in Recent Runes, the Senior Wrangler, and so on.

One other character is introduced in passing who will be recurring in later stories set at the University: Ponder Stibbons. In *Moving Pictures*, he graduates with his degree in wizardry through a fortunate turn of events involving his friend Victor's absence from their final exam; he'll be back as a graduate student.

---

[89] Okay, Poons is not really *permanent*.

And why, then, you might ask, do I not consider this a part of the series about the wizards of Unseen University, when they appear and play a significant role, and the hero is a student at the University?

Because, for one thing, Rincewind is never mentioned.

For another, there are brief appearances by Sergeant Colon and Corporal Nobbs of the Watch, by the Patrician, by Death, and so on, but none of them are what the story's *about*, and neither are the wizards. They're just a plot element. What the story is *about* is the line between illusion and reality, the mad world of movie-making, and Victor, Ginger, and Gaspode.

It's about a new idea upsetting the status quo (one can't really call anything so disorganized and bloody-minded "the peace") of Ankh-Morpork, a theme that Mr. Pratchett will return to again in half a dozen volumes, as described in Chapter 20.

The next volume, though, returns to the series about Death.

13

Reaper Man (1991)

THIS IS ONE OF THE STRANGEST of all the Discworld stories, right from the first sentence: "The Morris dance is common to all inhabited worlds in the multiverse." That sentence is a reminder of how thoroughly English Mr. Pratchett is, and must leave a great many American readers scratching their heads and wondering what on Earth a Morris dance is.[90]

We proceed from an explanation of how the only place that the

[90] You probably think I'm going to tell you, which makes it very tempting not to, to tell you to go look it up, but I am going to be a kind and generous soul and resist that temptation.

The Morris dance is an English folk dance with a lot of complicated traditions and garbled history behind it, obscuring its actual origins. Various English villages have their own versions, each with its own traditional tune, costume, steps, and schedule, but most commonly it takes the form of several men (always men until the 1970s, anyway, when women first began to participate) dancing in two lines facing each other, outdoors in the spring. In most villages the dancers wear white, with bells strapped to their legs and beribboned hats on their heads and various belts and other trappings, and wave either sticks or large white handkerchiefs about. Additional mummery characters such as fools, hobby-horses, and half-men-half-women (called "the Betty") may be involved—especially a Fool, complete with a pig's bladder on a stick, which he uses to whack dancers who he thinks are slacking off.

The Morris dance is often assumed to be an ancient fertility ritual, and treated as such, but its actual history is a hopeless tangle of myths, misunderstandings, and outright lies, overlaid with Victorian nonsense. Don't believe anything anyone (including me) tells you about its origins.

The name apparently comes from an eighteenth-century belief that the dance is Moorish in origin. It almost certainly isn't.

There are entire books about Morris dancing, and deservedly so, as it's an interesting phenomenon. In England it's just something everyone knows about, and the English are often startled to discover that nobody else has any such custom—unlike many British traditions, it failed to take root in the colonies, possibly because of the distaste of many American religions for any form of dancing whatsoever.

Of course, it may be that Morris dancing is one of the *reasons* that Southern Baptists and the like don't approve of dancing, as it has a definite pagan flavor to it.

At any rate, there are American Morris dancers now, just as there are American Zen Buddhists and American dashiki-makers, but they tend to be an urban phenomenon and not much like their English forebears.

It's actually a great deal of fun for both participants and spectators, though. It's rather too bad it isn't more widespread here on the western side of the Atlantic.

Morris[91] is danced properly is a village in the Ramtops to the first appearance of the celestial Auditors of Reality, and the vast, cosmic (and cosmically bored) being Azrael, the ultimate keeper of time and death.

The Auditors will be back; Azrael only appears in this one novel. I sometimes find it disconcerting how Mr. Pratchett will introduce a big chunk of cosmology, or a whole family of characters, and then only re-use the bits he finds amusing, without their original context.

At any rate, the Auditors like the universe to be orderly and bland, and have decided that Death—the being that represents death on the Disc, our old friend from lo these eleven novels to date—has become excessively eccentric and must be retired in favor of a new, less individual anthropomorphic personification.

Death is not happy with this decision, but there is no appeal. He is removed from his role.

Remember Windle Poons, the oldest member of the faculty of Unseen University?

Well, perhaps you don't, if you're reading this by following one series at a time and you're only looking at the books about Death at this point, but if you've been reading straight through, you really ought to have noticed the mention of him in the discussion of *Moving Pictures*. If you want to flip back and read it, you can, though you won't find it very interesting, as all I said was that he's the oldest member of the faculty and a part of the permanent cast of characters at the University.

I lied about one part of that, though. He's not exactly permanent. After all, he's a hundred and thirty years old, and in *Reaper Man*, he does exactly what you would expect of someone that age—he dies.

Unfortunately, he does so during the period between the forced retirement of the old Death and the arrival of his replacement. No scythe-wielding being appears to usher his spirit into the next world; instead he finds himself hanging around the University, and so he reinhabits his remains, becoming a zombie.

This turns out in many ways to not be what he expected, and much of the plot follows his adventures among the undead. It seems that Death's absence does not mean that nothing dies, it only means that the spirits of the dead do not depart, and the Discworld begins to experience a

[91] And also the *other* dance, the opposite of the Morris, which will turn up again much later, in *Wintersmith*.

serious excess of life-force. Ghosts start complaining of crowding; poltergeist activity reaches heretofore unheard-of levels.

So far, that all makes a certain amount of sense, and is entirely in keeping with what we know of the Discworld, but midway through the book, the story takes a bizarre left turn with the discovery that this excess life-force has triggered the breeding cycle of something that initially appears to be cities, but then turns out to be instead a parasite that preys on cities.[92]

While that's happening, the retired Death has taken up an ordinary life as a farmhand named Bill Door—a good man with a scythe, our Bill Door.

So we have two separate but related plots—the story of undead Windle Poons dealing with his new existence and defending Ankh-Morpork and Unseen University from a ferocious predator, and the story of Bill Door learning about life, death, and humanity.

It's traditional in such cases for the two plots to eventually merge, but these two don't, really. They remain distinct, to the point of being set in different typefaces. Ah, well; it happens.

At any rate, Bill Door finds his replacement unsatisfactory and takes his old job back, while Poons and company defeat the predatory hive creature, and the plots do sort of merge, after a fashion, when the restored Death belatedly shows up in Ankh-Morpork, but that's really after everything's over.

Along the way we have had a great deal of silly fun, and hints of things to come, though we might not have recognized them as such. There are references to the Amazing Maurice and His Educated Rodents, who appeared to be a throwaway gag back in 1991, but reappeared ten years later in a book with the curious title *The Amazing Maurice and His Educated Rodents*.

They aren't a throwaway gag in the latter.

We meet Reg Shoe, the militant undead-rights activist zombie; he'll be back, more than once. As will his landlady, Mrs. Cake—a medium, verging on small—though generally not in as large a role.

The Death of Rats and the Death of Fleas appear for the first time in *Reaper Man*.

It's established here that the Discworld has the full panoply of undead available—the story includes not just zombies, but vampires, werewolves (honorary undead), a bogeyman, a banshee, and although no

[92] This creature's rather complicated life-cycle obviously owes a great conceptual debt to the late, great Avram Davidson, and his award-winning story "Or All the Sea with Oysters."

golem appears *in propria persona*, Reg Shoe reports having known one at some point. (We'll see lots of golems in *Feet of Clay*, as described in Chapter 23, and in various places thereafter.)

The first mention of the University's High Energy Magic building, the only building on campus less than a thousand years old, is made. It will be back in later stories.

We discover that just as New York is the Big Apple, Ankh-Morpork is the Big Wahooni, a wahooni being a Discworld vegetable we've seen mentioned now and again.

There are, by the way, direct contradictions of previous events. We are told flat-out that Death has never killed, that he's only taken life when its user was finished with it—but in *The Colour of Magic* we saw Death fatally dispose of a nuisance or two.

Furthermore, it's stated that until the appointment of Mustrum Ridcully, the average term in office of an Archchancellor of Unseen University was eleven months, and that Unseen University has existed for thousands of years, which would mean thousands of Archchancellors, but we were told back in *The Light Fantastic* that Galder Weatherwax was only ("only," he says; ha!) the 304th Chancellor of Unseen University.

It really does seem as if those first two volumes weren't actually part of the series at all, but a sort of warm-up, a trial period. The inconsistencies keep piling up.

At any rate, by *Reaper Man* the series very definitely *is* a series, with cross-references and in-jokes and foreshadowings of stories to come. Not only do perennials like the Librarian and the Patrician have their usual roles, but Sergeant Colon makes a couple of brief appearances. Everything's becoming consistent.

Sort of.

We've come a long way from parodies of Fritz Leiber and Anne McCaffrey. Instead we have parodies of self-help groups and shopping malls and weekend warriors and spiritualists and any number of other real-world phenomena. How much of this is reality leakage, Discworld as "world and mirror of worlds,"[93] and how much is just human nature,[94] is hard to say.

At any rate, *Reaper Man* is a good one, and we'll have more about Death five volumes later in *Soul Music*, as seen in Chapter 20, but first we return to Mistress Esmerelda Weatherwax and her covenmates.

---

[93] A descriptive phrase from the opening page of *Moving Pictures*.

[94] And whether there's a difference.

14

Witches Abroad (1991)

THIS IS ANOTHER TALE of the witches of Lancre, but before we get back to Granny Weatherwax, Nanny Ogg, and Magrat Garlick, we get a little lecture (as we so often do) on the nature of the Discworld, including a mention that "... the Discworld exists right on the edge of reality. The least little things can break through to the other side."

Reality leakage.

And narrativium—except here we're told, "This is called the theory of narrative causality and it means that a story, once started, *takes a shape*. It picks up all the vibrations of all the other workings of that story that have ever been."

Or, "... if you prefer to think of it like this: stories are a parasitical life form, warping lives in the service only of the story itself."

Narrativium is presumably the element these parasitic stories are based on, just as we are based on carbon (well, me and my family and everyone I know; I don't know who *you* are, reading this, and for all I know you're a blob of ionized gas from somewhere in the Andromeda Galaxy that found this book in ancient ruins somewhere).

You know, Mr. Pratchett is rather fond of parasitical life forms—previously he's described ideas as parasites, here it's stories, in *Reaper Man* we saw a parasite that preyed on cities, and in later volumes we'll see parasitic elves and parasitic vampires. It's clearly an idea that resonates with him.

At any rate, the story does eventually get started, and Desiderata Hollow dies, leaving her duties as someone's fairy godmother to Magrat

Garlick, who we discover has not yet married King Verence as it appeared she would at the end of *Wyrd Sisters*.

Desiderata, it seems, opposed the schemes of someone named Lilith, who is using mirror magic to *encourage* stories. Which we have just been told are parasitic. This is clearly a bad thing.

So Magrat sets out for the distant and wondrous city of Genua, accompanied by Nanny Ogg and Granny Weatherwax, and after many amusing adventures they arrive there and deal with Lilith Tempscire.[95]

Genua, despite its Italianate name and instances in later books where Italian is the language spoken there, is remarkably like New Orleans in a good many ways, and is generously supplied with voodoo women, swamps, alligators, Carnival, and the like. Fittingly, our three witches get there partly by riding a grand paddle-wheel-driven riverboat, complete with crooked gamblers.

Various things appear along the way that we'll be seeing again in later volumes—dwarf bread, to name one, and Casanunda, the dwarf seducer and the Discworld's second-greatest lover,[96] for another. Something we probably won't see again is a cameo appearance by what appears very much to be Gollum—it would seem that bits can leak over from *lots* of different realities, not just our own. There are obvious references to Oz, too, though we are by no means back in the parodic territory mined by *The Colour of Magic*; these little details are more in the nature of brief and loving tributes than parodies.

We learn a great deal more about Gytha Ogg,[97] who comes across here as the absolute quintessence of the crass English matriarch. Esme Weatherwax, previously established as a determined and powerful witch with very strong opinions as to what's proper, is shown here as downright indomitable and on her way to becoming a force of nature.

Magrat Garlick is depicted as something of a wet hen, and even though she's nominally the fairy godmother, the other two have far more to do in the course of the story.

---

[95] "Temps," it should be noted, is a versatile French word that means, among other things, the weather. "Cire" is French (or Quirmish) for "to wax."

[96] We aren't told who's #1, but hey, #2 tries harder. (If you don't get the reference, you're too young to remember Avis Car Rental's most successful ad campaign.)

[97] Named for Gytha North (1951–2006), a British fantasy fan and enthusiastic singer of Mr. Pratchett's acquaintance. Her fondness for music is probably responsible for Nanny Ogg's penchant for breaking into bawdy song whenever she is able to get a drink or two into her, but otherwise the resemblance seems to have been rather slight.

Lilith, by the way, is working not with just *one* story, but several twined together, with Cinderella at the core.

Although it's hard to explain exactly why, I would point to this novel as the one where the Discworld series really attains its mature form. It developed plots back around *Mort*, and various elements fell into place thereafter, but this is where it all really begins working together smoothly. The story is complete and consistent and entirely within the Discworld milieu, while still having obvious reference to the real world and offering insights into human nature. Narrativium is not yet named, but the story is built around it. Where *The Colour of Magic* was about other stories, *Witches Abroad* is about the concept of story itself. It's not about the content of stories, but about how stories are used. There are stories within stories, stories about stories, stories played out and stories defeated, from the stories that Lilith uses to control Genua to the stories Nanny Ogg writes home to her son Jason, from the role Granny acts out with the riverboat gamblers to the role Ella rejects. The stories are mirrors, and the mirrors both reflect and shape reality.

Damn, I wish I could construct a story like that!

The Discworld series is all about stories, as I've said before, but this novel is where it becomes obvious and explicit.

And we'll be seeing more of the witches very soon, in *Lords and Ladies*, as seen in Chapter 17, but first there's another dose of Gods and Philosophers.

15

Small Gods (1992)

OMNIA IS A THEOCRACY ruled by the priests of the Great God Om, where Brutha is a novice who helps tend the gardens in the Citadel of the ruling priesthood. There are a few odd things about Brutha, though: He has an absolutely perfect memory, he never dreams, and he really, truly believes in Om.

This last, it turns out, is very unusual indeed. Most Omnians believe in the Church, in rules, in order, in Omnia, but not in the god himself; he just isn't very relevant. His Church has everything so firmly controlled that there's no call for divine intervention. (Later we'll see a similar but less extreme situation regarding the god Nuggan in *Monstrous Regiment*.)

Gods in Discworld *need* belief; it's their source of power. Om is therefore not quite the great and powerful god he used to be.

He is, in fact, a one-eyed tortoise, and his once-mighty lightnings are reduced to sparks that can barely singe a heretic's hair. He took that shape a few years back, and didn't have the strength to get out of it again. Finding a true believer in Brutha, though, has given him renewed hope.

And hearing his god talk to him has disturbed Brutha's placid existence, getting him caught up in the preparations for war between Omnia and Ephebe.

Ephebe, you will recall, is the land of philosophers we saw in *Pyramids*. It's basically a parody of ancient Athens. Here we get a much more extensive look at it, largely to contrast its rather easy-going ways and general flexibility with the rigid authoritarianism of Omnia.

Actually, as I said in Chapter 9, it's not a parody of ancient Athens; it's a parody of the popular conception of ancient Athens. Discworld is all about stories, not history, and about beliefs, not facts. Ephebe is a collection of all the stories told about ancient Athens, cranked up to the absurd—elected tyrants, labyrinths, philosophers arguing about tortoises, and leaping naked from the bath shouting "Eureka!"

Ancient Athens is often depicted in stories as a bastion of freedom in contrast to the military dictatorship of Sparta, or sometimes in contrast to the Oriental despotism of the Persian Empire, so it would be nice to be able to say that Omnia is standing in for Sparta or Persia, but alas, that doesn't work. Neither of those states was as theocratic, nor as fond of torture and as abhorrent of heresy, as Omnia; it just doesn't match either model even loosely enough for a Discworld parody. No, Omnia is more general than that, a depiction of a land where the need for certainty, for clarity, for rules and order, has superceded everything else, including evidence and sanity. The willingness of the Ephebians to say that they don't know, that they could be wrong, that circumstances might change, disgusts and horrifies the Omnians, who don't tolerate doubt.

The name "Omnia" obviously means "land of Om," but it's surely not a coincidence that it's also Latin for "everything." The Omnians want to control everything. They say they act in the name of their god, but it's clear that they want control for the sake of control, not for the sake of Om.

They want to be gods themselves, in a way—able to control everything around them. While the actual small gods do appear in the story, the title can also be taken to apply to the Omnian priests. They're determined to make reality conform to their beliefs, rather than adjusting their beliefs to conform to reality.

The Omnian church is a satire on every religion gone wrong, every church that's become obsessed with its own power and glory rather than the god it allegedly serves. You could draw parallels to the medieval church, the Spanish Inquisition, the Islamic theocrats—it's a bit depressing, actually, just how many real-world faiths match up.

Small Gods is one of the most *focused* of all the Discworld novels, with very few of the digressions and side-plots that usually complicate matters and provide much of the amusement. Brutha and Om are only rarely offstage for even a page or two, and when they are it's because some essential bit of plot is playing out.

Still, the novel manages to bring in the Librarian for a cameo, Death has a few scenes, and it does introduce us to the History Monks, the absurdly long-lived caretakers of the proper course of events. One of them, Lu-Tze, is sent to observe events in Omnia, and intervenes at a crucial point.

We'll see those fellows again, in time.

There's also the introduction of Cut-Me-Own-Hand-Off Dhblah. Previously, when discussing Cut-Me-Own-Throat Dibbler, Mr. Pratchett told us that such people can be found everywhere; well, he's demonstrating the truth of this assertion by showing us Dhblah, the Omnian equivalent and probable distant relative of Dibbler.

Small Gods is also the source of my title. One doctrine of the Omnian church is that they live on a globe, and this talk of a disc-shaped world supported by elephants atop a gigantic turtle is nonsense—heretical, blasphemous nonsense that can get you executed.

The Omnians who dare to rebel against the church hierarchy take part of their inspiration from stories about people who have seen the edge of the world that the church says doesn't exist; they believe that the Disc *does* rest on Great A'tuin's back, as described by travelers and in an Ephebian book entitled *De Chelonian Mobile*—"The Turtle Moves."

The rebels adopt that as their slogan and rallying cry. After all, if the church is demonstrably wrong about a basic fact like that, how can anything they teach be trusted?

This is clearly based on the famous report that after Galileo had formally renounced his heretical view that the Earth moves around the sun, he muttered, "*E pur si muove*"—"And yet it moves." The Omnian church is more drastic than the Catholic church of Galileo's time, but the similarities are obvious—as I said, lots of real-world religions match up with it.

And the rebels, like Galileo, may pay lip service to the Omnian faith in public, but among themselves they remind one another, "The Turtle moves!" As John Morley said, "You have not converted a man because you have silenced him." The truth will out in time. When the stories people live by become too far distanced from reality, they break down. Regardless of what anyone may teach, regardless of what anyone may want, the Disc *does* rest atop four elephants, who *are* standing on Great A'tuin's back.

And the Turtle moves!

If you think about it, it doesn't really matter to your ordinary Omnian in the street that the Turtle moves, but it's a short, catchy phrase that sums up the extent of the church's lies. It works.

And I'm hoping it works as a catchy book title, too.

Anyway, *Small Gods* is mildly unusual in that Ankh-Morpork and the wizards of Unseen University play almost no role whatsoever in the story; they're barely mentioned, other than as a place Brutha might want to flee to. *Pyramids* included an extended depiction of Teppic's training as an assassin in Ankh-Morpork, even *Witches Abroad* had several passing references to wizards and the Big Wahooni, but in *Small Gods* there's almost nothing—basically just Om's suggestion of taking refuge in Ankh-Morpork, and the Librarian's brief appearance from L-space.

But there's plenty to say here about human nature, religious belief, ways of thinking, and the like. If the Discworld series as a whole is about stories, *Small Gods* is about stories used to oppress and destroy, stories that cannot be questioned.

Pretty heavy stuff for a bunch of funny fantasy.

Which may be why we don't see any more of the Gods and Philosophers series until *Thief of Time*, more than a dozen volumes later—if then; *Thief of Time* is one of those hard-to-classify ones, as described in Chapter 32.

Instead, there's a brief interruption in the form of a short story, and then it's back to Lancre and the three witches.

16

"Troll Bridge" (1992)

YES, THERE ARE SHORT STORIES about Discworld. The earliest is "Troll Bridge," written in 1992 for *After the King*, an anthology of stories paying tribute to J.R.R. Tolkien.

Obviously, if it's set on the Disc it's not set in Middle Earth; in his introduction, Mr. Pratchett explains that he didn't want to trespass in Prof. Tolkien's world, and instead tried to reflect something of the *feel* of *The Lord of the Rings*—great things passing out of the world and leaving it poorer in some ways, even though it's safer and saner.

He had an obvious character to star in such a story: Cohen the Barbarian. Who I've arbitrarily decided isn't the hero of a series, largely because he's a secondary character in all his appearances up through *Interesting Times* and never has a full-length novel to himself, but who is the protagonist of this story, and arguably of *The Last Hero*, though the latter is really more of an ensemble piece where Cohen could equally well be considered the villain.

At any rate, in "Troll Bridge" Cohen is looking under bridges for a troll to slay, and finally finds one, but matters do not proceed as expected.

The story does exactly what Mr. Pratchett says he set out to do—to show a world that's changing, that no longer has a place for warriors even though some of the old heroes are still around. It doesn't really add much of anything to the Discworld as a whole, and it doesn't add to any of the sub-series except perhaps "Beyond the Century of the Fruitbat," but it's a good little story all the same.

And like all Discworld stories, it's about stories—Cohen and the troll swap stories of the old days, and find common ground in their shared stories. They know the story they want to play out, and the roles the story expects of them, but in the end they don't follow it. The time for that story is past.

They don't make 'em like that anymore.

We'll see Cohen again in Chapter 20, but for now it's back to Lancre.

17
Lords and Ladies (1992)

THIS IS THE FIRST DISCWORLD NOVEL to start with an acknowledgment that it's a sequel to previous stories and may not stand on its own. The Author's Note at the front says, "I can't ignore the history of what has gone before," specifically the events of *Wyrd Sisters* and *Witches Abroad*. This story begins, once the preliminaries are out of the way, with the return of Granny Weatherwax, Nanny Ogg, and Magrat Garlick to the kingdom of Lancre, after their wanderings in foreign parts.

They aren't the only ones returning, unfortunately. It seems that beings generally referred to by euphemisms, because to use their true name is to summon them—the Gentry, the Lords and Ladies, the Fair Folk—are trying to get back through an opening barred to them long ago by a ring of meteoric iron. The barrier is wearing thin, and the elves are able to influence events, and lure people to open the door for them.

This gets tangled up with the preparations for a royal wedding—Magrat is to marry King Verence II—but Granny and Nanny do their best to prevent disaster, and partially succeed.

Matters are further complicated by the arrival of certain wedding guests, including Mustrum Ridcully, Archchancellor of Unseen University; the Librarian; the Bursar (whose nerves have now cracked completely); young Ponder Stibbons, who now holds the title Reader in Invisible Writings; and Giamo Casanunda, the womanizing dwarf who took an interest in Nanny Ogg in *Witches Abroad*. We learn that Ridcully and Mistress Weatherwax have some unexpected history, and the coincidence of Unseen University having had an Archchancellor named Weatherwax is finally addressed.

There's more about Morris dancing—quite a bit more, actually. There's more about high-energy magic, more about quantum universes, and the first appearance of a Discworld unicorn.

One tidbit, trivial but amusing, is that in one of the Bursar's fits of madness, he says, "Millennium hand and shrimp." This phrase will be seen again.

And at the heart of the story are the elves, who are not at all the benevolent creatures of Tolkien or his many imitators, but more like the terrifying creatures of old folklore. Not the cleaned-up nursery version the Victorians wrote about, not even the stronger but still sanitized version Shakespeare gave us, but the *real* old stories about baby-snatching monsters under the hill, all glamour, illusion, and cold-hearted whim.

Not that Mr. Pratchett ignores the Shakespearean approach; his Queen and King are not totally unrelated to Titania and Oberon, and there are at least two direct references to *A Midsummer Night's Dream*. That's not even counting the fact that the elves get loose on a Midsummer Eve.

Story and belief—the elves lure their prey with stories created by editing what's remembered, and defeat their foes by manipulating their beliefs. They're parasites using stories to control their hosts.

And as always, the witches stand up for the right of people to run their own lives—or at least, to *mostly* run their own lives, since of course it's different when it's witches doing the meddling.

Other than establishing elves as villains, and providing firm connections between the witches and the wizards (and on the witches' home ground, unlike the earlier meeting in *Equal Rites*), this novel does not really represent any real change in Discworld as a whole. It's a fine, funny story, with some good scary moments, but it doesn't really stand out from the crowd, so I find myself without much to say about it.

That's the last we'll see of the witches of Lancre as the stars of a book until *Carpe Jugulum*, nine volumes later; for now it's back to Ankh-Morpork for another look at the resurgent Night Watch under the command of Samuel Vimes.

18

"Theatre of Cruelty" (1993)

THE SECOND DISCWORLD SHORT STORY, originally written for a bookstore giveaway, was published after *Men at Arms*, but from internal evidence is very clearly set between *Guards! Guards!* and *Men at Arms*, so I'm inserting it here, one place out of publication order.

The story opens with Sgt. Colon and Nobby investigating a suspicious death. They report to Captain Vimes, and tell him they've sent Corporal Carrot to find a witness.

Carrot being Carrot, he finds the one witness there is to *every* death on the Disc, and the investigation proceeds from there.

How it is that Carrot can see Death, when Carrot is neither a wizard nor a cat nor otherwise psychically advantaged, is not explained; perhaps heirs to thrones get special privileges, or perhaps he has the same sort of knack for seeing what's really there that witches do.

"Theatre of Cruelty" is quite short, and although it has some good funny bits, its real impact as a story depends on being familiar with *Punch and Judy*, which many people these days are not. Its major contributions to the Discworld canon are to provide another example of Carrot's curiously simple way of thinking, to establish the existence of gnomes, and to provide a sort of origin for *Punch and Judy* shows. It can be read online, on Lspace.org, if you're really interested, but if you can't find it or can't be bothered, I don't think you're really missing much.

19

Men at Arms (1993)

THE ANKH-MORPORK NIGHT WATCH, under the command of Captain Samuel Vimes (at least for the moment), is back.

It hasn't been long since the end of *Guards! Guards!*, and matters are much as we left them, except that Captain Vimes is about to be wed to Lady Sybil Ramkin, and intends to retire to a life of leisure after the wedding. At least, he *thinks* that's his intention, but clearly he's not entirely in agreement with himself about the idea.

The question of who will succeed him as Captain is not settled, and is of some concern to Corporal Carrot and the other Watchmen, though not really very urgent—until dead bodies start turning up, bodies with holes through them not like the wounds left by any traditional weapons. It seems that an invention of Leonard da Quirm's, a weapon called the gonne, has been stolen, and is being used—or perhaps is using the thief. The gonne is clearly *not* simply a gun of the sort we find in our world, but something with a will of its own.

I'm sure the author's intent was that this would be a metaphor for the temptations of lethal power, but nonetheless, in the story the gonne does have its own thoughts and desires. Its exact mechanism is apparently not quite like a real gun's, either. It uses six-shot clips rather than single cartridges, and seems to have a hair-trigger trigger and remarkable range and accuracy for a device that's the first of its kind.

This doesn't appear to be a case of reality leakage, of ideas bleeding through from our world, but simply of Leonard of Quirm being a creative genius, and producing something like a gun, but adapted to the Disc. The result is a weapon that literally *wants* to be used, and which, despite being the first of its kind, is as lethal as the guns it took our world a couple of centuries to develop.

Discworld, after all, has a very strong magical field and a shortage of reality.

The Patrician, Lord Vetinari—and now we learn that his first name is Havelock, as Lady Sybil addresses him by it—warns Vimes not to involve himself in investigating the mysterious deaths, knowing full well that such a warning will simply make Vimes more determined to find the truth. As indeed it does.

The Patrician has miscalculated matters slightly, but nonetheless, Vimes and company do find and destroy the gonne and dispose of the murderer, and all ends well—in fact, *very* well—for the Watch, as Carrot finds himself in a position to more or less blackmail the Patrician, and dictates terms that merge the Night Watch with the Day Watch and restore the result to its full establishment, rather than leaving it the pitiful, useless remnant it had been. Actual detectives will be trained. Carrot is promoted to Captain, and rather than being retired, Sir Samuel Vimes is to be the Commander of this enlarged Watch.

That's the core of the plot, but really, the more important and entertaining elements of the story are elsewhere. The man who steals the gonne intends to restore the monarchy in Ankh-Morpork and has identified Carrot as the rightful heir to the throne, which he definitely is, and part of the book's point is the realization that, contrary to literally thousands of years of storytelling, such a restoration would be a bad thing. This king is not interested in returning; he knows he does more good for the city as a Watchman than he would sitting on its golden throne.

Carrot has, in fact, learned how the city actually works in the gap between *Guards! Guards!* and *Men at Arms*. He still knows the ancient laws by heart, and uses them when it's appropriate, but he's come to understand the Patrician's system of balancing Guilds and power blocs against one another, the function of the Thieves' Guild in keeping crime under control, the rather broad local definition of "suicide," and so on.

And he's taken to heart Vimes's total distrust of arbitrary authority, and Vimes's hatred of class distinctions.

Samuel Vimes, it turns out, is very determinedly anti-monarchist. He doesn't like the Patrician much, either, but at least Vetinari doesn't claim any sort of divine right, or put on all the pomp a king would.

Early in the book, Vimes describes to Carrot how the old kings were overthrown, how someone got fed up at the atrocities committed by the last king, Lorenzo the Kind, and led a rebellion. This rebel leader was Commander of the Guard, a man called Old Stoneface.

Toward the end of the book, the Patrician mentions that the Commander of the Guard at the time of Lorenzo's overthrow was a man named Vimes, and Carrot confirms that the present-day Vimes is his descendant. In short, anti-monarchism is a very old Vimes family tradition.

This, of course, contradicts *Guards! Guards!*, where the kings have been gone for millennia and Vimes was virtually unaware they'd ever existed, but hey, it makes a better story, and Discworld is all about stories.

And this story is the heart of the Watch series, really. Vimes believes that life ought to be fair and sensible, that everyone deserves a decent life, and the fact that this is clearly not the case has him perpetually awash in anger and despair. Anger is his driving force.

Carrot believes that life ought to be fair and sensible, that everyone deserves a decent life, and that if everyone would just *try*, then this could be made to happen, at least briefly and locally.

That's the core; the plots of the various stories in the series are elaborations on that.

Men at Arms introduces or continues a great many other elements. The Ankh-Morpork Post Office is described in passing—still nominally functioning, after a fashion, but not well. We'll eventually see that addressed[98] in *Going Postal* (see Chapter 41). Leonard of Quirm, first mentioned in *Wyrd Sisters*, is properly introduced; it seems that his mysterious disappearance came about when the Patrician locked him away where he wouldn't be quite so dangerous.

Bloody Stupid Johnson, the Discworld's worst landscape architect and designer,[99] is described, and several of his creations mentioned.

Gaspode the Wonder Dog, who lost his ability to talk at the end of *Moving Pictures*, has regained it by sleeping too close to Unseen University and its intense magical field; he's back, and essential to the plot.

---

[98] Yes, of course the pun is intentional.

[99] Later on we'll learn that he designed and built lots of things besides landscaping, from organs to plumbing.

Mrs. Cake and her undead lodgers appear briefly; she still has a problem keeping her precognition in check.

Foul Ole Ron is introduced, mumbling to himself, saying things like "Millennium hand and shrimp"—a phrase that the Bursar of Unseen University said in *Lords and Ladies*. Having two different befuddled characters say it does leave one wondering whether it might actually *mean* something.

More likely, though, Mr. Pratchett just liked it and wanted to use it again, and Foul Ole Ron was handier than the Bursar of Unseen University. He does this, taking some bit of business and moving it from one character to another, as he's had Rincewind and Mort both looking for logic that isn't there (and will later assign this to Ponder Stibbons), and he's taken the literal-mindedness of the Zoons and transferred it to the dwarfs. Now "millennium hand and shrimp" has leapt from the Bursar to a new and permanent home in Foul Ole Ron.

An ongoing subplot that will continue throughout all future books set in Ankh-Morpork is the Patrician's decision to integrate all the city's various populations, and to use the Watch as a tool for this purpose. At the start of the book, Vimes has been ordered to recruit a dwarf and a troll, so that those species will be represented in law enforcement and become full participants in Ankh-Morpork's community, rather than considering themselves oppressed minorities in a human city.

The detail that dwarfs and trolls hate each other complicates this, but that hardly deters Lord Vetinari. There are several references to the long-ago Battle of Koom Valley, where armies of dwarfs and trolls managed to ambush each other; we'll hear more about that in books to come, especially *Thud!*, as described in Chapter 44.

Accordingly, in line with the Patrician's edict, Vimes has enlisted a dwarf named Cuddy, and the troll Detritus, previously seen working as a bouncer—well, a splatter—at the Mended Drum in *Guards! Guards!*, and as a bodyguard and gofer[100] in *Moving Pictures*.

And then there's Angua, also recruited in response to the Patrician's demand for inclusion, and there's a running gag in which people say, "But she's a w—" and never finish the word, so that the unsuspecting first-time reader thinks the word is "woman."

---

[100] "Go fer this, go fer that..." But you knew that, right?

Actually, of course, it's "werewolf."[101] Lord Vetinari wanted the undead represented, and a werewolf is considered to be close enough.

Angua and Detritus are a permanent addition to the cast of the Watch novels, and will be back many times, along with Vimes, Carrot, Sgt. Colon, Nobby Nobbs, and the rest. The trend of recruiting new varieties of watchmen will also continue in *Feet of Clay*, as described in Chapter 23, and in *Thud!*, as we'll see in Chapter 44, but first there's a multi-volume interruption, beginning with a return to the Death series.

---

[101] Fine, I blew another gag, and without warning you. Sorry. But it's really pretty essential to know that Angua's a werewolf in several later stories.

20
Soul Music (1994)

DEATH HAS ABANDONED HIS JOB AGAIN—this time because he's remembering something he doesn't want to. He wants to be able to forget, but as an anthropomorphic personification, that ability has been denied him.

So he goes off to join the Klatchian Foreign Legion under the name "Beau Nidle,"[102] and his granddaughter Susan of Sto Helit inherits his duties during his absence.

We haven't met Susan before, though her parents, Mort and Ysabell, were prominently featured in *Mort*. She's sixteen, attending a school for sensible young women of good family, and is at least temporarily unaware of her curious ancestry, until the Death of Rats shows up, demanding her attention.

She has vague early-childhood memories of her grandfather, but had never really grasped what they meant, partly because her parents actively discouraged her from doing so. They expected her to live in the normal human world—well, as normal as Discworld gets, anyway—and thought her peculiar background could only make things difficult, so they encouraged her to have as little to do with the mystical as possible.

"As little as possible," though, isn't none, for anyone on the Disc, and especially not for Death's granddaughter. Despite her relentless common sense and lack of education in matters mystical, Susan has managed to inherit some of her grandfather's nature—other people often

[102] I am embarrassed at how long it took me to recognize that as "bone idle." Usually I pick up puns fairly quickly, but that one went right by me for ages.

have trouble seeing her, or remembering that she's present, and she's able to see things and do things that ordinary mortals can't.

When she objects that adoptive children don't inherit physical characteristics, and that acquired traits aren't inherited either, Death explains that it's morphic resonance at work, rather than genetics. The Disc's magical field is presumably responsible.

Meanwhile, something's gotten loose in Ankh-Morpork, much as in *Moving Pictures*—an idea, or rather, a whole package of ideas. This time it isn't movies, though; it's Music With Rocks In. A young man named Imp y Celyn,[103] from the nation of Llamedos,[104] arrives in Ankh-Morpork, planning to make his living as a musician. Alas, he breaks his harp, and replaces it with a strange guitar from a mysterious little shop near Unseen University.[105]

He then falls in with a dwarf named Glod Glodsson, and a troll named Lias Bluestone, and together they form the Band With Rocks In.

When this comes to the attention of Archchancellor Ridcully, he immediately recognizes what's happening: "Stuff leakin' into the universe again, eh?" A bit later he adds, "And then there was those moving pictures," just to make very clear that this is the same sort of reality leakage. But this time it's not Hollywood; it's rock 'n' roll.

The story is awash in references to, and puns based on, things from our world, far more than the Discworld norm; in particular, there are dozens of homages to scenes and dialogue in *The Blues Brothers*, *Back to the Future*, and *Terminator 2*, and several James Dean and Elvis jokes, as well as puns on and quotes from any number of band names, song titles, and lyrics, and an extended set-piece based on the teenage death songs of the 1950s. When I first decided I was going to write this book, I expected to have a lovely old time annotating them all, but then I discovered that the clever folks at Lspace.org had beaten me to it, so there's no point in rehashing all their work. I can, however, at least say that I e-mailed them about a couple they'd either missed or deemed unworthy of mention.

At any rate, rock 'n' roll is loose on the Disc, and I'd think it's obvi-

---

103 Welsh for "sprout of holly"—except Pratchett prefers "bud" to "sprout." Yes, it's real Welsh and means what he says it does.

104 Not real Welsh. Read it backward, as three words. Or two and a half, anyway. Mr. Pratchett presumably got this trick from the Welsh poet Dylan Thomas, who set his prose piece "Quite Early One Morning" (later expanded into a play for voices, *Under Milk Wood*) in a town called Llareggub.

105 We've seen mysterious little shops before, and will again. Quite a nuisance they can be, sometimes.

ous how this involves Death—and in his absence, his heir. Mr. Pratchett references James Dean's "Live fast, die young, and leave a good-looking corpse," but there's also the Who's "Hope I die before I get old," and any number of other relevant quotes—some of which seem a bit quaint now that the Rolling Stones are in their sixties and still going, though plenty of rock stars *did* die young, from Buddy Holly to Kurt Cobain.

But the music itself will *never* die. That's part of the mythology, and we all know by now how powerful myths and stories are on the Discworld.

So the legend plays itself out—or maybe it doesn't. As we saw at the end of *Mort*, in a scene that we're explicitly reminded of in *Soul Music*,[106] Death sometimes bends the rules. He arranges a happy result here, where certain things didn't happen after all. As he puts it, "HISTORY TENDS TO SWING BACK INTO LINE. THEY ARE ALWAYS PATCHING IT UP."

He doesn't say who "they" are. In *Mort* he'd made arrangements with some gods, but that doesn't seem to be what happened this time.

This may be a hint of things to come several books later, involving the History Monks.

Other hints are in references to several other anthropomorphic (more or less) personifications other than Death—we learn a little more about the Hogfather, Tooth Fairies, the Sandman, Old Man Trouble, and the like. There's even a mention of the Soul Cake Tuesday Duck, which would seem to be the Disc's approximation of the Easter Bunny.

We also see inside the High Energy Magic building at Unseen University, which has been mentioned before, but has not really been described. It seems Ponder Stibbons and several students have been conducting experiments there, and constructing devices that are the Discworld equivalent of computers. Their big machine uses ants rather than electrons, and glass tubes instead of wires, but it reads punch cards and can do simple arithmetic.

Stibbons thinks it can do more if they get more bugs into it, in a reversal of our own world's attempts to *remove* bugs from computers.

A good many familiar faces return in this novel. C.M.O.T. Dibbler once again attempts to cash in on strange phenomena, and the wizards of Unseen University try to make themselves useful without much suc-

---

[106] Unlike *Lords and Ladies*, there's no warning in *Soul Music* that it's a sequel and can't stand on its own, but in fact it would be very, very hard to follow some bits if one hadn't read *Mort*. A look at *Moving Pictures* wouldn't hurt, either.

cess, though the Librarian does have a hand or four in the eventual outcome. Sgt. Colon and Nobby put in a brief appearance; the more effective members of the Watch are noticeably absent, though Mr. Downey's presence as master of the Assassins' Guild establishes that this does take place after *Men at Arms*. The Patrician is not very involved, though he appears and we learn something about his musical tastes and his use of informers. In general, Ankh-Morpork has the same inhabitants we see in every story.

At this point in the series as a whole, it seems as if the supporting cast remains the same regardless of which sub-series we're in, but lead characters from other sub-series—such as Rincewind, Vimes, or Granny Weatherwax—do not appear if they don't have a major role. The supporting characters accumulate, too. We see Foul Ole Ron again, and Cumbling Michael, as well as the Librarian, the Patrician, and so on. Gaspode has a cameo.

It's Susan who takes the lead, though; from now on Death is never really the protagonist, and his granddaughter takes over the series from him.

There's an animated adaptation of this book; alas, despite multiple attempts, I haven't been able to obtain a copy, so I can't comment on it.

Death and Susan Sto Helit won't be featured again until *Hogfather*, four books later, as seen in Chapter 24. First it's time to see where Rincewind came out at the end of *Eric*.

21

Interesting Times (1994)

WE LAST SAW RINCEWIND climbing a stairway out of Hell at the end of *Eric*; the story did not tell us where he emerged, but he's been noticeably absent from all the subsequent scenes at Unseen University. In *Interesting Times*, we learn that he came out on a desert island some six hundred miles from Ankh-Morpork, and he's been living there ever since.

Alas, Fate and the Lady are playing a new game, as they did in "The Sending of Eight," back in *The Colour of Magic*, and the Lady has once again chosen Rincewind as her pawn. Accordingly, Lord Vetinari meets with the Archchancellor and asks him to find Rincewind and send him to the Agatean Empire, which Ridcully does.

The Agatean Empire, which had seemed fairly American in *The Colour of Magic*, is now definitely based largely on legendary Imperial China, though there are bits from Japan thrown in, such as Noh plays, ninjas, and Disembowel-Meself-Honorably Dibhala's habit of calling everyone "shogun." (The Chinese have never made a habit of ritual suicide, so D.M.H. Dibhala's name also implies a Japanese background.)

The Empire is a land of starving peasants, jammed cities, and unthinking obedience to authority—and that last bit is why I specify *legendary* Imperial China, since the real historical China saw plenty of peasant revolts and demonstrations of individual initiative.

As the famous line has it, when fact and legend disagree, print the legend. Mr. Pratchett's parodies are almost always drawn from legends, rather than actual history.

It seems that Twoflower returned home to Agatea and wrote up his adventures in the outside world as a book called *What I Did on My Holidays*, which has been circulating as samizdat for years. This has become the basis for simmering unrest and talk of revolution, as Twoflower's rosy and largely fictional depiction of Ankh-Morpork has a great many Agatean peasants thinking about how much more pleasant it sounds than their everyday lives.

Stories again.

The Grand Vizier, Lord Hong, has used this to stir up a small and inept rebellion he intends to crush to help in securing his own ascent to the throne when the ancient and ailing Emperor dies. Defeating the Great Wizard whom Twoflower described will add a good flourish to the tale, so Lord Hong has asked the Patrician to send Rincewind along so that he can be suitably thrashed.

Meanwhile, Genghiz Cohen, also known as Cohen the Barbarian, has gathered half a dozen other elderly barbarian heroes into the Silver Horde[107] to invade the Empire and steal... well, everything.

Rincewind is flung into the middle of this, and as usual manages to save the day without intending to.

This version of Rincewind is the later, less-interesting one we first saw in *Eric*, the magicless wizard who is the Disc's greatest expert on surviving by running away. Cohen the Barbarian, on the other hand, is fleshed out a little, and even Twoflower, who reappears, has more depth here than he did in the first two volumes.

It's not unusual in Discworld stories to see things mentioned that aren't relevant immediately but will be developed further in later episodes, and there's some of that here. For example, the computer analogue that Ponder Stibbons and his students were building in *Soul Music* is now much larger and more powerful, and has acquired the name Hex, punning on "hex" as in "curse" as well as "hex" as in "hexadecimal," the base-16 code computers are programmed in. It is now magically designing and building additions to itself, as well as being expanded by the wizards, and is capable of highly sophisticated calculations and starting to show signs of self-awareness. In *Interesting Times* it's really only of secondary importance, but we'll see more of it later.

We also have a loose end or two tied up; not only do we find out what's become of Twoflower, but there's also a passing mention of Hrun

[107] A reference to the Golden Horde, of course, but silver as in "silver-haired."

the Barbarian, last seen in *The Colour of Magic*. He's given up heroing and taken up a job in the Guard somewhere.

The story ends with Rincewind transported to EcksEcksEcksEcks, the mysterious continent that is Discworld's approximation of Australia; we'll see more of that a few books from now in *The Last Continent*, as described in Chapter 26. It's a bit unusual for Mr. Pratchett to so obviously set up a sequel, but this time he did exactly that.

For now, though, it's back to Ankh-Morpork, by way of Lancre.

22

Maskerade (1995)

In *LORDS AND LADIES*, Magrat Garlick married King Verence II and became Queen of Lancre. That rather took her out of her previous line of business as a witch; the two roles, while not totally incompatible, don't mesh well if one isn't trying to be a C.S. Lewis villain.

There's also the detail that witches are supposed to come in triads: maiden, mother, and crone. The Lancre witches had Nanny Ogg (mother, we now learn, of fifteen) for the second role and Granny Weatherwax for the third, but Magrat's marriage has left her unqualified for the first, so there's a vacancy to be filled.

The most promising candidate is young Agnes Nitt, last seen in *Lords and Ladies*. Unfortunately, she's gone to Ankh-Morpork specifically to avoid the job, and landed a role in the chorus at the Opera House.

From that start we find ourselves thrust into a plot that clearly leaked through from Gaston Leroux's *Phantom of the Opera*, though it mutated en route. One might think that this sort of murder mystery/thriller would be more suited to Commander Vimes and the Watch than to the witches of Lancre, and a couple of Watchmen do make brief appearances, but mostly it focuses on Agnes Nitt, who does indeed take up her place as the third member of the coven at the end.

Maybe it's just that the witches fit better into pre-existing stories than the Watch does; after all, previously we've seen them tackle *Macbeth* and *Cinderella*, and not slipping into the Hansel and Gretel role is a constant worry for the Disc's witches.

At any rate, Granny is initially not inclined to go to Ankh-Morpork in pursuit of Agnes, as it wouldn't look fitting, but when she learns that Nanny has written a rather indecent cookbook called *The Joye of Snacks* that's been wildly successful, and that Nanny has been severely underpaid for this, well, clearly a trip to Ankh-Morpork to discuss matters with the publisher is in order, and if they then happen to stop in at the Opera House, well, there'd be nothing unsuitable about *that*.

The Joye of Snacks provides for a good many double entendres and the like, and also served as the inspiration for *Nanny Ogg's Cookbook*, one of the many spin-offs from the Discworld series. Many of these spin-offs aren't sold in America, unfortunately, and I had to spend a great deal of money to have them shipped over from Britain while researching this book, and I'll have you know (especially if you're from the Internal Revenue Service) that I was *forced* to obtain them *purely for purposes of research*, and of course I didn't enjoy reading them a *bit*, not one little bit, so those were entirely and completely business expenses, not at all for my own use. So there.

But as it happens, I was able to find *Nanny Ogg's Cookbook* in the U.S., though only as an import. It includes a great many fine recipes, most of which might even work, though I wouldn't necessarily count on it in all cases, and it also includes some very educational materials on etiquette and other matters, and several memos accidentally left in the front by the publishers. It's highly entertaining, and if you've wondered whether it was worth buying, here's my vote saying yes, it definitely is. And Mr. Pratchett isn't even paying me to say that, nor is Stephen Briggs (who seems to have co-authored it or even written pretty much the whole thing), nor is Tina Hannan (who provided the recipes), nor even one of the publishers. *No one* is paying me to say that;[108] I just like the book. So there.

At any rate, this little side-venture (*The Joye of Snacks*, not *Nanny Ogg's Cookbook*) allows Mr. Pratchett to get in a few gentle jabs at the publishing trade, something almost any writer is likely to do when given a chance, and also leads to the statement that moveable type was known in Ankh-Morpork, but forbidden by the wizards, for unknown reasons, which is why the city has no newspapers. This will change later, in *The Truth*, as seen in Chapter 31, but what the heck; it's true for the moment.

---

[108] Unless you count BenBella Books, who are paying me to write this whole book and not telling me what to say in it, which I think is very generous of them.

Death appears toward the end of the story, elaborately dressed in red rather than his customary black; this references a scene that's in pretty much every version of *Phantom of the Opera*, but perhaps most impressively in the silent film starring Lon Chaney. The movie is in black and white, of course—except for one scene, at a ball in the opera house, where the Phantom appears in red....

That probably impressed the heck out of movie-goers back in 1925.

So the witches are three once again, and will return four volumes from now (in Chapter 28) in *Carpe Jugulum*, but for now we remain in Ankh-Morpork with the Watch.

23

Feet of Clay (1996)

SIR SAMUEL VIMES IS SETTLING into his role among the rich and titled, and overseeing the greatly-expanded Watch, when a string of mysterious murders comes to his attention. He's hardly started on that when Lord Vetinari is (non-fatally) poisoned. Vimes, Captain Carrot, Angua the werewolf, Sgt. Colon, Nobby Nobbs, and the rest of the Ankh-Morpork City Watch must investigate.

This is the first time golems make a real appearance, though they've been mentioned before, and they're all over this novel—as you might have guessed from the title. We also get a little more about vampires than we've seen before, and further consideration of werewolves such as Angua.

Überwald,[109] a vast region of gloomy forested hills and backward villages, is mentioned for the first time, as the land of origin of both Angua (whom we've met before) and a dwarf named Cheery Littlebottom (whom we haven't). We'll be seeing much more of Uberwald.

A character named Igor appears, as bartender of Biers,[110] a bar frequented by the undead, but he doesn't appear to be the sort of Igor we'll see in Uberwald in later books. In fact, much, much later, in a footnote in *Thud!*, we will be informed that he definitely is not one, and that he doesn't appreciate attempts at humor based on this coincidence of names.

---

[109] "Überwald" is German for "beyond the forest." "Transylvania" is Latin for "the land beyond the forest." This is not a coincidence. Incidentally, the umlaut in the name of the Discworld country comes and goes; technically it ought to be there, according to Uberwald's inhabitants, but the people of Ankh-Morpork often can't be bothered with the fiddly little thing, so usually it's omitted. I intend to follow the example of the Ankh-Morporkians and save myself the typographical hassle of including it hereafter. Its effect on pronunciation is only discussed much later, in *The Amazing Maurice and His Educated Rodents*.

[110] Yes, it's a pun on *Cheers*.

We meet Wee Mad Arthur, a gnome rat-hunter, who bears some resemblance to the Nac Mac Feegle, who haven't been introduced yet but who will turn up later and be of some importance. This is the first gnome to play a role in one of the novels, though we did encounter a family of them in "Theatre of Cruelty."

Mostly, though, *Feet of Clay*, like most of the Watch stories, is about Vimes and Carrot solving crimes and pursuing justice and racial tolerance in Ankh-Morpork. This series is probably the most coherent and consistent of all the various segments of the Discworld oeuvre, and I don't really feel a need to say much more about the individual volumes. They've settled into their mature form by this point. We'll be returning to the Watch in a couple of volumes, with *Jingo*, in Chapter 25.

But first we see what's up with Death and his granddaughter.

24

Hogfather (1996)

THE AUDITORS OF REALITY, last seen in *Reaper Man*, are back. This time they're trying a somewhat subtler approach in their attempts to remove illogic from the universe, and have engaged the Guild of Assassins to put an end to the Hogfather, Discworld's equivalent of Santa Claus—or rather, given Mr. Pratchett's nationality, I should probably say Father Christmas.

Death undertakes to foil the scheme, filling in for the Hogfather on Hogswatch while his granddaughter Susan, now working as a governess, tackles the actual assassination plan.

The Guild of Assassins has sent a psychopath named Mr. Teatime ("Teatime" is four syllables, not two—each vowel is pronounced individually) to handle the job, on the theory that he's the most likely to succeed, and that they'll be glad to be rid of him if he doesn't make it back. Teatime has, in turn, recruited a few helpers, and taken them to carry out his ingenious plan for destroying the Hogfather.

That plan takes them to places Death cannot go,[111] so Death tries to keep things under control elsewhere by playing the role of Hogfather while Susan deals with the killers. Death's appearance as the Hogfather at a department store, replacing their hired actor, is marvelous. There are good bits with the Death of Rats and his interpreter raven, as well.

We learn much more about the Hogfather, the Tooth Fairy, and other anthropomorphic personifications in the course of the story. Susan was only sixteen in *Soul Music*, when we last saw her, and has since grown

[111] Yes, there are some.

into a formidable young woman; here we get to know her better. She's working as a governess and has become something of an expert on childhood fears, which serves her well in dealing with the Tooth Fairy's tower and various other things.

The wizards of Unseen University and their thinking machine Hex have their share of the story, as well, though Rincewind is absent—presumably still on EcksEcksEcksEcks.

The Hogfather himself is off-stage for almost the entire book, though. He doesn't have a single line of dialogue.

Mr. Pratchett demonstrates in this novel that he understands children very well indeed. But then, by this point in the series he's demonstrated that he's got a pretty good handle on the entire human race, and children generally qualify as human. Not that it's always obvious.

Britain's Sky One television network has made a live-action adaptation of *Hogfather* as a four-hour miniseries, but as of this writing I've only been able to see brief excerpts, since I'm on the wrong side of the Atlantic. The bits I've seen look very well done, though, and the producers seem to have done an especially fine job with Susan.

Death and Susan are featured again in *Thief of Time*, as seen in Chapter 32, and of course Death continues to appear wherever appropriate in the various other series. Next in the overall series, though, it's back to Commander Vimes and the Watch.

25

Jingo (1997)

THE LOST ISLAND OF LESHP has resurfaced in the Circle Sea, midway between Ankh-Morpork and the empire of Klatch, and both nations find themselves determined to control this rather soggy bit of real estate. A peace mission from Klatch arrives in Ankh-Morpork, where someone promptly attempts to assassinate the ambassador. Sir Samuel Vimes, Commander of the Watch, sets out to investigate this crime, and finds himself entangled in politics, intrigue, patriotic fervor, and war.

The Patrician, Havelock Vetinari, prefers not to oversee the actual war, and hands control of the city over to Lord Rust for the duration of the conflict; in company with Leonard of Quirm, he then undertakes some investigations of his own.

Klatch is invaded, though not very successfully.

Along the way, Nobby gets in touch with his feminine side, we learn a little about the species known as Curious Squid, and the usual sort of shenanigans go on. It all ends with order restored, the mysteries solved, and Vimes made a duke.

Reg Shoe, the zombie first encountered in *Reaper Man*, has joined the Watch, as have representatives of various other exotic species—though no Curious Squid.

We discover that Lord Vetinari can juggle. Given his training as an Assassin and his generally high level of competence, this does not come as much of a surprise.

At one point a reference is made to "The monstrous regiment of watchmen," perhaps anticipating a novel yet to come—or perhaps just playing around with the English language a little, since John Knox's oft-quoted phrase[112] has been around for a long time.

Yet another Dibbler parallel appears in Klatch, a fellow named al-Jibla. Alas, we never learn his forenames.

While in general I don't try to provide detailed annotations, since the fans online have already done such a thorough job, the L-space annotations on Nobby's disguise as "Beti" fail to mention one of the possible reasons that name was chosen—the Betty in mummers' plays and Morris dancing is a half-man, half-woman.

The target of Mr. Pratchett's satire here is obvious right from the title. He's attacking the sort of belligerent, unthinking "patriotism" known as "jingoism," and its tendency to bring about pointless wars—usually ineptly run wars, at that. This makes this one of the less-subtle novels in the series, but it's still both highly entertaining and thoughtful, and at least as relevant now as when it appeared ten years ago.

At this point in the series, we really aren't seeing much real change from one book to the next; Samuel Vimes is still ferociously egalitarian in his beliefs, moving up the social ladder but not happy about it, and convinced that the world would be a far better place if people minded their own business. He sees everything from the point of view of the honest policeman, including considering war to be a crime worthy of arresting all concerned for breach of the peace. The other members of the Watch are also set on their paths—Captain Carrot as the natural leader who declines to assert his authority, Angua as the Watch's secret weapon and Carrot's devoted companion Detritus as the one-troll heavy weapons squad, Sgt. Colon as the fat and stupid old copper, Nobby as . . . well, as Nobby, and so on.

By no means am I saying that the Watch books are getting repetitive, because they aren't; it's just that the pattern for them is set. And we'll see it continue in *The Fifth Elephant*.

First, though, we last saw Rincewind arriving on the continent EcksEcksEcksEcks.

---

[112] *The First Blast of the Trumpet Against the Monstrous Regiment of Women* is the title of a book by John Knox, first published in 1558, denouncing the existence of female monarchs.

26

The Last Continent (1998)

IT'S NOT AUSTRALIA. Mr. Pratchett has stated that explicitly.

EcksEcksEcksEcks is, however, very *reminiscent* of Australia, which nobody denies. When Rincewind lands there (as we saw him do at the end of *Interesting Times*), he finds that it's cut off from the rest of the Discworld, and appears to have been added after the rest was built, rather than being part of the Disc's original creation. It doesn't *fit* with the rest. It's magically separated from the rest of the Disc, to the point that the weather systems that ought to reach it don't, and it never rains there.

Not rarely. *Never*.

Time is also somewhat damaged in its vicinity. Rincewind keeps stumbling across things that have been there for thousands of years, but that hadn't been there for thousands of years a few hours ago.

Before going further, there's something I feel it necessary to mention here. Obviously, I love the Discworld stories—I'd hardly have read them all, let alone decided to write a book about them, if I didn't. But naturally, some I like more than others.

The Last Continent is my least-favorite novel in the entire series. Some people think the first two are the worst, or point to various others as a bit lacking, and maybe I'm missing something, but to me, *The Last Continent* seems very definitely the weakest entry.

Where the novels before and after it in the series have nicely constructed plots, rich characterization, and everything else necessary for the creation of an entirely satisfactory reading experience, *The Last Continent* seems more a series of gags strung together by a series of *dei ex machinae*—literally, as Rincewind survives and is guided on his way through the direct intervention of a divine being that manifests itself through cave paintings, posters, billboards, and the like. This being may be the continent's creator, though that's not established definitely; it usually appears in the form of a kangaroo that tells Rincewind he can call it "Scrappy."

In the course of the story, Rincewind makes his way across a good bit of EcksEcksEcksEcks, encountering mystical kangaroos, Mad Max references, beer, ballads about bush rangers, beer, drought, and more beer. He's aware, as he travels, that EcksEcksEcksEcks has severe long-term problems caused by its failure to fit properly into its place on the Disc, and that the lack of rain is one of these problems, but he's not making any attempt to solve them; he's simply trying to run away and get off the continent and back to Ankh-Morpork.

Meanwhile, the senior faculty of Unseen University is trying to find a way to treat the Librarian, who has fallen magically ill. His incapacity has made the university's library impossible to use safely. It's suggested that Rincewind, once the Librarian's assistant, might be able to help, and so, led by Archchancellor Mustrum Ridcully, the wizards set out to retrieve Rincewind.

However, they're almost immediately sidetracked by a discovery in the rooms of the Egregious Professor of Cruel and Unusual Geography, who, they realize, has been missing for some time without anyone having noticed. They wind up on an island some distance off the coast of EcksEcksEcksEcks, more by happenstance and authorial fiat than by planning or reason, where they encounter an interesting god and have a few adventures.

In the end, Rincewind and the senior faculty all wind up beneath a brewery in the Ecksian town of Bugarup, where they are led to perform the magic necessary to screw the continent properly into place on the Discworld.

They are not there through any skill, daring, or pluck of their own, but only because divine forces have *put* them there. Rincewind completes the ritual not because he's figured anything out, or made a conscious choice at all, but because Scrappy has guided him to do it.

For me, this is a thoroughly unsatisfactory way to structure a novel.

Yes, there are lots of funny bits along the way, especially if one is familiar with Australia, and Rincewind does display some cunning here and there, but all in all I consider the story a disappointment. After reading it the first time, I pretty much concluded that the character of Rincewind had been played out.

That was before I read *The Science of Discworld*, though. That's where we see Rincewind next, and where he redeemed himself in my eyes, as described in Chapter 29.

First, though, let us return to Lancre and its witches.

27

"The Sea and Little Fishes" (1998)

THE LONGEST OF THE SHORT prose-only Discworld stories, originally written for the anthology *Legends*, "The Sea and Little Fishes" introduces the Witch Trials, which we'll see again in the Tiffany Aching series. It also gives us a first look at Letice Earwig, who will return in *A Hat Full of Sky*.

The Witch Trials, it should be noted, are nothing like the infamous witch trials of our own world, but are, rather, modeled on sheep trials, or time trials, or whatever—they're an annual competition in witchcraft, they are not court trials.

This story is about Granny Weatherwax and Nanny Ogg—Agnes Nitt, the third in the Lancre coven, has only the very smallest of roles. Really, it's a character study of Granny Weatherwax, as seen from Nanny Ogg's point of view. It establishes once and for all that Granny is the most powerful witch on the Disc—and, like the wizards of Unseen University, an important part of her power is knowing when *not* to use magic.

She's also not a nice person. A good person, someone who does what's right, but not a *nice* person.

She's a *proud* person. She demands respect.

Which is a plot point in our next novel.

28

Carpe Jugulum (1998)

THE KINGDOM OF LANCRE is celebrating the birth of an heir to the throne, and King Verence has invited the neighbors in. Unfortunately, those neighbors include a clan of vampires from nearby Uberwald, the Magpyr family, who decide to make themselves at home.

Permanently.

Lancre, of course, is protected by its witches, but the vampires have planned for that. These are not your traditional, easily handled vampires; these are *modern* vampires, who have overcome the traditional thinking that has held their kind back for so long. Garlic, sunlight, religious symbols—those can all be survived with a little training. There's no need for all that skulking about in the dark, being warded off by holy symbols, turning to dust, or whatever; with the right mindset and some careful practice, these vampires know that all these weaknesses can be overcome.

And witches can be handled.

Or so they think. Planning has its limits. Agnes Nitt, the youngest of Lancre's four witches, turns out to have unsuspected depths. Granny Weatherwax, who they recognized as by far the most dangerous, is even a little more clever than they realized. Queen Magrat comes out of retirement to protect her daughter.

As for Nanny Ogg—well, they did a fairly solid job of handling her witcheries, but they weren't quite so thorough with her role as head of the Ogg family.

Nor did they count on a phoenix turning up in Lancre, or the pict-sies[113] known as the Nac Mac Feegle, or the growing dissatisfaction of Igor, their traditional and tradition-loving servant, with their newfangled ideas.

All of those play a part, along with an Omnian priest by the name of Mightily Oats,[114] King Verence himself, and assorted others, but it's mostly the witches who settle things.

In *The Last Continent*, we got a lot of events and inventions that didn't particularly fit anywhere or lead to anything; in *Carpe Jugulum*, we have just as much innovation[115] and just as much happening, but it *does* all fit in and go somewhere. We'll be seeing more of Uberwald, more about vampires, more of the Nac Mac Feegle, and more of Igor and his family (all of whom seem to be named Igor) in later books. In this story, we see Magrat and Agnes maturing and Nanny and Granny developing. We see Granny discussing religion at some length with Oats, and summing up her beliefs on right and wrong thusly: "And sin, young man, is when you treat people as things." While it's always dangerous to assume that any character is speaking for his or her author, that summation seems to match Mr. Pratchett's beliefs pretty closely, going by everything in the series so far.

Mightily Oats, as shown here, is an interesting character. He's a follower of the Omnian Church, but the humane version that the Prophet Brutha left behind after the events of *Small Gods*, rather than the ferocious and militant church that preceded him.

A lesser writer than Mr. Pratchett might have presented the latter-day Omnian faith as an unalloyed improvement on the old, but Pratchett is better and truer than that. Instead he gives us an Omnian church that's undergone hundreds of schisms, and an Omnian priest in the midst of an extended crisis of faith—Brutha's reforms made it acceptable to question, which made it possible to doubt. The unity and strength of the old, dangerous, bloodthirsty Omnian church has been lost. Oats is a man hag-ridden by doubt.

Granny Weatherwax is not one to be troubled by doubts, and there's a very powerful scene where she tells Oats why he should be glad she doesn't believe in his god.

And then there are the Nac Mac Feegle, the little red-haired, blue-tat-

---

[113] Note spelling. These aren't pixies, exactly; they're gnomes or fairies with pictish roots, meaning they speak like Scottish hooligans, are covered in blue tattoos, and have red hair.

[114] Mightily-Praiseworthy-Are-Ye-Who-Exalteth-Om Oats, in full.

[115] If not more.

tooed men with their barely comprehensible Scots dialect and their penchant for fighting and theft. The first impression is that they're a cross between Smurfs and soccer hooligans, but they're more than that. Right from this first appearance, it's established that they live underground in matriarchal clans, with dozens of males serving a witch-mother called a kelda,[116] who is absolutely nothing like Smurfette. They have a social structure that makes sense, in its own bizarre way. They'll be back in the Tiffany Aching stories, several volumes later.

There's also the phoenix—or phoenices;[117] it's clear that, mythology to the contrary notwithstanding, the Disc has more than one phoenix. While it has a role to play in the story, its part doesn't seem entirely essential, and we don't really learn all that much about it, except that it's an actual bird and a bane of vampires.

As for the vampires themselves, these are the vampires of low-budget horror films, not of Rumanian folklore. Like the Hammer Studios version of Dracula, they're relatively easy to kill, but they don't *stay* dead. They dress in evening clothes, have gothic names like Lacrimosa and Morbidia, and have extensive hypnotic and shape-shifting abilities. The Magpyrs are rebels in that they would rather not have cobwebs and dust everywhere, and prefer doors that don't creak, much to Igor's chagrin. They *do* drink wine. They have rebelled against the foolish old stories, and, they think, triumphed.

But they're still vampires—bloodsucking, undead monsters. It takes all the witches can do to remove them from Lancre, once and for all.

They do succeed in the end, though. Of course.

The next novel in the regular series will take us back to the Ankh-Morpork City Watch, and we won't see the witches of Lancre again except as supporting characters in the Tiffany Aching stories. First, though, we have a curiosity—it's a story of Rincewind and the faculty of Unseen University, but not exactly a novel. . . .

---

[116] This appears to come from a word meaning "a deep spring, or source."

[117] Since there's only one phoenix at a time in mythology, either on Earth or on the Disc, there's no firmly-established plural. If you'd prefer "phoenixes," write your own book; I'll go with the Greek "phoenices."

29

The Science of Discworld (1999)

(with Ian Stewart and Jack Cohen)

IF YOU'RE AN AMERICAN, you may well not have known this book existed; now that you do, you may well be asking, "*What* science? The Discworld doesn't *have* any science!"

And you'd be more or less right. As the authors explain right up front, "Discworld does not run on scientific lines." It runs on the power of story.

What this book does is intersperse a new Discworld story with essays on science—not some contrived Discworld science, but the science of our own world. A world which, it seems, the wizards of Unseen University accidentally created in a squash court, and sent Rincewind to investigate.

The story of the wizards creating and investigating Roundworld, as they call it, alternates chapters with actual science and history of science. Ian Stewart is a professor of mathematics at Warwick University, and Jack Cohen is a professor of biology there. They know their stuff, and write well, so the science chapters are good reading, and tie in well to the story.

The authors provide a sort of compact history of the universe, covering cosmology, astronomy, physics, and chemistry, but as you might expect, given their specialties, the science in the three volumes of this sub-series, especially the latter two, is heavy on biology, particularly evolutionary biology—and if you've been reading Discworld stories for long, it shouldn't surprise you that Mr. Pratchett chose a biologist as one of his collaborators. Evolution, in one form or another, has long been a recurring element in the series. We've met a god of evolution, we've seen discussions of how natural selection has operated in producing the current faculty of Unseen University and the Disc's remarkable crop of barbarian heroes, and we've had comments on the evolutionary value of tortoises learning to fly, on the survival value of stupidity in vampires, on the reproductive strategies of the phoenix, and on any number of similar subjects. Yes, evolution on the Disc is distorted by the intense magical field and the author's sense of humor, but it's obviously a topic near and dear to Mr. Pratchett's heart.

So perhaps it's not surprising—though it's undoubtedly frustrating for American fans who haven't bought *The Science of Discworld* through Amazon.co.uk or the like—that it's in a supposed science book that much is revealed about the nature of Discworld. It's here that such vital elements as chelonium,[118] deitium,[119] and narrativium[120] are explained, as the wizards try to figure out how a universe can operate without them.[121] It's here that the law "As above, so below" is presented, explaining why there are so many links between Roundworld and Discworld—the reality leakage is inherent in the system.

The basic story here is that Ponder Stibbons, the faculty member of Unseen University who's too bright for his own good, has devised a thaumic reactor—that is to say, a magical device that breaks down the elementary particles of magic to produce energy. He's built it in the university's squash court.

He's also misjudged a few things, and in an attempt to bleed off excess magic, he and the other wizards (with the aid of Hex[122]) create a universe. Like many magical things, it's much larger on the inside than on the outside, so that even though its exterior is only a foot in diameter, the interior is our own full-sized universe.

The wizards find this new universe fascinating in its complete lack of

---

[118] Necessary for the creation of cosmic turtles.

[119] Necessary for the creation of gods.

[120] Necessary for the creation of pretty much everything, from the Discworld point of view—it's what stories are made of.

[121] It's also mentioned that the Disc's traditional five elements are earth, air, water, fire, and surprise. Apparently Discworld, like our own world, has both the classical short list and a much larger modern table of elements.

[122] You remember Hex; that's the magical computer equivalent introduced in *Soul Music*, named in *Interesting Times*, and last seen in *Hogfather*.

magic, and watch it develop over a few billion years of its internal time—which is conveniently only a matter of days for Unseen University. With the aid of Hex and the omniscope, they're able to study it closely, and even to project themselves into it.

Poor Rincewind is named Egregious Professor of Cruel and Unusual Geography[123] and sent in as their scout, but he doesn't have it all to himself; eventually most of the familiar faces on the faculty take a look around. They find it baffling that a reality lacking in basic elements like narrativium can develop life, and equally baffling that once that life exists, it doesn't immediately produce wizard-level intelligence. They watch various promising species, hoping they'll evolve into something that can hold interesting conversations, and are repeatedly disappointed as trilobites and dinosaurs and assorted mammals all fail to oblige them.

No one happens to be watching when certain apes finally get the hang of this "intelligence" thing.

I won't give away the ending, but there is one, and a pretty satisfactory one at that. The thaumic reactor is eventually shut down, and the universe tucked safely away on a shelf.

And Rincewind, who was so unsatisfying as the protagonist of *The Last Continent*, is a much better character here than he has been in some time, displaying intelligence and compassion as well as his usual cowardice. It works.

All in all, it's a shame that the book has no American edition. It was a bestseller in Britain, and deservedly so. Where most of the other spin-offs unavailable on the western shores of the Atlantic—such as the *Discworld (Reformed) Vampyre's Diary*, or the Mapp *Death's Domain*—are merely entertaining trivia, the science volumes are real Discworld stories, quite possibly novel-length even without the science chapters.

Not to mention having lots of good popular science.

At the end, though, we leave Rincewind in his place at Unseen University, with Roundworld's universe on its shelf, until *The Science of Discworld II: The Globe*, which we'll consider in Chapter 35.

For now, though, it's time to see what Samuel Vimes and the Watch are up to.

---

[123] The former occupant of that post was found to be missing in *The Last Continent*, and never did turn up. Rincewind was chosen to fill the vacancy because that would mean he was the appropriate person to explore this hostile new universe.

He wasn't given a choice, of course.

30

The Fifth Elephant (1999)

BY THIS POINT IN THE WATCH SERIES, Samuel Vimes and company have Ankh-Morpork fairly well sorted out,[124] but Mr. Pratchett clearly isn't done with the character. There's obviously more to be said about Sir Samuel Vimes, Commander of the City Watch.

The only reasonable thing to do, then, is to send Vimes somewhere else. Accordingly, Lord Vetinari appoints him ambassador to Uberwald, to represent the city at the coronation of the Low King.

Up to this point, we haven't been told much about the dwarfs' system of government; now we learn that they have an elected Low King, who is crowned on the Scone of Stone[125]—a sixteen-pound chunk of dwarf bread dating back some fifteen hundred years—in their largest city, which is underneath Uberwald. Ankh-Morpork is eager to get trading concessions from the Low King, so the Patrician wants a good showing at the coronation.

One would hardly think that sending a notorious anti-monarchist cop would be an appropriate representative in such circumstances, but Lord Vetinari has a complex mind, and there are complications that he thinks Vimes can simplify.

---

[124] Well, except for the measures introduced in passing at the end of *Jingo*, when the Watch was charged with relieving traffic congestion and using the resulting fines to help finance itself. This was perhaps not the best idea the Patrician ever had, and we see some of the consequences in the early scenes of *The Fifth Elephant*, such as the Discworld equivalent of traffic cameras and the boot.

[125] I had assumed that the pun on the Stone of Scone, whereupon the kings of Scotland are crowned, was too obvious to need mentioning, but at least one advance reader felt I should point it out. So now I have.

The casual reader might wonder what the politics of dwarfs and werewolves have to do with elephants. Well, first off, the title almost certainly originated simply as a pun on *The Fifth Element*—the Bruce Willis SF movie was in theaters right about the time this novel was starting to gestate.[126] Secondly, the Disc rests upon the backs of four elephants. Legend has it there was once a fifth,[127] but it slipped off Great A'tuin's shell, orbited around, and smacked fatally into the Disc in what later became Uberwald. The impact was responsible for much of the mountainous terrain in the area, and the elephant's buried remains have provided the dwarfs with gigantic fat mines.

Those trade concessions Lord Vetinari is hoping for are for some of that fat.

Since this is a Vimes story, there are crimes to be solved and criminals to be apprehended, and class issues to be dealt with. Vimes is sent to Uberwald not as Commander of the City Watch, but as Duke of Ankh-Morpork.[128]

He hates that.

Someone has robbed a museum in Ankh-Morpork, and a tradesman has been murdered, but Sir Samuel must leave that to others as he sets out for Uberwald with his wife and a few selected escorts.

That leaves Carrot Ironfoundersson in charge of the Watch—but then he, for reasons of his own, also leaves the city, bound for Uberwald.

That leaves Fred Colon as Acting Captain. Yes, Fred Colon.

This is, of course, a disaster, though that's incidental to the main story. It does make for some very entertaining scenes, some of them curiously reminiscent of *The Caine Mutiny*.

Our primary narrative, though, follows Vimes to the Uberwald town of Bonk, where he unravels a conspiracy between a clan of werewolves and certain disgruntled dwarfs. We learn a great deal more about Angua's family, about dwarf society, and about Igor—and Igor, and Igor, and all their clan. Vampires make only a rather small (though significant) appearance; perhaps Mr. Pratchett wanted to avoid repeating too much from *Carpe Jugulum*.

---

[126] Note that the wizards of Unseen University consider the fifth element to be surprise, according to *The Science of Discworld*.

[127] I mentioned this back in Chapter 2, in musing about Great T'phon's name.

[128] You may recall he was made a duke at the end of *Jingo*, complete with coronet. It's worth mentioning, perhaps, that in *Jingo*, Lord Vetinari said the coronet would have knobs on; in *The Fifth Elephant*, Vetinari says, "The ducal coronet, if I remember my heraldry, does not have knobs on. It is decidedly... spiky." I have no idea why this contradiction exists.

Gaspode the talking dog has a role, as do several other familiar characters—the Librarian doesn't appear, which is unusual, though he's mentioned once in passing, but Death has a few scenes, and pretty much all the established Watchmen appear.

In the course of the novel, Lady Sybil informs Vimes that she's pregnant, which isn't significant here but obviously will be in the future.

And we get our first look at the clacks.

These are signal towers, using semaphore arms by day, lights and shutters by night, to send coded messages from one tower to the next, faster than a horse can gallop. This is obviously well within the technological capabilities of the people of Discworld, even without magic, but it just wasn't anything anyone had a real reason to build until now, when it finally occurred to someone that it would be useful to know what various commodities are selling for in Ankh-Morpork *before* sending a shipload of goods there.

This parallels our own world, where semaphores have been possible for a couple of thousand years, but hardly ever got built except for a few military signaling systems and traffic control on railroads.

We'll see more of the clacks in later books, including the very next one, which does not star any of our established heroes, despite being set in Ankh-Morpork. Oh, plenty of familiar faces appear, but the protagonist is new, and at least so far, only featured this once, in *The Truth*.

Samuel Vimes won't have the lead again until *Night Watch* (see Chapter 36).

31

The Truth (2000)

THE CENTURY OF THE FRUITBAT has been a time of great change in Ankh-Morpork, and those changes include the arrival of lots of dwarfs looking for ways to make money. One bunch of them has built a printing press, complete with moveable type.

It was established in *Maskerade* that moveable type isn't allowed in Ankh-Morpork—the wizards of Unseen University forbade it because they were afraid that type used to print anything remotely magical might pick up some of the magic, which could have unfortunate effects when the type was re-used for something else.

In the waning years of the Century of the Fruitbat, though, Archchancellor Ridcully decides that this restriction has outlived its usefulness, and that the value of moveable type in dealing with the growing flood of paperwork required in a modern university outweighs any dangers. Lord Vetinari reaches a similar conclusion. The dwarfs are allowed to retain their machine.

And one William de Worde, a gentlemen of limited means who has heretofore made his living by sending newsletters to half a dozen wealthy foreign clients who wish to be kept abreast of developments in Ankh-Morpork, happens upon the dwarfs on his way to the engraver, and finds himself becoming one of their first customers. At the urging of the dwarfs, who want more business for their press, he keeps increasing the size, frequency, and circulation of his newsletter, transforming it from a private letter into the *Ankh-Morpork Times*.

Meanwhile, yet another plot to depose Lord Vetinari is under way.

In previous volumes, the defeats of such conspiracies have always been stories about Sam Vimes and the Watch, and indeed, Commander Vimes does investigate this one, but only in the background. Our viewpoint instead follows de Worde as he invents both the newspaper and the occupation "investigative reporter," and uncovers the details of the scheme.

It's interesting to see the Watch from the outside, and to get a new angle on Lord Vetinari. The actual story is mostly familiar material—powerful families unhappy with the city's modernization under Vetinari, hired thugs, complicated schemes, dwarfs, trolls, and a vampire or two. The story doesn't break much new ground, but revisits such favorites as Foul Ole Ron, Gaspode the talking dog, and Mr. Slant the zombie lawyer. We see the Black Ribboners, the vampire temperance movement, in action, and the Ankh-Morpork equivalents of photography and PDAs.

There are a few relatively subtle publishing in-jokes—for example, all the dwarf printers except Gunilla Goodmountain are named for typefaces, though with modified spellings (e.g. Boddony for Bodoni)—and a good bit of commentary about the nature of the newspaper business that reminds the reader that Mr. Pratchett has considerable first-hand experience in journalism.

All in all, it's a satisfactory Discworld novel, but not one that seems especially important or innovative in anything but its choice of protagonist—and even there, although most of the stories have featured recurring characters like Rincewind, Granny Weatherwax, or Sam Vimes, we've had one-off heroes before, in such books as *Small Gods* or *Pyramids*, and of course Victor in *Moving Pictures*, the previous novel about new technology changing Ankh-Morpork. William de Worde fits fairly comfortably into that company. He reappears in a minor role in *Monstrous Regiment*, but is not the hero of any other stories, as yet.

The next book in the series is rather drastically different; where *The Truth* was content with comfortable settings and plot elements, *Thief of Time* is not—but that's the next chapter.

32

Thief of Time (2001)

THIS NOVEL is one of the more difficult to fit into a sub-series; it could be considered part of the "Gods and Philosophers" set, but since Death and his granddaughter Susan have major roles, I decided to class it as a Death novel.[129]

Thief of Time[130] introduces us once again to the History Monks of Oi Dong, who live high up in the central mountains of the Disc, where the magical field is strong. We encountered them briefly back in *Small Gods*, you may recall. The Order of Wen the Eternally Surprised manages the flow of time on Discworld and, we learn in the course of the novel, had to reconstruct their world's history once, when it was broken.

This is, as Mr. Pratchett has admitted[131] in interviews, a handy device for explaining away any discrepancies that might crop up among the various books and stories in the series. The histories of Ephebe and Omnia are particularly damaged, which explains why their timelines often don't match the rest of the Disc, sometimes being off by several centuries. Some bits were used several times in patching things up, as well, which explains why certain events appear to have happened in more than one era.

The History Monks have a rather troublesome apprentice by the name of Lobsang Ludd, who is assigned to the sweeper Lu-Tze for training. Lu-Tze is not exactly the standard issue sweeper, of course.

[129] If you don't like that, you can class it however you please, of course, in the privacy of your own mind. If you want it classed differently in print, though, write your own damn book.

[130] The title comes from a proverb: "Procrastination is the thief of time." Since the story involves devices called Procrastinators that literally steal time....

[131] Or perhaps bragged.

This all provides Mr. Pratchett with an opportunity to mock Eastern mysticism and martial arts—not so much the real things, perhaps, as the way they're presented in western fiction, especially the products of Hollywood. There are references to the old TV series *Kung Fu*, the James Bond movies, and a variety of other such entertainments.

Meanwhile, the Auditors of Reality, previously seen in *Reaper Man* and *Hogfather*, are once again trying to put an end to messy, illogical humanity, this time by convincing Jeremy Clockson, a brilliant young clockmaker in Ankh-Morpork, to build a device that will stop time.

Naturally, that attracts the attention of the History Monks, since Time is their major interest, and also of Death, since endings are his concern. The History Monks send Lu-Tze and his apprentice to deal with the matter, while Death calls upon his granddaughter, Susan Sto Helit, now working as a schoolteacher, to try to prevent the success of the Auditors' scheme.

Susan, it seems, is one of those wonderfully intimidating schoolteachers who actually *teaches* her students, rather than bullying or babysitting them. This suits her well, and she resents being dragged off to deal with incarnations, anthropomorphic personifications, apocalypses, and the like. But she does go.

No explanation is given, by the way, of why Susan is a schoolteacher and not the reigning Duchess of Sto Helit. Her ancestry seems to have been quietly forgotten—or perhaps the title she inherited no longer carries any actual power, after the fashion of present-day European nobility.

Death himself does not try to stop the clockmaker, but instead prepares to ride out at the end of time with his fellow Horsemen, as he is expected to.

Naturally, it does all work out in the end, though not quite the way one might expect. The Auditors learn a good bit about being human, Nanny Ogg plays a small but important part, an Igor gets to help build an infernal device, Jeremy Clockson and Lobsang Ludd find their place, the Five Horsemen ride out, and everything is more or less put right.

Yes, five Horsemen. The identity and nature of the fifth is a significant plot element that I really shouldn't reveal here. I will mention, though, that I don't think I'm just imagining the parallels between the Horsemen and the Beatles; I'm pretty sure they're deliberate.

All in all, *Thief of Time* is a very satisfactory entry in the series, even though it lacks any mention of the Patrician, Sam Vimes, Granny Weatherwax, the Librarian, or the wizards of Unseen University. The recurring cast has now gotten so large that it really isn't practical to fit anywhere near all of them in every volume, and even the favorites need a rest sometimes.

Lots of regulars will be appearing in the next book, though.

33

The Last Hero (2001)

THIS IS A LAVISHLY ILLUSTRATED volume that's labeled "A Discworld Fable," featuring lots of spiffy art by Paul Kidby. It's also a story of Cohen the Barbarian, last seen in *Interesting Times*, where we left him as ruler of the Agatean Empire. It seems he's become discontented with the emperor business, and is leading the remaining members of the Silver Horde on a final adventure, one that they have no intention of surviving. Specifically, he's planning to reverse the action of the very first of Discworld's heroes, Mazda, who stole fire from the gods. Cohen intends to *return* fire to the gods, in the form of a fifty-pound keg of the most powerful explosive he can find.

The Agateans aren't sure this is a good idea, and have informed the Patrician of Ankh-Morpork, who investigates the matter and is told that, while this isn't going to do anything irreparable to the gods, it *will* temporarily collapse the Disc's magical field, thereby destroying all life on Discworld.

This is, understandably, seen as a bad thing, and an expedition is launched to intercept the Horde.

We therefore have two storylines to follow: Cohen's progress toward the home of the gods, and the expedition's creation and progress to that same destination. They do eventually merge, of course.

Rincewind is included, naturally; he's pretty much always there if Cohen's involved, and is about as close to being the protagonist as any character herein. We also get Leonard of Quirm, Lord Vetinari, the faculty of Unseen University, Captain Carrot, and the Librarian, in a tale about the nature of heroes and their legends that manages to include some magnificent scenery along the way.

I have a suspicion that to some extent this story was designed to include whatever Mr. Kidby felt like depicting. It provides us with entirely unnecessary but enjoyable extras such as a pictorial guide to thirty-seven varieties of swamp dragon, and diagrams of several of da Quirm's creations, annotated in his own rather elegant hand. While not a full-length novel, it's really quite a satisfactory package for any Discworld fan. And it does wrap up Cohen's saga.

I am informed, by the way, that the paperback edition includes additional illustrations that were not ready in time for the hardcover. Alas, I haven't seen the paperback edition and can say no more about that.

34

The Amazing Maurice and His Educated Rodents (2001)

THIS WAS THE FIRST DISCWORLD NOVEL to be marketed as a "young adult" title. What this apparently means is that it has chapters and the protagonists are young. Other than that, it's pretty much your basic Discworld story. There are dark scary bits—it's not toned down for young readers. The vocabulary isn't reduced, either.

It's maybe not as funny as most of the adult ones.

At any rate, we first heard of the Amazing Maurice and his educated rodents as a throwaway gag in *Reaper Man*, back in 1991; now we meet them.

Maurice is a cat. It should be mentioned for our American readers that in England, "Maurice" is pronounced "Morris"—I've heard Mr. Pratchett say the title, and he definitely pronounces it that way.

And my English readers, if any, are now probably saying to themselves, "Well, how *else* would you pronounce it?" Indeed, some Americans may pronounce it after the British fashion, but more common on this side of the Atlantic is to pronounce it like the French, "Maw-REESE."

But Mr. Pratchett is, as previously mentioned, undeniably English, so the correct pronunciation here is "Morris," and it's presumably a reference to Morris the Cat, the spokesbeast for Nine Lives cat food and an advertising icon of the 1970s.

The educated rodents are self-taught, for the most part. They're a clan of rats who ate from the garbage heap behind Unseen University, where the wizards discarded leftover magic, and this thaumaturgically enhanced diet has given them roughly human-level intelligence and the ability to speak. Maurice, too, has acquired super-feline intelligence.

This newfound ability to reason has led Maurice and the rats to conclude that there's a better life to be had than eating garbage in an alley. Maurice has recruited a young musician[132] to play the role of a piper, and the lot of them have been traveling across the Disc, scamming villagers.

The Amazing Maurice: The Series

The Amazing Maurice and His Educated Rodents doesn't seem to fit anywhere else, so it gets to be a series all by itself. If you really insist on disagreeing with some of my other classifications, then you can call this series "one-offs," or "singletons," or something along those lines, and move other titles into it. If you *insist* on being difficult.

I don't have a chapter about the series as a series, for reasons I hope are obvious.

It's a simple enough ruse. The rats arrive in a new town, make themselves as visible and obnoxious as they safely can, and then the kid shows up and offers to get rid of the plague of rats for a fee. He plays his pipe, leads the rats out the town gates, gets paid, and then kid, cat, and rats all pack up and move on to the next town.

The rats have a dream of using their share of the money to buy a boat and then finding themselves a deserted island to live on, peacefully ever after.[133] Maurice intends to get rich, and has perhaps been misleading the rats as to just how much money a boat costs. They've worked their way from Ankh-Morpork across the plains and into Uberwald, where we join them shortly before they arrive in the town of Bad Blintz.

The rats want this to be the last town they defraud; they're developing ethics, and beginning to realize that their little scheme is dishonest. Maurice would prefer to keep going. The kid doesn't much care.

---

[132] We only find out that his name is Keith several chapters into the story. And it only now occurs to me to wonder whether this has any connection to the suggestion in *Soul Music* that Death ought to have a first name, such as Keith.

[133] I wonder—am I the only one who sees this as reminiscent of the Lilliputians in T.H. White's *Mistress Masham's Repose*?

But it all becomes moot when Bad Blintz turns out to be a very strange and unhappy town indeed, one in the midst of a famine that's being blamed on rats, even though most of the rat tunnels underneath are deserted. . . .

Our heroes tackle the mystery, and confront the source of the trouble, and in the end, Bad Blintz becomes a very different place and the rats find a permanent new home.

Along the way, Keith and Maurice fall in with Malicia Grim, a girl who dresses in black and has an unhealthy fondness for stories—unhealthy in that she keeps expecting events to follow a proper storyline.

Which, this being a story, they often do. It being a Pratchett story, though, they often aren't the events Malicia expects. She was raised on classic fairy tales—her grandmother and great-aunt were the Sisters Grim, famous Discworld authors of fairy tales—and the story Malicia finds herself in isn't exactly one of those.

The rats, too, have a story they believe in, a children's book called *Mr. Bunnsy Has an Adventure*. It's a good bit less grim than the stories Malicia loves, and has become a symbol of hope for the rats.

And of course, their entire livelihood—the scam Maurice invented for them—is a reenactment of a famous story.

The disparity between stories and reality is an ongoing theme here. Almost all the characters have stories guiding them, but not the same stories. They strive to fit their lives into stories, or fit stories into their lives. Some of them, like Maurice and the piper, hope to exploit other people with the stories they tell, while others primarily influence themselves.

In interviews and talks, Mr. Pratchett has mentioned several times that the book that first turned him into a reader himself, and set him on the path that eventually led to the creation of Discworld, was *The Wind in the Willows*, by Kenneth Grahame. He has also pointed out how utterly absurd much of *The Wind in the Willows* is, even on its own terms—the characters change size as needed to suit the plot at any given moment, issues of predation are ignored, and so on. Despite this lack of logic, he and millions of other readers love the book.

I think it's a fairly safe assumption that *Mr. Bunnsy Has an Adventure* owes a great deal to *The Wind in the Willows*—it's an absurd, idealized story set in a world lacking in real conflict that everyone agrees is ridiculous, but people love it anyway.

Of course, Discworld itself is also absurd, but not so much idealized as exaggerated, and it's far more consistent than *The Wind in the Willows*, even if the version in *The Colour of Magic* does have a lot of details that don't match the current one. (It *has* been developing for more than twenty years, after all.)

Incidentally, none of the regular Discworld characters appear here except Death and the Death of Rats. (It would be pretty silly to tell a story like this and *not* mention the Grim Squeaker.) There's no mention of the Librarian, Granny Weatherwax, the Patrician, Sam Vimes, or Archchancellor Ridcully—none of them appear, presumably because this book is aimed at younger readers who haven't read any of the other Discworld stories. There are mentions of familiar places, such as Sto Lat, Bonk, and of course Ankh-Morpork, but virtually the entire story takes place in, around, and under Bad Blintz. It's a self-contained story, with little room for connections or sequels; it doesn't fit into any of the Discworld series. When I first read it, I wondered whether that would be the pattern for all the Discworld "young adult" stories—assuming there were more.

Well, there were more, and it wasn't. So far, all the other YA Discworld stories have been about Tiffany Aching, starting with *The Wee Free Men*, as seen in Chapter 38.

But before we get to that, it's back to Rincewind and books aimed at adults.

35

The Science of Discworld II: The Globe (2002)

(with Ian Stewart and Jack Cohen)

ONCE AGAIN, WE HAVE A DISCWORLD STORY about Rincewind interfering with the evolution of Roundworld, also known as Earth, interspersed with essays on science.

In this case, most of the faculty of Unseen University has been off playing the wizardly equivalent of paintball[134] when they find themselves transported to Roundworld. They send a message in a bottle to Rincewind,[135] who hadn't come along; Rincewind, Ponder Stibbons, and the Librarian then venture through L-space to sixteenth-century England to rescue the other wizards—and Roundworld—from elves.

In the first *Science of Discworld*, the wizards managed to miss the entirety of human history; they studied the apes that would become humans, and looked at Earth after humanity's departure, but completely missed the period between. Just didn't happen to be looking.

Fortunately, Hex determined that it was possible to observe any time

---

[134] One might reasonably wonder why wizards were participating in anything so active that didn't involve food. It's a team-building exercise instigated by Archchancellor Mustrum Ridcully. Of course, it wasn't working.

[135] Who is now, we are informed, not merely Professor of Cruel and Unusual Geography, but also Chair of Experimental Serendipity, Reader in Slood Dynamics, Fretwork Teacher, Chair for the Public Misunderstanding of Magic, Professor of Virtual Anthropology, and Lecturer in Approximate Accuracy, thanks to the Archchancellor's realization that Rincewind was a handy place to dump unwanted posts that for one reason or another had to be filled.

on Roundworld, not just the apparent present, so that intervening in the sixteenth century wasn't particularly difficult.

The elves are the same interdimensional parasites we saw in *Lords and Ladies*. The inhabitants of Discworld had driven them off and established protections against them, but Roundworld was unguarded, and they found it eventually. In order to reach it, they passed *through* Discworld, though, and the wizards were drawn along in their wake.

Once Rincewind, Stibbons, and the Librarian arrive, simply rescuing the other wizards would be easy, but it's agreed that the elves must be stopped, and that Roundworld, too, must be rescued.

Using Hex as their time machine and semi-omniscient guide, the wizards travel back and forth through human history, meddling as they go, until they manage to arrange things to their satisfaction and remove elves from our present lives—though not from our history.

The story alternates with chapters discussing information theory, language, human evolution, and assorted other science—though this time around the science is somewhat more speculative than in the original *Science of Discworld*. The authors argue that what makes humans special is that we tell stories; they then suggest that this is at the heart of science itself, when we tell ourselves a story (i.e., create a hypothesis), and then check it against the real world to see whether it's true.

In fact, they argue that stories are the basis of civilization, of the entire human species—that it's storytelling that has made us humans, rather than just a relatively hairless variety of ape.

And meanwhile, the wizards are conferring with John Dee, making sure William Shakespeare gets born and writes the right plays, and so on, all while discussing the nature of stories, and how they work in a world where there's no narrativium, no actual magic.

Rincewind saves the day, and this time around, as in the first *Science* book, he's far more appealing a character than he was in *Interesting Times* or *The Last Continent*. He's still a coward and an expert on running away, but that's not *all* he does.

Granny Weatherwax has a brief cameo, but it serves little purpose other than to remind us that she exists, that Discworld runs on narrativium, and that the clacks are in operation.

All in all, it's a good story and an entertaining book, and we'll see more of Rincewind and Roundworld in Chapter 43, but for now it's back to Ankh-Morpork and Sam Vimes.

36

Night Watch (2002)

WHEN YOU'VE FOLLOWED A CHARACTER through a tough climb up the social ladder, from a drunk in the gutter to the well-respected Duke of Ankh,[136] it starts to get tricky to find good things to do with him. One of the best tricks is to take away all those hard-won accomplishments.

So in *Night Watch*, as Lady Sybil nears her delivery date, His Grace Commander Sir Samuel Vimes is in pursuit of a really nasty serial killer by the name of Carcer, and has chased him onto the roof of Unseen University's library, when a thunderstorm blows in from the Hub and a bolt of magical lightning flings Vimes and Carcer thirty years into the past.

I think it's arguably possible that this was the same storm that powered up the glass clock in *Thief of Time*, though I haven't worked out whether the chronology for that entirely fits. Whether it is or not, it certainly seems to be connected somehow to the damage that one did to the Disc's history. Once he's in the Ankh-Morpork of his youth, before Lord Havelock Vetinari became Patrician, before Mustrum Ridcully became Archchancellor, and before Samuel Vimes himself was much more than a raw recruit, Lu-Tze the sweeper intervenes, and gives Vimes four days to make history come out right—or be removed from it. Carcer has already caused significant damage to the history Vimes remembers, and that has to be repaired; if Vimes can't fix it, the History Monks will have to erase it, and Vimes with it.

---

[136] In *The Fifth Elephant*, he was Duke of Ankh-Morpork. Now he's Duke of Ankh. Clearly, the History Monks have been meddling. But in *Thud!* the "Morpork" is back.

And he has no help, no well-organized, well-manned, well-equipped Watch, no cooperative Patrician, no money, no family—just his own wits and thirty-year-old memories.

Well, that, and a healthy supply of narrativium, which is to say, the author's on his side. Still, it's a lot of fun watching it all play out.

There are hints of things to come; early on, before being transported back in time, Vimes is told that Borogravia has invaded Mouldavia. We'll see more of Borogravia's military adventures, and Sam Vimes's involvement in them, in *Monstrous Regiment*.

There are also references to what's gone before, as *The Times*, William de Worde's newspaper from *The Truth*, is still going.

There's at least one odd little error, when a torturer who is described as "naked to the waist" shortly thereafter has "blood on his shirt," when he very definitely hasn't had a chance to put a shirt on.

And there's a great deal of seeing how Ankh-Morpork came to be as we know it. We meet a much younger Havelock Vetinari, the legendary Rosie Palm[137] and the Agony Aunts[138] (often referred to but not seen until now), and so on.

Mostly, though, we watch Sam Vimes doing his job—protecting the people of Ankh-Morpork from each other, and from their own rulers.

He does, of course, survive and return to his own time, where his son, little Sam, is born. We'll see more of them in *Thud!*, as described in Chapter 44.

But there are a few other stories to look at before we get there.

[137] I feel a little silly sometimes explaining these names, but you never know who might be missing them. For those of you so innocent that it's not obvious, the name "Rosie Palm" is an old joking euphemism—"a date with Rosy Palm and her five sisters" means masturbation.

[138] "Agony aunt" is an old slang term (more British than American, in my experience) for an advice columnist.

37

"Death and What Comes Next" (2002)

WRITTEN FOR AN ONLINE GAME called *TimeHunt*, this very short story is simply a conversation between Death and a dying philosopher. The philosopher is trying, by means of quantum uncertainty, to talk his way out of dying. Death replies with some of the logical results of such thinking.

A good bit of the theorizing here closely matches discussions between Ponder Stibbons and the other wizards in *The Science of Discworld II: The Globe*.

There really isn't much to say about it; it's a cute bit of persiflage, and not much more than that. If you feel it necessary to read it, it's online at Lspace.org.

38

The Wee Free Men (2003)

THE NAC MAC FEEGLE, whom we met in *Carpe Jugulum*, are back, and responsible for the title of this first book about Tiffany Aching.

This is the second of the nominally-for-kids Discworld novels, after *The Amazing Maurice and His Educated Rodents*, and it's much closer to the standard "young adult" model, in that it describes a young person starting on her path in the world. In this case, Tiffany Aching, age nine, learns that she's the hereditary protector and designated witch of the Chalk, an area of the Disc that bears a very, very strong resemblance to the English Downs.

Tiffany's baby brother Wentworth has begun attracting the attentions of monsters, and simultaneously Tiffany finds herself being aided, for unknown reasons, by the Nac Mac Feegle. After receiving some initial guidance from a witch, Miss Perspicacia Tick, Tiffany is left to make her own way—and when the Queen of Fairyland steals Wentworth, it's up to Tiffany and the Feegles to rescue him.

This Queen, while clearly an elf of the usual parasitic sort, is not quite what we've seen in *Lords and Ladies* or *The Science of Discworld II*, but instead leans a little more toward the version presented in traditional fairy tales, or the Queen of Faerie described by T.H. White in *The Once and Future King*, or even the Goblin King in the movie *Labyrinth*.

In fact, the plot is similar to *Labyrinth* in its most basic outlines, though very different in its particulars.

Tiffany is a very likeable character, though the people around her mostly don't find her very likeable. That's because they aren't inside her head, as we're privileged to be. She, like other Discworld witches, has the knack of seeing what's really there, rather than what *ought* to be there, and of thinking about it rationally, rather than just following rules, traditions, habits, and patterns. She's a thoroughly grounded character, with roots deep in her ancestral home.

At the end of the book, Nanny Ogg and Granny Weatherwax make a brief appearance, and it's no surprise that Granny approves of Tiffany's no-nonsense approach.

The Education of Tiffany Aching

The Education of Tiffany Aching is presented in:

The Wee Free Men..Chapter 38
A Hat Full of Sky..Chapter 40
Wintersmith..Chapter 45

A fourth and probably final volume, *I Shall Wear Midnight*, is forthcoming. The series as a whole is discussed in Chapter 58.

In outline, this is one of the most traditional plots in any of the Discworld stories—a girl's baby brother is stolen by the fairies, and with the help of magical allies but mostly by means of her own determination, wits, and courage, she's able to rescue him from the Queen of the Fairies, and return home, a stronger person than when she left. There's no parodic or satirical twist, just the story as it is. If not for the appearance of Mrs. Ogg and Mistress Weatherwax, and the fact that we've seen the Nac Mac Feegle before, this wouldn't need to be a Discworld story at all—there's no mention at all of Ankh-Morpork or any of the other familiar lands, nothing involving cosmic turtles or gigantic elephants, no trolls or dwarfs. This could have been set in Sussex, or Terry Pratchett's adopted home county of Wiltshire, with only the most trivial of changes.

Of course, then it couldn't have cashed in on the immense popularity of the Discworld series, and these *are* unquestionably the same sort of witches we've seen in Lancre, and the same Nac Mac Feegle we met in *Carpe Jugulum*, and the links do become somewhat stronger in the subsequent Tiffany Aching stories, so it's just as well that it's on the Disc.

And it's a very fine story, no matter how traditional it may be. I was very pleased, after reading it, to learn that we would see more of Tiffany Aching, who returns in *A Hat Full of Sky*, as described in Chapter 40, and in *Wintersmith*, as described in Chapter 45—and we're promised a fourth and final Tiffany Aching story, *I Shall Wear Midnight*, to be out in a year or two.

But first, it's off to the mountains of Borogravia....

39

Monstrous Regiment (2003)

THIS IS ONLY BY AN EXTREME STRETCH of the definition a part of the Vimes sub-series; our protagonist is a Borogravian girl named Polly Perks, an innkeeper's daughter who disguises herself as a boy and joins the army. Sam Vimes does appear, though, as the representative of Ankh-Morpork and the voice of reason, and since I prefer not to acknowledge the existence of singleton novels that don't fit into the eight categories I listed initially, I'm declaring this an honorary Vimes novel.

He *is* in it, after all.

One might argue that it fits in the "Beyond the Century of the Fruitbat" series because it's partly about social change, but I think that's stretching it even more than calling it a Vimes novel, so I won't say that.

We've seen Vimes as an envoy before, in *The Fifth Elephant*, and in the early chapters of *Night Watch* he was being kept informed on the conflict between Borogravia and Mouldavia, so it's not a surprise to see him sent out there to represent Ankh-Morpork's interests. It's mildly amusing, though, to see what the Borogravians think of him—they call him "Vimes the Butcher," correctly acknowledging him as the second most powerful man in Ankh-Morpork.

William de Worde and Otto Chriek also put in appearances, as does Sergeant Angua, but none of the other established characters show up—unless you count Death, but his only visible or audible manifestation here is apparently a hallucination.

One rather interesting detail is that there's no overt magic in this story at all—well, unless you count vampires, werewolves, Igor's surgery, divine intervention, or other normal Discworld phenomena. There's no wizardry or witchcraft, as such.

At any rate, most of the story closely follows Polly Perks as she and her fellow recruits are flung into Borogravia's current war—which is not, despite what I said above and what Vimes was hearing in *Night Watch*, primarily with Mouldavia. So far as Polly knows, the war is against those vile Zlobenians, who have dared to trespass on the sacred soil of Borogravia.

Borogravia is not a happy place. The state religion is the worship of Nuggan, a god who has taken to pronouncing any number of ordinary objects and activities to be Abominations.[139] The ruler is a Duchess no one has seen for years, who is rumored to be dead; her generals actually run things. The war is not going well. Most of the young men have gone to be soldiers, and haven't come back.

One of those young men is Polly's brother Paul, and she intends to find him and bring him home. She has it all planned out.

Naturally, events don't follow her plans. It seems that matters are far worse than she had realized—Borogravia is at war with *all* its neighbors, and (thanks to Nuggan declaring the clacks towers to be an Abomination) Ankh-Morpork is backing the Alliance.

It also seems that she's not the only girl who's signed up to fight, for one reason or another.

Way back in *Equal Rites*, as I said in Chapter 5, it looked as if Mr. Pratchett intended to mock either feminism or sexism, but he didn't really do either one. Here, though, sixteen years later, he finally does take up the subject of sexism and really consider it. In the interim, the Discworld series has transformed itself from light parody to serious satire, if one can use such a phrase, so instead of mere mockery he gives us an insightful, funny, and sometimes bitter look at the relationships between the sexes, the perception of women, and the roles forced upon them. And perhaps some commentary on the effects of testosterone, though it's never described in those terms.[140]

He also gives us a look at soldiering, and the proper roles of officers and NCOs. This is a subject he's touched on before, notably in *Jingo*, but he tackles it in more depth here.

---

[139] Nuggan and some of his Abominations appeared in *The Last Hero*. No one there seemed to consider him especially good company.

[140] It's described in terms of socks.

He also takes a look at war in general, and plainly does not like what he sees.[141] There's not much light-hearted humor here; the subject isn't one where that would be appropriate. He presents us with a character who seems to pretty much sum everything up: Sergeant Jackrum, a red-coated blend of mother hen and murderous fiend. Jackrum has been at war for decades, and has absorbed all the lessons war can teach: Rules don't matter. Laws don't matter. Chains of command, nationality, age, sex—none of that matters. What matters is staying alive, protecting your own, and killing anything that threatens you. Jackrum has gotten very good at what matters. Compared to Jackrum, the vampire Maledict is a harmless nothing.

But Sergeant Jackrum isn't cruel or sadistic or evil, just horribly, monstrously pragmatic—which is what's needed in war.

There's a lot of red in *Monstrous Regiment*, reflecting the bloody nature of the enterprise—red faces, red skies, and the Borogravian uniforms include red coats, just as the old English ones did for centuries. It's probably for much the same reasons: a red coat looks grand on parade, it stands out on the street, and it doesn't show the blood when someone gets shot.

Pragmatic, that. Very English. Like Mr. Pratchett.

While everyone knows that historically, there have been women who disguised themselves as men in order to serve in the military, there may be some who find it unlikely that any could do as well as some of the women in this story. I would suggest that these doubters look into the life of, say, Nadezhda Durova. I suspect Mr. Pratchett was familiar with her history.

In a Usenet post on the subject, he said, "... I do know a little about Colonel Gauntlett Bligh Barker who was, believe me, only one of thousands if not tens of thousands of women who fought as men during the past few centuries—I've seen estimates of as many as 1,100 in the American Civil War alone. She was probably one of the last to be able to get away with it." So he had certainly read up on the subject.

Stories and belief are behind much of the trouble in this book, just as they are in so many Discworld novels. The Borogravian rulers have been relying on propaganda to keep the fight going long past the point where a sane government would have quit, and the people's belief in Nuggan and the Duchess has let them get away with it. It's only when Polly and

[141] Not a big surprise.

company can bring the truth to light that the war can be brought to an end.

Sergeant Jackrum uses stories as weapons; the mere mention of Jackrum's name is enough to cow most foes because of the stories everyone's heard about the fearsome Jackrum.

And of course, the enlisted women all have their own stories driving them. No one here is fighting for truth, or ideals, or wealth, or power; they're all playing out their individual stories.

This novel is noteworthy for its lack of outright magicians, as I mentioned, and also for its intermittent failure to pretend that Discworld is distinct from our own world. Over the course of the series, there has been a gradual shift from the use of fantasy-novel details to real-world details—names such as Bravd have given way to the likes of Susan, for example—and in *Monstrous Regiment* this progresses to citing actual songs from eighteenth- and nineteenth-century Britain, such as "The World Turned Upside Down" and "Johnny Has Gone for a Soldier," rather than inventing their Discworld equivalents.[142]

I mentioned in the last chapter that *The Wee Free Men* could almost have been set in Sussex; well, *Monstrous Regiment* could have been set in seventeenth-century Germany or Napoleonic Europe with only slight modification. Mr. Pratchett long ago stopped writing about fantasy in favor of writing about humanity; now even the fantasy trappings are wearing thin in spots, letting some very dark things show through.

Monstrous Regiment is a low point in that regard. Not in quality, as it's a good (if sometimes depressing in its view of our species) story, but in its fantasyness. The fantastic elements are back in subsequent volumes.

Sam Vimes will return in *Thud!*, as seen in Chapter 44.

Next, though, Tiffany Aching and the Nac Mac Feegle are back.

---

[142] I find it interesting that British songs about war are almost all depressing stuff like "Johnny Has Gone for A Soldier." Other countries have rousing battle hymns like the Marseillaise or "*Deutschland Über Alles*" or "Battle Hymn of the Republic," while Britain has "The Cruel War" and "The Deserter," even though it was the British who conquered a fourth of the world in their day. This may be related to Sgt. Jackrum's pragmatism.

40

A Hat Full of Sky (2004)

THE EDUCATION OF TIFFANY ACHING, hereditary witch of the Chalk, continues into a second volume. This time she's leaving home at age eleven to learn witchcraft properly, apprenticed to a Miss Level, whom we have not encountered previously and who happens to be a rather remarkable person in ways beyond merely being a witch.

The first "young adult" Discworld novel, *The Amazing Maurice and His Educated Rodents*, was complete in itself and did not lend itself to sequels; the story of Tiffany Aching, though, was clearly still just starting at the end of *The Wee Free Men*. She remains only a girl, with much to learn.

In *A Hat Full of Sky*, she sets out to learn some of it.

Alas, she's attracted the attention of a creature called a hiver, an intangible thing that takes over the mind and body of its victim. Rob Anybody, Big Man of the Chalk clan of the Nac Mac Feegle, follows her, along with several of his men, hoping to protect her from this monster. He isn't terribly successful at this, though he does help.

This novel is obviously a direct sequel to *The Wee Free Men*, but rather oddly, it's also a direct sequel to "The Sea and Little Fishes" in some ways. Letice Earwig and her apprentice Annagramma are among the new acquaintances Tiffany encounters during her stay with Miss Level, and there are important scenes at the Witch Trials.

And of course, Granny Weatherwax is back. Her appearance at the end of *The Wee Free Men* was brief, and she didn't really do much beyond acknowledging Tiffany's successes, but in *A Hat Full of Sky* she plays a major role throughout the second half of the book, and teaches Tiffany a good bit about being a witch—and about being human.

There's an interesting semi-inconsistency in that in "The Sea and Little Fishes," Granny has traditionally always won the Witch Trials, while in *A Hat Full of Sky*, she doesn't really compete at all—but then, she doesn't compete because she's accepted as being so good that she no longer has anything to prove to anyone, so it could easily be argued that she's simply moved up to the next level between stories. Or perhaps in the course of "The Sea and Little Fishes."

Some of the apprentice witches compete in the Witch Trials; we get a scene relatively early on where Annagramma and company are discussing what they'll do for their entries.

There are amusing consistencies, if that's the right term; Zakzak Stronginthearm's not-really-a-wizard assistant Brian, for example, attended Unseen University, but he didn't study magic there, he studied fretwork—and one of Rincewind's titles, as reported in *The Science of Discworld II*, is "Fretwork Teacher."

And the theme of story is strong here. Granny explains to Tiffany that people need stories to tell them what to do, stories to believe. "Change the story, change the world," she says. Tiffany finds an important clue to dealing with the hiver in remembering stories, specifically the story of the three wishes. (Exactly which story of three wishes doesn't really matter, since on some level they're all the same. Except maybe *Eric*.)

There's also stuff about evolution, which is obviously a topic that interests Mr. Pratchett, and which he'll tackle head-on in *The Science of Discworld III*, as seen in Chapter 43.

I consider this book one of Mr. Pratchett's best works; his knack for the telling phrase is well displayed here, as when he describes Tiffany's room in Miss Level's home: "It smelled of spare rooms and other people's soap."

I was delighted to hear that two more books about Tiffany Aching were planned—and disappointed that it's only two. *I Shall Wear Midnight*, which takes its title from a line in *A Hat Full of Sky*, isn't out yet, as of this writing, but the third one, *Wintersmith*, is covered in Chapter 45.

First, though, it's back to Ankh-Morpork....

41

Going Postal (2004)

THE MORIBUND ANKH-MORPORK POSTAL SERVICE was first mentioned in *Men at Arms*, way back in 1993, but it took more than a decade to bring us this tale of the unfortunately named Moist von Lipwig and his efforts to restore the post office to its proper functions.

To do this, of course, he must first survive being hanged. Lipwig is a con man, forger, thief, and swindler who fell afoul of Ankh-Morpork's unexpectedly effective City Watch.

Fortunately for him, Lord Vetinari sees to it that he *does* survive being hanged, and offers him a choice: take over as postmaster and restore the post office to functionality, or die. Not *much* of a choice, but technically, it's still a choice.

Lipwig's a survivor. He takes the job, and after a few attempts at escape, gets caught up in the challenge. Public relations isn't really that different from fraud, and he's very good at fraud. . . .

There are several problems facing the post office. Its original collapse, decades earlier, was brought about by the use of a temporally complex mail-sorting machine designed by our old friend Bloody Stupid Johnson. The accumulated undelivered mail is responsible for other difficulties; just as the magical properties of books create L-space, all those words wanting to be read are causing distortions in time and space.

Most of all, though, the major clacks company, the Grand Trunk, sees the postal service as a competitor. The Grand Trunk has fallen into the hands of a group of unscrupulous businessmen led by one Reacher Gilt, whose cost-cutting measures have impaired the effectiveness of the clacks service, leaving an opportunity that Lipwig's postmen leap at.

The clacks, while really just a semaphore system, serve as a Discworld parallel of the Internet, where tech-obsessed young clacksmen are so happy to be playing with hardware and coded data that they barely notice how they're being exploited by ruthless businessmen.

Reacher Gilt is the epitome of all that's bad in venture capitalism; he's taken over the Grand Trunk through financial maneuvers so complex that no actual money was involved. He's a pirate—and that's made explicit in his description. He is, in fact, Long John Silver, right down to his name. He has a bird, a pet cockatoo that says "Twelve and a half percent!" in imitation of Silver's parrot chanting "Pieces of eight!" (I'd have been happier if Mr. Pratchett hadn't felt it necessary to actually explain, in the story, that "Twelve and a half percent!" means "Pieces of eight!"[143])

Moist von Lipwig recognizes Reacher Gilt as a swindler like himself, and one reason that he sets out to succeed in the job he's been forced to take on is to demonstrate that he's not the monster Gilt is. Lipwig employs golems, invents postage stamps,[144] and does everything he can to move the mail and give the public a good show. Where Sam Vimes sees the newspaper as a dangerous nuisance, Lipwig sees it as a tool to be used and a battlefield to be won.

Incidentally, although Lord Vetinari is a major character in *Going Postal*, Sam Vimes doesn't appear at all. He's mentioned in passing, nothing more. We do see that Dr. Lawn's Lady Sybil Free Hospital, established at the end of *Night Watch*, is functioning nicely, and Lipwig does get interviewed by Captain Carrot at one point, but Vimes himself is kept out, probably to keep him from stealing the spotlight.

We are informed of the existence of Anoia, Goddess of Things That Stick in Drawers; we'll get to meet her in person in *Wintersmith*.

Ponder Stibbons appears and makes a punning reference to "phase space," a concept explained in the previous *Science of Discworld* volumes. Archchancellor Ridcully has a significant role. And there's a small Tolkien tribute, of sorts, in a scene with an omniscope—that's a magical device not totally unlike a crystal ball, or Tolkien's *palantir*.

---

[143] Yes, it does. "Pieces of eight" were each one-eighth of a Spanish gold dollar; hence the name. They were also known as "bits," as in "Shave and a haircut, two bits!"

[144] Which means, contrary to the evidence of their publication dates, that *Nanny Ogg's Cookbook* was written by Mrs. Ogg well after the events of *Going Postal* happened, since Nanny includes in her etiquette section a guide to the significance of stamps.

Oh, the title deserves comment. Every American I've ever spoken with knows what "going postal" means—going berserk, like the handful of postal workers in the 1980s and '90s who went on shooting sprees. In online discussions, though, it appeared that many British or Australian readers had never encountered the phrase until the publication of this novel, and really weren't clear on its derivation. That startled me, since as I've mentioned before, Mr. Pratchett is a very English writer, and clearly *he* knew the phrase, and thought it was familiar enough that his readers would get the joke.

One of the more interesting features of *Going Postal* is that it has chapters. Up until now, and excluding the four divisions of *The Colour of Magic* and the four books of *Pyramids* as really being something different, only the "Science of" books and the "young adult" novels featuring the Amazing Maurice and Tiffany Aching have had chapters. Oh, there have been prologues (*Going Postal* has two) and epilogues (there's one of those here, too), but not chapters. *Going Postal* has fourteen chapters, each of them headed by a list of the scenes to be found therein, in the manner of a nineteenth-century novel—for example, Chapter 1 opens as follows:

In which our hero experiences Hope,
the greatest gift * *The bacon sandwich of regret* *
Somber reflections on capital punishment
from the hangman * *Famous last words* * *Our hero dies* *
Angels, conversations about * *Inadvisability of misplaced*
offers regarding broomsticks * *An unexpected ride* *
A world free of honest men * *A man on the hop* *
There is always a choice

There's nothing like that in any of the previous Discworld novels.

Each chapter also features (at least in the editions I've seen) an illustration of an Ankh-Morpork postage stamp.[145]

And unlike the "young adult" novels, *Going Postal* acknowledges the old Discworld idea, much neglected in the later novels, that the number eight has magical significance and should therefore be avoided; the chapter between Chapter 7 and Chapter 9 is Chapter 7a.[146]

---

[145] And I'll have more to say about those stamps in Chapter 49.

[146] An idea which, you'll have noticed, I shamelessly stole.

Also, I believe (though perhaps I just missed it earlier) that *Going Postal* is the first novel where the men of Ankh-Morpork wear neckties. The faux-medieval trappings of the early novels have given way to something far more modern—though not *exactly* modern, as women's fashions, we are informed, currently include bustles.

In an interview publicizing the Sky One adaptation of *Hogfather*, Mr. Pratchett explained that various aspects of Discworld tend to mirror whatever Roundworld era he thinks most suitable for that particular feature; apparently he sees the Post Office as late Victorian.[147] At any rate, it's plain that we've long ago left behind the generic faux-medieval setting of traditional fantasy novels.

All in all, *Going Postal* is a bit of a change—and the beginning of a new sub-series featuring Mr. Lipwig, as Moist von Lipwig is also the protagonist of the latest novel, *Making Money*, wherein Lipwig takes over Ankh-Morpork's Royal Mint.[148] Moist von Lipwig seems to make a habit of taking things over, and has apparently taken over the "Beyond the Century of the Fruitbat" series, as well.

Making Money has chapters, like *Going Postal*, but *Thud!*, as described in Chapter 44, does not.

The board game of Thud is introduced in *Going Postal*, as it happens—Lord Vetinari is playing a game by clacks. Thud involves a battle between dwarfs and trolls. Again, Mr. Pratchett is hinting at things to come.

But first we have a short story, and then another book with chapters, lots of them, as the Science of Discworld series reaches its third volume.

---

[147] Since postage stamps were invented during Victoria's reign, this isn't unreasonable.

[148] The Mint is mentioned in the epilogue of *Going Postal*, so apparently he had this planned for some time.

42

"A Collegiate Casting-Out of Devilish Devices" (2005)

IT COULD BE ARGUED that this isn't really a short story at all, but it looks like one to me, so I'm including it. "A Collegiate Casting-Out of Devilish Devices" first appeared in the *Times* Higher Education Supplement for May 13, 2005; that was well after the publication of *Once More* with Footnotes*, which is why it isn't included therein.

It's an account of a faculty meeting at Unseen University where the wizards deal, in their usual fashion, with certain suggestions from the Patrician's representative, A.E. Pessimal. Readers will see more of Mr. Pessimal in *Thud!*, when he's assigned to review the operation of the Watch, but here he's been sent to see if he can improve the University.

The wizards don't think the University needs improvement, but it doesn't do to simply ignore the Patrician, so they give Mr. Pessimal's questions some attention.

Like many of the scenes at Unseen University, it's a parody of academia, and a good one. It stands on its own as such, but definitely ties into the series as a whole—besides Mr. Pessimal, there are references to Braseneck College, which was introduced in *The Last Continent*.

It's a shame it isn't more widely available.

43

The Science of Discworld III: Darwin's Watch (2005)

(with Ian Stewart and Jack Cohen)

ONE MORE TIME, THE WIZARDS of Unseen University descend upon Roundworld to prevent the eventual extinction of the human species. This time an outside force has been tampering with Charles Darwin's history. Instead of writing *Origin of Species*, he's written *Theology of Species*, which results in a more peaceful twentieth century—and slower scientific and technological progress, leading to disaster.

This is really quite a clever idea, and depends on a good understanding of Darwin's life and background. He was brought up in the Church of England and took it seriously, and almost certainly would have preferred to find a theological explanation for the diversity of life he observed, but instead reported honestly what he saw, and what he concluded from that.

In *Darwin's Watch*, something, it would seem, has prevented this.

The cause of the tampering is less obvious this time than was the interference by elves in *The Science of Discworld II*, and is not discovered until halfway through the story, so I'll only name it in a footnote,[149] so those of you who prefer not to be told can avoid it.

It's the footnote to this paragraph.[150]

---

[149] Not this one, the next one.

[150] It's the Auditors of Reality, as seen in *Reaper Man, Hogfather, and Thief of Time*. They're defeated largely by the methods seen in *Thief of Time*.

There.

Now, moving on, the science in the even-numbered chapters in this volume, unsurprisingly, includes a great deal about evolution, but not merely Darwinian natural selection; it also discusses social evolution and technological evolution, how particular social situations led to certain results. Sociology and history can be considered science, right? There's a good bit about how and why nineteenth-century Britain saw such a tremendous surge of development, compared to most of the rest of the world.

But since you're reading about it here, I assume you're more interested in the Discworld elements, rather than the science.

In the previous *Science* volumes, Rincewind was more or less the hero; in this one it's really an ensemble effort, with Ponder Stibbons taking the lead more than Rincewind. Oh, Rincewind (who has now accumulated a total of nineteen posts on the UU faculty, rather than the mere seven he had in *The Science of Discworld II*) is certainly present and active, but it's Stibbons, Hex, and Archchancellor Ridcully who take charge of dealing with the situation.

They (and we) learn a great deal about the life of Charles Darwin, and about just how unlikely it was that *Origin of Species* actually got written.

Charles Darwin, incidentally, learns far more than he wanted to about the Discworld when the wizards transport him there briefly. His stay includes a visit to the God of Evolution, whom we first met in *The Last Continent*. Fortunately for his sanity and our history, Darwin's memory of this is magically removed before he's returned to his own world, where he does indeed write *Origin of Species*.

So far, this is the final *Science of Discworld* volume, and I rather suspect it will stay that way. It holds up well, but one rather gets the impression that the authors have pretty much said what they had to say on their various subjects. Dragging the faculty of Unseen University into yet another adventure on Roundworld would really seem to be stretching the premise too far.

Fortunately, there's still plenty to be said about Discworld, so it's back to Ankh-Morpork for another look at the adventures of His Grace Sir Samuel Vimes, Duke of Ankh-Morpork and Commander of the Watch. . . .

44

Thud! (2005)

THE ENMITY OF DWARFS and trolls has been an established feature of the Discworld for many a volume at this point, and there have been several mentions of the infamous Battle of Koom Valley. At long last, Mr. Pratchett sees fit to tell us more about that fabled conflict, while setting Commander Vimes another mystery to solve, and another disaster to stave off.

The title comes from the board-game Thud, which was introduced in *Going Postal*; in it one player plays dwarfs and the other trolls, in a battle between the two species.[151]

There are other echoes of *Going Postal*, as well—the expression "go postal" comes up more than once, in contexts where "go spare"[152] would have been more likely a few volumes back, and the Post Office's fondness for collectible stamps manifests itself in two different Koom Valley commemoratives that serve to fan the flames of dwarf/troll hostility.

And there's the painting, *The Goddess Anoia Arising from the Cutlery*—Anoia was first mentioned in *Going Postal*, and will turn up in person in *Wintersmith*.

These little consistencies are part of what gives the Discworld its charm. Little details of all sorts add to the flavor, as when we learn that Carrot Ironfoundersson's actual first name is Kzad-bhat, meaning Head Banger. "Carrot" is presumably merely a rough approximation of the correct pronunciation, as well as describing his appearance.

---

[151] And yes, of course someone has actually designed the game—primarily Trevor Truran, a professional game designer, under Mr. Pratchett's guidance. The game has its own website, in fact, at www.thudgame.com/.

[152] For my American readers: "Go spare" is British slang, roughly equivalent to "go nuts."

And then there are the little inter-universal references, such as the dwarfish symbol for the Long Dark, i.e., a mine tunnel. It's a circle with a horizontal line across it—which happens to be the logo of the London Underground.

At any rate, things are tense in Ankh-Morpork as the anniversary of the Battle of Koom Valley nears. A group of very conservative, very respected dwarfs have settled in the city—or under it, really—and are stirring up trouble.

Then one of the most provocative of the lot is murdered, and the dwarfs say a troll is responsible, and Sam Vimes investigates. He wants to prevent open warfare, and he wants to find the killer; he *hopes* these goals aren't incompatible.

Matters, of course, get complicated. It turns out there was more than the one murder, there are strange things going on in the troll community, the Watch has taken on a vampire as a recruit, Nobby has acquired a girlfriend. . . .

And Sam Vimes has a son, Young Sam, and every day at six he *must* read Young Sam the boy's favorite book, *Where's My Cow?*[153] He's made this an absolutely inviolable rule, in order to make sure that he never allows himself to neglect his child; it's *important*. Allowing anything to interfere with this daily ritual will be conceding defeat, admitting that the world can force him to give up parts of himself he does not intend to give up.

Non-parents may not empathize easily with the importance of the ritual.

Carrot, interestingly, *does* appreciate its importance, and cooperates with Vimes to ensure that the ritual happens on schedule, even though Carrot has previously said that "Personal isn't the same as important."

Some things, it would seem, are both.

All in all, it's a Vimes novel on the usual pattern—a crime has been committed that Vimes is determined to solve, no matter what or who might get in his way, and in the course of solving it he finds himself dealing with matters far larger than mere murder. Along the way, we see the various members of the Watch being themselves—Carrot, Angua,

---

[153] *Where's My Cow?* has actually been published here in Roundworld, illustrated by Melvyn Grant, written (of course) by Terry Pratchett, but the book version is somewhat modified from the original, as it includes both the original rural material, and urban material Vimes added. The result provides an entertaining look at a handful of Discworld characters, though perhaps not entertaining enough to justify the cover price.

Fred Colon, Nobby, Detritus, Cheery Littlebottom, Corporal Visit, and the rest. There are meetings with Lord Vetinari, interludes with Lady Sybil and her dragons, and more. It's a very satisfactory package indeed. The addition of Young Sam and the revelation of the secret of Koom Valley are new, of course, but they fit in nicely. Willikins, the family butler Vimes acquired when he married Lady Sybil, returns and develops some wonderful new depths.

There are certain new elements here of which I confess I'm not immediately enamored; the dwarfish culture seems to be getting even darker and more unpleasant than it was in *The Fifth Elephant*, for one. The Devices, pre-human artifacts the dwarfs collect, strike me as potentially a bad idea, and not entirely in keeping with Discworld's history as we know it.

A couple of lines hark back amusingly to much earlier books. For example, at one point Vimes remarks, "It's been a long time since this city was last burned to the ground."

Not *that* long, really, since it happened at the beginning of *The Colour of Magic*.

And Igor, the bartender at Biers, first and last seen in *Feet of Clay*, appears, with a footnote clarifying that he's not one of *those* Igors.

There are some nice subplots that have very little to do with the central story, but which are thoroughly entertaining all the same, such as Nobby's romance with Tawneee, and the "girls' night out" that Angua, Sally, Cheery, and Tawneee share. It's amusing to see that the Disc has cocktails just as ridiculously named as ours, including its own version of a Screaming Orgasm.[154] And it's good to see that Mr. Pratchett can still find stories to tell about Sam Vimes that don't involve dragging him off to Uberwald or Borogravia, or flinging him into the past, or having him be anything other than the copper he is.

I hope we'll see more of Mr. Vimes in the future, but so far, *Thud!* is his last starring role. The next book is another "young adult" title featuring Tiffany Aching, and then after that it's Moist von Lipwig again.

---

[154] 1 oz. vodka, 1½ oz. Bailey's Irish Cream, ½ oz. Kahlua. The Discworld recipe is somewhat different.

45

Wintersmith (2006)

TIFFANY ACHING IS BACK.

She's been learning witchcraft under various mentors, and as her thirteenth birthday approaches, she's living with Miss Eumenides[155] Treason, a very old witch, who takes her to observe the Dark Morris, the silent one described near the very end of *Reaper Man*, the one that balances out the ordinary Morris that ushers in the springtime.

The Dark Morris ushers in the winter.

Tiffany, in a moment of teenage rebellion, gets caught up in it and joins the dance, bringing her to the attention of the spirit of winter itself, the elemental known to the witches as the Wintersmith.

The Wintersmith never really noticed human beings as individuals before, but you can't ignore someone who's dancing with you, and he takes a very definite interest in Tiffany. After all, she usurped the role of his usual partner in the dance.

As Granny Weatherwax points out, Tiffany has put herself into a story, a very old, very powerful story, and the only way out is to see it through to the end, and to make sure the story comes out right.

Tiffany does her best—and since this is a Discworld story, she succeeds, with the help of the other witches, the Nac Mac Feegle, and a designated Hero.

Along the way, she learns more about people, witchcraft, and the world in general. The other young witches introduced in *A Hat Full of Sky*—Annagramma, Petulia Gristle, Dimity Hubbub, Lucy Warbeck,

[155] In Greek myth, the Eumenides are the Furies, the spirits of vengeance. Literally, though, "eumenides" means "the kindly ones"—the Greeks used it (not entirely without sarcasm) as an appeasing euphemism, rather the way the English called elves "the Fair Folk."

It's not accidental that Miss Treason is named Eumenides.

and the rest—appear, and advance in their respective careers. (We learn in passing that Petulia's Pig Trick was considered the winning magic at the Witch Trials in *A Hat Full of Sky*. I suspect we'll see more of Petulia. I hope we do, anyway; I like her.)

We see quite a bit of Granny Weatherwax and Nanny Ogg.

Throughout the Discworld series, we've had snatches of dog-Latin popping up, and a few bits of Welsh; in *Wintersmith* we also get Greek—not transliterated, but in the original alphabet—and a single phrase in Russian.[156] The series continues to evolve, and the Disc bears more and more resemblance to Roundworld.

And speaking of Roundworld, there's an explicit reference to narrativium, the element first named in *The Science of Discworld*. It's described as one of the components of people. Stories are what make us people, as set forth in *The Science of Discworld II: The Globe*.

Another cross-series reference is a scene of Rob Anybody reading *Where's My Cow?*, the book Sam Vimes reads to his son in *Thud!*

Anoia, a minor goddess first mentioned in *Going Postal*, gets a scene with Tiffany.

And there's a pun that I rather grudgingly admire. We learn that the name of Nanny Ogg's home, in the village of Slice, in the kingdom of Lancre, is Tir Nani Ogg. "Nanny Ogg," of course, is a familiar name to Discworld readers. "Tír na nÓg," on the other hand, is a familiar name to anyone who knows anything about Irish myth—it means "Land of Youth," and is the magical, other-worldly isle somewhere far to the west where the *sidhe* live, where there's no disease or aging.

I'd never made the connection between "Tír na nÓg" and "Nanny Ogg" before. I rather suspect that Mr. Pratchett originally hadn't, either, since if he had I'd have expected to see "Tir Nani Ogg" before this, but it's an amusing one, all the same, whether coincidental or planned.

While on the subject of Mrs. Ogg: We also meet one or two of Nanny's daughters-in-law, and (rather frustratingly, if you ask me) still don't learn any of their names.

This is primarily Tiffany's story, though. She's coming into her own—no longer just a girl, but a young woman; no longer a potential witch, but a practicing one.

I look forward to reading more about her—and about the rest of Discworld.

One more book to consider—the return of Moist von Lipwig.

---

[156] Allegedly from *Überwald Winter*, by Wotua Doinov, and meaning, "It's getting cold again."

46

Making Money (2007)

IN *GOING POSTAL*, we got to know former(?) con artist Moist von Lipwig, and watched him resuscitate the Ankh-Morpork postal service. In *Making Money*, Lord Vetinari offers him the opportunity to do the same for the Royal Bank of Ankh-Morpork, and the Royal Mint. Lipwig is not at all enthusiastic about the idea, but Fate and the Patrician conspire to see that he does eventually tackle the job—and Lipwig is forced to admit that, once prodded into it, he relishes the challenge.

And a challenge it is; Ankh-Morpork is in the midst of a banking crisis, and the Mint is horrendously outdated. Furthermore, while nobody else had any interest in running the Post Office, there are people very interested indeed in controlling the Royal Bank, and eager to wrest it away from Lipwig.

Like *Going Postal*, *Making Money* has complexly named chapters with illustrations at the start of each, though the illustrations aren't as consistent as the stamps in *Going Postal*. The chapter between Chapter 7 and Chapter 9 is simply Chapter 8 this time. While it's clearly following the model of the previous book, it doesn't seem as if the details are quite as well handled.

Likewise, the story itself seems a little less perfect than the magnificence of *Going Postal*. Some of the subplots, such as the hydraulic model of Ankh-Morpork's economy, while amusing, don't seem completely necessary, and Cosmo Lavish is a less effective villain than Reacher Gilt—it's fairly clear all along that Lavish carries the seeds of his own destruction, which was much less a foregone conclusion with Gilt.

Still, it's a lot of fun watching Lipwig invent paper money, try to take Ankh-Morpork off the gold standard, and give the banking business a healthy dose of showmanship. We learn a little more about Igors, meet a figure from Lipwig's past, and resolve some lingering old issues. We even learn C.M.O.T. Dibbler's full name. All in all, a worthy addition to the series, and one that leaves me eager for the next—whatsoever that may be.

47

Stories Yet to Come

THE DISCWORLD SERIES is not finished; it isn't anywhere *near* finished. As Terry Pratchett said at a book-signing I attended, a few years down the road he might retire, but if he does, he's not sure what he'd do. Maybe write a book.

Or two.

But I want to get *this* book finished, so I can't wait around to see what becomes of it all. I will, however, mention what I know of what lies ahead.

I Shall Wear Midnight, the fourth and probably last Tiffany Aching story, is in the works. Throughout the first three books, she's insisted on wearing blue or green, the colors of the Chalk, rather than proper witchy black; it would seem this is finally going to change.

Making Money ends with Lord Vetinari suggesting that Moist von Lipwig might consider revamping Ankh-Morpork's system of tax collection; presumably Lipwig will eventually accept the job. A working title of *Raising Taxes* has been mentioned. It seems Lipwig has taken over the "Beyond the Century of the Fruitbat" series, or perhaps he's becoming another series, like Sam Vimes or Granny Weatherwax. Launching another sub-series some thirty volumes in is . . . interesting.

Beyond that—I don't know. As of October 2006, Mr. Pratchett said he didn't, either, though he had a few ideas forming. The story goes on.

PART FOUR
More Comments

48

The Discworld Phenomenon

So THAT'S THE SERIES TO DATE. It started out as clever but fairly simple parodies of fantasy novels, but grew and changed, gradually shifting from parody to satire, and gradually turning its focus from fantasy to the real world, growing darker in the process. It's still changing—Moist von Lipwig has become a series, for example.

It keeps expanding and diversifying. The first two novels followed a standard series model, featuring the same protagonists, but with the third book, *Equal Rites*, those protagonists were nowhere to be seen. New series-within-series kept cropping up; old series mutated, as when Susan took over from her grandfather. Short stories were added to the mix, as were illustrated volumes, and "young adult" novels, and science books.

Early on, there seemed to be a deliberate effort *not* to repeat details—the perpetually shifting Archchancellors, for example, or place-names that appeared once and then vanished forever. But this changed, and what comic-book fans call "continuity" started to accumulate, sometimes becoming in-jokes—minor characters would pop up in unexpected but logical places, lines of dialogue would recur, and so on.

Where Mr. Pratchett found it necessary in *Lords and Ladies* to include a warning that the book was a sequel and best understood if one had read *Wyrd Sisters* and *Witches Abroad*, by the time of *Thud!* it seems to be taken for granted that readers are thoroughly familiar with much of what's gone before. Nowadays novels even include the hooks on which future volumes will hang, as the epilogue of *Going Postal* sets up *Making Money*. It's all growing ever more varied, but also more interconnected.

And that's just Mr. Pratchett's stories themselves, which are no longer the entirety of the Discworld phenomenon. There are now add-ons, lots of them, by other people, working from the base Mr. Pratchett has provided. They aren't new *stories*, as such, but they're all about Discworld. It seems as if there's a compulsion many readers feel to make various elements of the series more real.

To start, there's Stephen Briggs, who has been billed as the "cartographer of Discworld." He started off by adapting *Wyrd Sisters* to the stage for an amateur drama troupe, the Studio Theatre Club of Oxford; that went well enough that, at Terry Pratchett's suggestion, he started adapting other novels, and became fascinated with the series. He started compiling information and adding to it, with Mr. Pratchett's blessing, resulting in a series of three maps (*The Streets of Ankh-Morpork*, *The Discworld Mapp*, and *A Tourist Guide to Lancre*), a reference book entitled *The Discworld Companion* (followed by a second edition and then by *The New Discworld Companion*, with each version differing in several respects beyond simply having material about later volumes added), a spin-off I've mentioned before called *Nanny Ogg's Cookbook*, a series of at least eight diaries based on Discworld (most recently *Lu-Tze's Yearbook of Enlightenment 2008*), a graphic novel of *Guards! Guards!*, and an assortment of merchandise such as badges, T-shirts, and scarves based on various Discworld features. (There are also graphic novel adaptations of *The Colour of Magic*, *The Light Fantastic*, and *Mort*, but those don't seem to have involved Mr. Briggs.) The non-book merchandise is offered on his website at www.cmotdibbler.com/.

Oh, and his series of adaptations for the stage had reached fifteen, at last count. It's been suggested by some that Mr. Briggs may know more about Discworld than Mr. Pratchett does.

Then there are the two cover artists for the series—the late Josh Kirby, whose work adorned the British covers for almost two decades, and his successor, Paul Kidby. Mr. Kirby also provided the artwork for the original illustrated version of *Eric*, and his art was featured in Discworld calendars and elsewhere. For many British readers, Kirby's art was a significant part of what gave Discworld its flavor.

Paul Kidby first came to the series through the spin-offs—his first published Discworld art was a flyer accompanying a computer game based on the books. From there he went on to produce the art for *The Pratchett Portfolio*, depicting several of the characters from the novels, and then provided the illustrations for *The Last Hero*, *Nanny Ogg's Cookbook*, the various diaries, Discworld Christmas cards. . . .

There's also a fourth map, of sorts: *Death's Domain*, with Paul Kidby's depiction of Death's home. It's really more an illustration than a map, unlike the three Stephen Briggs did.

You know, when I started working on this book, I had the idea that I would assemble a complete set of all the available Discworld merchandise. I gave that idea up fairly quickly, as there's just too much of it. Christmas cards? Badges? T-shirts? Computer games? Cut-out books?

And then there's the Cunning Artificer, Bernard Pearson. He is a sculptor and artist who created the stamp designs in *Going Postal*—and who then went on to produce the actual stamps. Yes, if you're interested in both philately and Discworld, you can collect the stamps of Ankh-Morpork, a truly astonishing variety of them, complete with various errors to make them more interesting to collectors.

He'll also happily sell you sculptures of everything from the Fools' Guild to one of Mr. Dibbler's pies. Or a Tiffany Aching mirror frame, or an official Thieves' Guild coat-hook.

His central website is at www.artificer.co.uk/. He's also the creator of the pieces used to play the board game Thud, though game designer Trevor Truran devised the rules.[157]

And then there was Clarecraft, which created over 150 authorized models and other things, which are now collectors' items.

For most multimedia phenomena, licensed merchandise is largely cheap junk, mass-produced somewhere in Asia and sold through toy stores. Discworld merchandise, on the other hand, tends to be lovingly produced by individual craftsmen. People get *obsessed* by this stuff!

And these are just the ones who are doing authorized work, and selling the results; who knows what else fans may have created? There are Discworld conventions. There are undoubtedly Discworld costumes out there; a group of fans in the Chicago area created and danced the Dark Morris, the *other* dance mentioned in *Reaper Man* that later became central to *Wintersmith*. There is a CD entitled *From the Discworld*, by a musician named Dave Greenslade, who wrote theme music for various elements of the series and provided words and a tune for "A Wizard's Staff Has a Knob on the End," one of the songs that gets mentioned a few times in the course of the series.

---

[157] Based on an Old English or Norse game called Hnefatafl, apparently.

This isn't the only extant version of "A Wizard's Staff Has a Knob on the End"; in fact, there are at least three, written by various musically-inclined fans. Other fans have also, of course, written "The Hedgehog Can Never Be Buggered At All," and probably any other song Mr. Pratchett referred to that didn't already exist.

Besides Thud, there are Discworld computer games, and a Discworld version of the strategy game Diplomacy. The Discworld card game Cripple Mr Onion has existed in our world since 1993.

In short, fans seem determined to make real as much of Discworld as they can, or to find ways to spend more time there.

That's not unique, of course; there are plenty of people who do their best to recreate their favorite fantasies. Thousands of people in the world today speak Klingon or Elvish. Still, it takes a special sort of story to evoke this kind of loyalty; you'll find people making replicas of items from *Star Trek* and *Lord of the Rings* and *Harry Potter* and other immensely popular epics, but not from just any ordinary novel.

Discworld isn't an epic, though, it's *satire*. And for the most part, the heroes aren't kings or captains or princesses trying to save entire worlds; they're just people trying to get by. Yes, they sometimes *do* save the entire world, but that's not the *point*.

Or perhaps it is. After all, isn't it a bit easier to identify with a tired copper or a grouchy old witch than with the pride of Starfleet, or the Heir of Isildur, or the Boy Who Lived? It's not Rincewind's *job* to save the world, but he does it anyway. (I was going to say "despite not having any fancy titles," but he *is* the Egregious Professor of Cruel and Unusual Geography. And the Fretwork Teacher. Neither of which carries a great deal of implied nobility or a responsibility of world-saving, so far as I can see.)

All in all, Discworld is a rather different series from those others, and the fannish accoutrements available are rather different, as well. From *The Lord of the Rings* you can get swords and jewelry; from Discworld you can get an Unseen University scarf, or an official Thieves' Guild coat-hook. From *Star Trek* we have an invented alien language; from Discworld we have bawdy drinking songs.

They all have games based on them, but come on, game designers will base a game on *anything*. Anyone remember Burger Chef?

So we have wands and weapons from other fantasies, and we have household goods from Discworld. We have spaceship designs from *Star*

Trek, and postage stamps from Discworld. There's a different sort of emphasis there. It's not on heroes, but on settings; not on grand adventure, but on everyday life.

How appropriate! After all, as I've said from the start, Discworld is about people and stories, not heroes and adventures.

So why does anyone think that's worthy of going to the trouble to create or obtain the bits and pieces of such a world? It's not particularly uplifting or inspiring.

But it's comforting. It's fun. Discworld is a world of stories, and what's more, they're old stories, familiar stories—nursery tales and Hollywood clichés and favorites from childhood, all put together, where we know they'll all turn out right, because they always have.

The people of the Disc may complain that their world doesn't make sense, that there's no logic to it, but still, they all know the stories. They know million-to-one chances always come out—and so do we. It's just a matter of making sure we're in the *right* story.

Discworld is comfortable and funny and charming, like a good vacation, and readers want to bring back souvenirs. People come back from *Star Wars* or the War of the Ring with wartime souvenirs, weapons, and loot; people come back from Discworld with the sort of knickknack you'd pick up in a village gift shop. Nobody's selling replicas of Sam Vimes's sword or Granny's broomstick, but the stamps Moist von Lipwig had printed up, a scarf to keep out the winter chill of the Ramtops—those *fit*.

People admire Aragorn and Frodo and Captain Kirk; they *sympathize* with Sam Vimes.

So Discworld attracts fans, like the other great fantasy phenomena, but they're a rather different sort of fan.

Like those other creations, Mr. Pratchett's Discworld has built up the sort of detailed reality that people enjoy visiting. It's a world, not just a bunch of stage sets where the stories play out. It has details like stamps and coat-hooks. It wasn't created all of a piece before the stories began, the way Middle Earth was, though; it has accumulated.

A good many of those details were undoubtedly originally included not as serious world-building, but as jokes—the name of Death's horse, "one man, one vote," and so on—but they've added up into something much more than a bunch of throwaway gags. One way to make people laugh is to extend a process or metaphor to the point of absurdity, following something out to its logical but ridiculous conclusion, and Mr.

Pratchett has done that repeatedly. Discworld is awash in metaphors made literal and jokes carried too far. They're ridiculous, yes, but they're still *logical*—they fit together, they make sense, they're *satisfying*.

Another source of humor is repetition, bringing things back in unexpected ways, so we've seen themes develop as things recur. We learn, eventually, that cackling is a serious issue for witches, not just a joke.

And then there are the characters. Character is the root of most of the very best comedy, and Mr. Pratchett is a master of character. Discworld is rich in wonderful characters, many of whom fall into two categories: those who fit their role perfectly, to the point that they understand it in ways we've never seen before, like Granny Weatherwax or Genghiz Cohen or Havelock Vetinari, and those who are unsuited to a role, but either learn it, or force the role to fit *them*, such as Rincewind, or Captain Carrot, or Magrat Garlick.

Sometimes all three of these combine, as when we learn the Way of Mrs. Cosmopolite from Lu-Tze the Sweeper in *Thief of Time*—the exaggerated wisdom of martial-arts masters is parodied by taking it to the extreme of banality, the platitudes mouthed by the most tedious and stereotypical of middle-class matrons. We learn more about it as it's repeated, as more and more of her inane sayings are presented.

And we see Lu-Tze *make it work*, because he's so much the martial arts master that he can find the true wisdom he needs even in these appalling clichés.

It *all fits*.

And it gives Discworld that reality that makes us want to return there over and over.

There's an old saying, "It's funny 'cause it's true." Well, Discworld is true because it's funny. In assembling things we readers would laugh at, Mr. Pratchett has put together enough truth to bring his creation to life.

If there were just one or two books, I don't think we'd see any fan merchandise to speak of, no reference books or maps or art books, even if it/they sold in huge numbers. There just wouldn't be enough to base them on; there are no obsessive appendices or maps in the first couple of books, no grand plans outlined, nothing like that.

But there aren't one or two books, there are more than thirty. Once there were half a dozen and the background had accumulated some depth, fans began to take note, and the spin-offs started to appear.

There have been other series in fantasy and science fiction that ran dozens of volumes, but most of them didn't sell as well as Discworld, and perhaps more importantly, most series didn't get *better* from one book to the next. It's more common for the quality to deteriorate slightly, as the author runs out of ideas. Mr. Pratchett didn't run out of ideas, but he *did* get better at writing about them.

And *funny* series? No others have lasted anywhere near as long.[158] Usually the author's jokes have all been run into the ground after three or four books, at most. As I said right at the beginning, in my first introduction, this whole world-on-a-turtle thing should've only been good for a couple of books, three at the outside. What's kept Discworld going—well, there are two things, fear and surprise. . . . I mean, there are two things:

First, it's not all one series. We'd have all been very sick of Rincewind after a dozen books if we never saw anyone else's view of the Disc—or really, we'd have gotten tired of any of the others, too. If it had just remained parodies of other fantasy books, it wouldn't have worked. The Disc itself is a parody of a fantasy world, but it's not *about* the Disc, it's about various people *on* the Disc, and a key word there is "various." The multiple series keep everything fresh; they allow the author to run variations, rather than having to come up with something completely fresh each time—for example, having shown us the vampires in *Carpe Jugulum*, and introduced us to the Igors in Lancre and Uberwald, he can then show us vampires and Igors in Ankh-Morpork in subsequent books. Play with one idea with the witches, and then pit it against the Watch; try another on Rincewind, then throw it at the witches. You can get more mileage out of each invention, and generate new ideas in the process.

Second, Terry Pratchett is a fuckin' genius. He just is. Very annoying of him. And he's not your chortling, world-conquering sort of genius, either. He's a very pleasant sort of genius, the kind you want to sit and listen to endlessly.

Very annoying.

So he gets to be a phenomenon.

And I don't.

It's so unfair.

---

[158] No others have been anywhere near as funny, either. Nor as good in other ways. At least, in my personal, unsupported, but absolutely correct opinion.

49

The Nature of Pratchett's Genius

IT SEEMS AS IF I need to have a chapter about this, but really, what do I know about what makes someone a literary genius? If I knew how it was done, I'd bloody well do it myself, wouldn't I? And without having to write an entire book about Discworld first.

There's a book out there called *Terry Pratchett: Guilty of Literature*, edited by Andrew M. Butler.[159] I haven't read it, because I didn't want to risk stealing anyone's ideas, or worse, finding that an idea I'd come up with on my own had already been used so that I couldn't use it without *looking* like I stole it. Besides, the book is a bit hard to find and fairly expensive. Also, it's literary criticism, or purports to be, and I don't like to think I'm doing literary criticism.[160] I write for a living, which means I want to please editors and book-buyers, not critics. The two groups look for different things, and I don't want to be distracted by the critics' set.

Anyway, the book exists, and is a collection of essays about various aspects of Mr. Pratchett's work, not all of them related to Discworld.[161] The title is suggestive, though. Whoever came up with it thinks Mr. Pratchett is committing literature.

---

[159] First edition published in 2000 by the Science Fiction Foundation; U.S. edition published in 2004 by Old Earth Books.

[160] Oh, fine. Yes, technically, this book you're reading is literary criticism. I admit it. But it's light and fluffy literary criticism, not deep and scholarly. It's not intended as a textbook, and not intended for English professors. This is a book about the Discworld™ series, aimed at the casual reader. I'm not doing anything remotely like formal analysis here, I'm just talking about stories I love. It's like the difference between analytical chemistry and chatting about cooking, or the difference between surveying land and admiring the view.

[161] Yes, he's written other stuff. I've mentioned that before. Some of it is quite good, but it's not what this book is about.

I'm not convinced. He might be. Mostly, though, I think he's just really damn good at telling stories, which isn't the same thing.

I also think people have been trying to figure out how to tell really good stories for a few thousand years now, and nobody's really managed to determine exactly why some people are really good at it, and others . . . well, aren't.

I'm not going to pretend I know what the difference is. All I know is that Terry Pratchett's really damn good at it.

50

The Foundation on Which the Stories Stand

I'VE SAID SEVERAL TIMES NOW that the Discworld series is about stories, that that's my grand theory about the whole thing. I think it's time to explain that in a little more detail. Let me begin by quoting a bit from Chapter 2, "The Umpty-Umpth Element," from *The Science of Discworld II: The Globe*:

> Discworld runs on magic, and magic is indissolubly linked to Narrative Causality, the power of story. A spell is a story about what a person wants to happen, and magic is what turns stories into reality. On Discworld, things happen *because people expect them to.*[162]

Discworld is a world constructed of stories. It's not just a place where stories are set; it's *about* stories.

It started out in *The Colour of Magic* as being about a specific sort of story: fantasy adventures. Discworld was constructed out of all the clichés and exaggerations of existing stories—the absurdly dirty and violent cities, the vicious and venal inhabitants of those cities, the indomitable barbarian heroes, the impossible geography, the gods and monsters and magic, the dreams and dragons. In most fantasy stories, the characters take all that for granted, and fit right in, but in *The Colour of Magic* we were presented with all this familiar material as seen by

[162] Emphasis in the original.

two people who did *not* take it for granted and fit in. For Twoflower the tourist, it was all new and exciting, and while Rincewind did generally take it for granted, as a wizard with no magic and a cowardly hero, he didn't fit in very well. These two let us see the absurdity of the whole thing, and laugh at it.

The same approach continued in *The Light Fantastic*, and if that had been all there were to the series, it wouldn't have been anything special. However, with *Equal Rites*, it started to become something more. *Equal Rites* isn't a parody of fantasy novels; instead it's what happens when a story goes wrong, and someone is born into the wrong role.

Mort is about what happens when people refuse to follow the story they're in.

Stories. It's all about stories. Right from the start, Discworld ran on stories, and the stories we were told were the ones where something didn't go the way it was meant to, where the stories played out *because people expect them to*, even though something had not gone according to plan, or a character had wound up in the wrong role.

Mr. Pratchett has said several times that Discworld is a place that doesn't have much reality to it; it's a place where pretty much *everything* can go away if people stop believing in it. As such, it's almost the opposite of our own world where, as science fiction writer Philip K. Dick famously said, "Reality is that which, when you stop believing in it, doesn't go away." What the Disc *does* have is an intense magical field, and as Messrs. Stewart, Cohen, and Pratchett tell us, "Magic is indissolubly linked to Narrative Causality, the power of story."

That is, "…magic is what turns stories into reality."

So the Disc's magical field builds Discworld's reality out of stories. Narrativium is what makes it all go. It's all about stories.

Each series takes its own approach, but they're all about stories. It's stories all the way down. Just as what Ankh-Morpork is mostly built on is Ankh-Morpork, Discworld stories are mostly built on stories. Where much modern fiction tries to base its story on reality—well, reality is thin on the Disc, so the stories have to be built on something else.

Other stories.

51

Your Questions Answered

NOTICE THAT DOESN'T SAY *ALL* your questions answered, but I do want to respond to a few that I suspect some of you fine readers would like to ask, especially those who haven't already read several Discworld stories.

Let's start with, "I haven't read anything by Terry Pratchett. Will I like Discworld?"

Obviously, I don't know, since I don't know your tastes, but *I* sure like it, as do millions of other people. There's a very broad appeal here.

There's humor. Every book has plenty of funny moments of varying kinds. If you don't like puns, there are character bits; if character bits don't appeal, there are double entendres; if those do nothing for you, there's slapstick. In-jokes. Running gags. Grotesque exaggeration. Mordant wit. Clever banter. There isn't a trick in the comic writer's arsenal that Mr. Pratchett hasn't tried at least once—except possibly fart jokes, and I may just not happen to remember those, since that's a form of humor that doesn't amuse me.

There are complex characters—Granny Weatherwax and Sam Vimes and Tiffany Aching are fascinating.

There's lovely prose. I'm not going to cite examples because everyone's tastes vary in this, too, but honestly, Mr. Pratchett can turn a phrase beautifully.

There are exciting plots. If your pulse doesn't quicken when Vimes is running down Carcer, or Granny confronts the vampires, well. . . .

So yeah, if you like reading any sort of humor *or* any sort of fantasy, I'd expect you to enjoy at least parts of the Discworld series.

But not necessarily the whole thing.

Where, then, to start?

The traditional answer for any series is to start at the beginning, but that's not necessarily the best approach here. The earliest books are noticeably weaker than later ones—though fans can argue endlessly about whether the best are the most recent, or whether there was some peak that we're now past and they've gotten too dark, or whatever. And the various series within the whole may appeal to different audiences; the Watch stories are almost police procedurals, Tiffany Aching's series is a coming-of-age story, and so on.

Discussions of where to start can get very long and complicated, but let me give you my own opinions:

Since there are eight series within the whole, there are eight obvious starting points—the first books in each series. Any of these would work. Those eight are:

The Colour of Magic
Equal Rites
Mort
Pyramids
Guards! Guards!
Moving Pictures
The Amazing Maurice and His Educated Rodents
The Wee Free Men

Of those eight, *The Colour of Magic* is short, so it's not a major commitment, and it's divided into four stories to make it even more accessible for those just wanting a taste, but it's generally considered atypical of the series as a whole as well as one of the weakest, and it ends on a cliffhanger that's resolved in *The Light Fantastic*. I therefore don't recommend it—though I am reliably informed that it sells the most copies, presumably simply because it *was* the first. If you really want to start with a story about the wizards, *Sourcery* is probably the way to go.

Equal Rites is a fun book and a decent starting place, but it's only loosely tied to the rest of the series, and I'd suggest starting the witches series with *Wyrd Sisters*, instead. It's a better story, it's more typical, and you really won't have missed anything by starting there instead of with *Equal Rites*.

Mort stands on its own quite well. Good starting point if you aren't bothered by its metaphysical nature—I mean, it's a book about Death. Some readers don't mesh well with that.

Pyramids is very much a stand-alone story, and a good starting point—but so is *Small Gods*, and all in all, *Small Gods* may be a better book. Many people suggest *Small Gods* as the best Discworld story for a beginner, and I can't gainsay that.

For the Watch series, you really do need to start at the beginning, which is *Guards! Guards!* It builds up from there.

If you're a fan of parody, *Moving Pictures* is a fine place to start. It stands on its own well, and contains lots of the best features of the series. The one drawback is that it doesn't lead naturally into the next, and after reading it you may find yourself saying, "That was great! Which should I read next?" and not having an obvious answer.

That's a possible issue with *The Amazing Maurice and His Educated Rodents*, too, but in that case I'll suggest going on to the Tiffany Aching series next, as the other "young adult" entry.

And like the Watch series, the Tiffany Aching books need to be read in order, starting with *The Wee Free Men*.

So there you have . . . well, eleven choices, which is still too many. Let me arbitrarily narrow that down.

If you're a kid, or a kid at heart, start with *The Wee Free Men*.

If you're not, I'd recommend starting with *Wyrd Sisters*, *Small Gods*, or *Guards! Guards!*, depending on which series seems most suited to your tastes.

And how do you know which series is best suited to your tastes? Well, if you've read this far, you might have figured it out already, but if not, the next seven chapters, Part Five, are further remarks about each of the series (other than the Amazing Maurice).

PART FIVE
The Series

52

Rincewind and Unseen University: The Virtues of Cowardice, Gluttony, and Sloth

WHEN MR. PRATCHETT INTRODUCED us to the nominal hero of *The Colour of Magic*, we did not find ourselves face to face with a sword-wielding hero, nor a farmer's son with a destiny, nor a young female outcast, nor any of the other standard fantasy protagonists; instead we met a rather bedraggled young wizard by the name of Rincewind, who was in the process of fleeing the burning city of Ankh-Morpork.

In fact, Rincewind spends most of the first two books fleeing one thing or another. Fleeing becomes his most salient characteristic. In *Sourcery*, he's relatively flightless, but through *Eric*, *Interesting Times*, and *The Last Continent*, he spends most of his time trying to run away from one something or another.

By the time we get to *The Last Hero* and the three volumes of *The Science of Discworld*, Rincewind is an acknowledged expert on running away, to the point that he no longer needs to demonstrate his mastery of the art. Instead it's recognized that despite his cowardice, he has a knack for not dying—he's a sort of mirror image of Cohen the Barbarian, who has survived to a great age by being very, very good at not dying while being direct, fearless, and violent. Rincewind has become very good at not dying by being sneaky, cowardly, and harmless. Both of them are survivors; they just take opposite approaches to the problem.

Most people would not send a coward off to save the world, but Mustrum Ridcully, with his skewed way of looking at things, has noticed Rincewind's talent for survival, and therefore does indeed repeatedly thrust poor Rincewind into various perils in *The Last Hero* and *The Science of Discworld*.

It's notable, though, that by that point Rincewind is no longer a solo protagonist. In *The Last Hero*, he's just one of a band of heroes, while in the three volumes of *The Science of Discworld* he's a member of the ensemble cast that is the faculty of Unseen University. Yes, he's the one that Ridcully sends into danger first at every opportunity, but the other wizards are there as well. Rincewind really needs other characters to play off; for one thing, left to his own devices, he wouldn't *do* anything. He is, as Mr. Pratchett has said, an observer by nature, rather than someone who makes things happen.

In the first two books, he has Twoflower to drag him into things. In *Sourcery*, he's forced into action by the world collapsing around him. In *Eric* it's Eric who pushes Rincewind, in *Interesting Times* he's summoned against his will, in *The Last Continent* it's Scrappy urging him on, and then finally, in *The Last Hero* and the science books, it's Archchancellor Ridcully thrusting Rincewind, with his knack for surviving, into danger.

By that point, the other wizards have become a regular cast, and Rincewind is merely their point man.

This logical but apparently backward approach of sending a coward to play hero is representative of the wizards of Unseen University as a group. Students come to Unseen University to learn magic, but generally learn that often the best way to use magic is *not* to use it. The University, ostensibly dedicated to disseminating magical knowledge, actually serves to restrain it; in fact, it exists largely to *suppress* magic, thereby preventing widespread devastation, not by any sort of crude ban, but by redirecting wizards' energies.

The typical wizard at Unseen University is not as interested in magic as he is in dinner.

In fact, the wizards expend much of their energy on eating. They're too busy stuffing their faces to cause trouble. They're greedy, fat, and lazy. Sloth, gluttony, and cowardice are not vices among the faculty, but merely the norm.

In a way, Rincewind is the ultimate wizard, even though he can't perform any magic; he no longer even *pretends* to be accomplishing anything.

And this is a good thing. Why? Well, in *Sourcery* we get a look at what happens when you have wizards who are energetic and inventive, and it's not pleasant. Keeping most of the Disc's most powerful magicians focused on their next meal is far safer than letting them focus on their spells.

When the wizards do tackle real difficulties, they very rarely defeat them through the direct application of magic. Magic almost always seems to cause more problems than it solves.

Ponder Stibbons and Hex may well be one of the greatest threats to the well-being of Discworld, even though they're utterly well-intentioned, because Stibbons has *not* let himself be distracted from his magical studies. They're messing around with Things Man Was Not Meant to Know.

In a way, Ponder Stibbons is Simon from *Equal Rites* reinvented.

Except for Granny Weatherwax, Rosie Palm, Death, the Librarian, and Mrs. Whitlow, none of the characters from *Equal Rites* ever appeared again, but several of their characteristics resurfaced later.[163] Simon's dangerous ability to understand and use powerful magic without seeing the risks involved reappeared in Stibbons, in a somewhat softened form. Where Simon was so focused on his theories that he barely noticed the outside world, Stibbons has the knack of telling Archchancellor Ridcully whatever portion of the truth will get Stibbons what he wants.

To some extent, Stibbons may be taking over the series from Rincewind, just as Susan has taken over Death's series; after a while, there's not much more to do with a character as limited as Rincewind. Stibbons, on the other hand, has great potential as a source of disasters.

In fact, the wizards have turned up in roles of varying importance in any number of other series, with Ridcully and Stibbons being particularly useful.

At any rate, the series that began as a mockery of fantasy adventure has gradually mutated into a satire on academia and Big Science—the

[163] I've already mentioned how the naiveté of the over-honest Zoons reappeared as a dwarfish trait.

Say, I'm not overdoing these footnotes, am I? I mean, I wouldn't want to run the joke into the ground.

academic angle is most obvious, perhaps, in "A Collegiate Casting-Out of Devilish Devices." Rincewind has gone from being a young wastrel to being a burned-out wreck. There are rumors that another Rincewind novel may be in the works, but I have no idea what else can be done with the character.

53

The Witches of Lancre: Telling the Story Where to Go

THE WITCHES OF DISCWORLD seem very English to me, each serving a village as midwife, veterinarian, nurse, and constable. These are not the isolated, forest-haunting old crones of the Brothers Grimm, or the cattle-cursing terrors of the Scottish witch trials, or Satan's handmaidens as described in the *Malleus Malificarum*, or the gossip victims of Salem, Massachusetts. They're clearly largely based on the witches in fairy tales, but only on the most benign sorts; they see cackling, poisoned apples, and gingerbread houses as occupational hazards best avoided.

They're a very *practical* sort of witches, and really, the whole series about them, including the Tiffany Aching books, demonstrates their practicality, along with their refusal to be bound by the stories other people unquestioningly accept.

In *Equal Rites*, Eskarina Smith is a female wizard, something that's never been seen before, but Granny Weatherwax accepts it—she doesn't force Esk to go on trying to be a witch once that's clearly not working, yet she refuses to give up when Archchancellor Cutangle fails to accept Esk. She deals with what's *there*, instead of what's expected, or what *should* be there.

This contrast between expectation and reality is far more pronounced in *Wyrd Sisters*, right from the opening scene: three witches gathered around a cauldron in the midst of a stormy night, straight out of *Macbeth*. One says, "When shall we three meet again?"

And the response, rather than being poetical or theatrical, is, "Well, I can do next Tuesday."

Which is not just funny, but sets the tone for the entire novel, which is constantly playing expectations off against reality, story against truth. The witches always see the truth, but they know that most people won't, that most people want the story—so they try to make sure that it's the *right* story, the one that will have the best outcome for the kingdom. The Duke is trying to promulgate the story of the hero deposing the wicked king and ruling happily in his stead, and initially the witches don't really have a problem with this, but when it turns out that the Duke is incapable of ruling competently, they substitute the story of the rightful heir returning to claim his birthright, even though they know that isn't any more true than the Duke's version of events.

The witches don't care who's king, as long as he's a *competent* king. They're utterly pragmatic. They know people will believe stories, rather than truth, but they want them to believe the stories that will treat them well—they want people to control the stories, rather than letting the stories control people.

They don't want stories that treat people as things—that's Granny Weatherwax's definition of sin in *Carpe Jugulum*, treating people as things, and it's a good one.

So in *Witches Abroad*, they reject and destroy the story Lily is presenting. In *Lords and Ladies*, they reject the fiction the elves impose. In *Maskerade*, they reject the fantasy of the Phantom they're given. In *Carpe Jugulum*, they reject the vampires' lies. In every case, they see through the story intended to lull people into the acceptance of evil, see to the truth underneath, and find a better story to put in its place.

In fact, Granny Weatherwax becomes a story *herself*, the story of the prideful, powerful witch who will defend Lancre against all threats. The vampires know that story, and try to get around it, only to find that the story is simpler than the truth.

And in "The Sea and Little Fishes," Letice Earwig makes it plain that she doesn't *like* Granny's story, and wants a nicer one, only to find that Granny's story is too firmly established to change—even *she* doesn't believe Granny can really change.

Granny is what she is, whether she wants to be or not—and she makes plain in *Witches Abroad* that it's not what she would have chosen, but if it's what she has to be, then she'll bloody well do it up right. And she'll have no truck with people or creatures who commit the sin of treating people like things, who put the stories in control rather than the people.

54

Death in the Family: The Very Model of a Modern Anthropomorphic Personification

ONE OF THE CHARACTERISTICS of the Disc's intense magical field, as explained in the *Science of Discworld* books, is reification—things that people believe in becoming actual *things*, rather than remaining abstract concepts. Foremost among those is everyone's final friend, the Grim Reaper, the man with the scythe: Death.

The idea of Death as a person, or at least a conscious entity, is ancient, of course. Death has turned up in stories for centuries, and is still turning up, in everything from Ingmar Bergman's *The Seventh Seal* to *The Grim Adventures of Billy and Mandy* on the Cartoon Network, from Edgar Allen Poe's "Masque of the Red Death" to Neil Gaiman's *Sandman* comics. The traditional representation has always been a tall, skeletal figure in a dark robe, so of course that's the form Death takes on the Disc—Discworld is home to every fantasy cliché, after all, and this is just one more. A seven-foot scythe-wielding skeleton in a black robe, bearing an hourglass and riding a great white horse through the sky—this is very much the classic figure of Death as he's been seen in western civilization at least since the plagues of the fourteenth century.

But this is Discworld, so when we look close, some of the details that aren't in the traditional tales turn out to be somewhat skewed. For example, the big white horse is named Binky.

Somehow, I doubt that anyone else ever gave Death's horse a name like Binky; not even Neil Gaiman, who represented Death as a perky goth girl, would have done that.

Death in Discworld is not quite the standard model in other ways; traditionally Death has been depicted as heartless, implacable, a cold and unfeeling monster, but Pratchett's creation is instead a working man who takes pride in his craft, and rather likes people—though he doesn't understand them.

That's one of the more interesting conceits Mr. Pratchett has come up with—Death is not bound by time or space, he exists in a higher reality than that perceived by mere humans, he never has very much contact with people,[164] so he doesn't really grasp how we think. He *tries*, since after all we're part of the job, but he just doesn't quite get it.

In a way, it's very similar to Arthur Weasley in J.K. Rowling's Harry Potter series, whose job is devoted to dealing with muggles (non-magical people). He handles muggle technology all the time, but because he himself has lived his entire life in the wizarding world, he really doesn't grasp how muggles think, or how the muggle world works. Even when he *thinks* he does, he gets the details wrong.

Likewise, Death gets the details wrong. He knows that a home should have a bathroom with towels in it, but he hasn't entirely grasped *why*, or what towels are for, so he's furnished his own home with a bathroom, and towels—but the towels aren't soft or absorbent, they're stiff and hard.

This is an amusing concept for a character, but it's not really an easy one to get a story out of. Death does his job, and it goes on constantly, day in and day out, and where's the story in that? Generally, Death shows up when a story has just ended, not when it's about to begin.

The most obvious way to use Death in a story is as the villain, the menace to be defeated, as Bergman did in *The Seventh Seal*, but that's been done, and it's really not very entertaining anymore.

Another approach is to look at what happens if Death *doesn't* do his job, day in and day out, as in the classic movie *Death Takes a Holiday*, or the more recent *Meet Joe Black*. But that, too, has been done, though Mr. Pratchett does do a sort of variant on it in passing in *Reaper Man*.

---

[164] He meets everyone, but for the vast majority of us, it's only once apiece, and generally not for long or under the best circumstances.

But—well, most of all, Death is someone doing a job. What can happen to a working man *other than* a normal day, or a day off?

He can train an apprentice, of course, with an eye to eventual retirement—someone to pass the family firm to. That gave us *Mort*.

He can be laid off by his bosses, replaced with a younger, less-experienced worker; that gave us *Reaper Man*.

He can have a bad day at the office, when things get a little crazy; that gave us *Soul Music*.

He can find out about threats to his job, and try to head them off; that gave us *Hogfather* and *Thief of Time*.

The thing is, though, that even with the quirky personality Mr. Pratchett has given him, Death is a limited character. He's not human, after all; he's an anthropomorphic personification. He's limited in what he can do, bound by rules that we mere mortals do not have, while at the same time he has powers far beyond ours, such as the ability to traverse time and space at impossible speeds. And just as he has trouble understanding us, we have trouble in getting inside his head and appreciating him as our viewpoint character.

This is why in *Mort* our viewpoint character isn't Death, but the title character, his apprentice.

In *Reaper Man*, we have multiple viewpoint characters, but Death isn't really one of them most of the time, even though he's at the heart of the story; Windle Poons has far more "screen time."

But then in *Soul Music*, we met Death's granddaughter Susan, who provides the sensible human viewpoint for the reader to identify with, while still having Death's concern with more cosmic matters. Susan has gradually taken over the series. She's the protagonist of *Hogfather*, and one of the protagonists of *Thief of Time*, battling her grandfather's old foes, the Auditors.

Death has the lead in "Death and What Comes Next," and continues to make appearances throughout the various other series, but he hasn't really been the star of a novel since *Reaper Man*.

So if the wizards' series is primarily parodies of heroics and academia, and the witches' series is about the need to stay in control of stories, what's the central conceit of the Death series?

The need for compassion, I would say. In both *Mort* and *Reaper Man*, the real threat is that Death's role will be taken by someone less suited to it, less compassionate, than the current Death. In *Soul Music*, the self-destructive nature of Music With Rocks In needs to be kept in check, and a personal tragedy needs to be accepted. In *Hogfather* and *Thief of Time*, it's the Auditors' schemes to rid the universe of the messy nuisance known as human life. Logically, Death perhaps ought to be a destroyer, a ravager, but in Discworld he's a necessary part of the system operating in a restrained and rather kindly fashion; he wants life in general to continue, even if he's responsible for the end of countless individual lives.

And Susan, of course, wants a great many individual lives to continue, including her own; she has rather more at stake than her grandfather, which is why she makes a better protagonist in most cases. She exists between the human world and the world of anthropomorphic personifications and interacts with both of them; she not only can deal with Death, but with the Hogfather, the Tooth Fairy, Old Man Trouble, and all the rest.

Not that she particularly *wants* to.

To some extent, the wizards deal with magic, the witches deal with stories, and Susan deals with belief.

She's not the only one, though. Belief is a rather vital concern for the gods, after all. . . .

55

Gods and Philosophers: Belief and Reason

NO ONE SANE ON THE DISC denies the existence of the gods; Mr. Pratchett tells us the gods have a habit of coming round and smashing atheists' windows. That isn't to say, however, that everyone exactly *believes* in them, any more than everyone believes in the current U.S. president. They're undeniably *there*, but that doesn't mean that anyone's putting any faith in them.

They're quite a varied lot. The chief god of the Disc, at least at present, is Blind Io, who isn't actually blind in the sense of being unable to see, he just doesn't happen to keep any of his eyes in his head. He's your basic thunder god, reminiscent of Jupiter or Zeus. Other popular deities include Offler the Crocodile-Headed God, the ichor-dripping Lovecraftian monstrosity Bel-Shamharoth, the sea-god Dagon, the wine-god Bibulous, Bast, Nuggan, Anoia, and of course Om, who spent virtually all of *Small Gods* in the shape of a small tortoise.

None of them created the Disc, though; the being responsible for that is simply called the Creator, and we met him in *Eric*: a workman doing his job, not some silly creature sitting on a mountaintop expecting to be worshiped.

FourEcks was apparently added later, by a different Creator, who may have appeared as the kangaroo Scrappy in *The Last Continent*. Again, he's not one of the gods hanging out on Cori Celesti.

Lots of gods turn up elsewhere; the god of evolution has his bizarre island, as seen in *The Last Continent*, and in *Small Gods* we learn that some gods are reduced to near-nothings living in the desert, hoping a worshiper will stumble upon them.

Throughout all the various series, gods have popped up occasionally. Bel-Shamharoth got the first major role for a deity in "The Sending of Eight," all the way back in *The Colour of Magic*, along with Fate and the Lady, and they've turned up here and there ever since.

Only a few stories *focus* on the gods and their priests, cults, and followers, though. "The Sending of Eight" does, to some extent, but it's not until *Pyramids* that we get a story that's actually about religion.

Even there, it's not the gods themselves who are meddling with human affairs; it's the ancient high priest Dios. He's locked the entire kingdom of Djelibeybi into an endless, pointless round of rituals and ceremonies, where the supposed god-king is permitted to do nothing but play out his assigned role. It's not the *gods* who are responsible for the kingdom's sorry stagnant state; it's their presumed followers.

Likewise, in *Small Gods*, the Omnian church is an oppressive, imperialist, totalitarian force—but Om himself is trapped in the form of a small tortoise, unheard by even his own priests, until Brutha saves him.

In between, *Eric* showed us the Creator, and the inhabitants of Hell, but just as a sidelight, not as a focus. Afterward, *Interesting Times* had Fate and the Lady back at their gaming, and *The Last Continent* had gods involved, but only rather incidentally. Om is not seen again, but his church reappears, represented by Constable Visit in various Watch stories, and by Mightily Oats in *Carpe Jugulum*. The edicts and followers of Nuggan are a major source of trouble in *Monstrous Regiment*. In a minor subplot in *Going Postal*, Moist von Lipwig uses religion as a cover, and Anoia, the goddess he credited with a miracle, appears in person in *Wintersmith*.

And of course, in *The Last Hero*, Genghiz Cohen sets out to return fire to the gods at their home, Dunmanifestin,[165] atop the impossibly high peak of Cori Celesti.

Throughout all of this, though, the gods are really something of an irrelevancy. They don't generally shape events; they simply stay up on

[165] I had assumed that this gag was too obvious to need explanation, but apparently that's my age showing. It used to be that a standard name for a retirement cottage or guest-house was "Dunroamin," or some variant thereof, which looks like a Gaelic place-name, and *might* actually mean something in Gaelic, but mostly means "Done roaming," as in, "this is where I'm settling down to stay." It was a kitschy sort of gag.

Well, the gods of the Disc named their home "Dunmanifestin," indicating that they're kitschy gods.

their mountain, enjoying the worship. Even in *Small Gods*, it's not Om, but Brutha, who transforms the Omnian church. Religion is supposedly directed toward the gods, but in practice it's designed and administered by men, men like Dios and Vorbis and even Constable Visit.

And as with the stories the witches master, what Teppic and Brutha and Cohen do is to make sure that religion serves people, rather than people serving religion—that the priests are not permitted to treat their people as things.

The gods sometimes treat people as *play*things, of course—in "The Sending of Eight" and *Interesting Times* and *The Last Hero*, the gods use people as game-pieces. They don't pretend they're serving any higher cause, though, and they recognize that they're dependent on people, that without human worshipers they would be reduced to tiny voices crying in the wilderness.

In both *Pyramids* and *Small Gods*, the rigidity of the old religions is contrasted with the freewheeling argumentation of the Ephebian philosophers—but that philosophy is mocked, too. While not as smothering and deadly as religion, it's still absurd and dangerous. The people of the Disc have a tendency to take things very literally, so the Ephebians don't settle for thought experiments when *actual* experiments can be performed. All the theoretical musings of the ancient Greeks are considered by the Ephebians, but do not remain mere theorizing; instead, arrows and tortoises and bathtubs are brought out to test each hypothesis, but somehow fail to resolve many of the arguments.

Mr. Pratchett gives us a rather different and haunting take on the whole matter of natural philosophy in Chapter 21 of *The Science of Discworld II: The Globe*, with the tale of Phocian and his attempts to demonstrate the truth of the teachings of Antigonus.

And then of course there's the mock-Asian philosophy of Lu-Tze in *Thief of Time*, where he tries to teach Lobsang Ludd the Way of Mrs. Cosmopolite.

In every case, it's not the source of the belief that matters, or the truth of it; what matters is how it's used.

In *Small Gods*, the rebels in Omnia take "The Turtle moves!" as their rallying cry. Now, we know they're right, Great A'tuin does indeed move, but does it really *matter*? How does the Turtle's existence and movement affect anyone?

It doesn't. All it means is that the Omnian Church is *wrong* about something, and that's enough, because the Church claims to be infallible. If it's wrong about anything, it might be wrong about *everything*. It's not important that the Disc is atop a cosmic turtle; what's important is that the Church says it *isn't*. The Omnian Church claims perfect certainty, and uses that as the justification for torture, murder, and war.

In Djelibeybi, Dios and his priests also claim to know everything they need to know. They aren't as brutal as the Omnians, but they aren't doing the kingdom any good, either.

In Ephebe, while each philosopher may claim to know the Truth, no one believes them, and they're constantly arguing with each other. There's no certainty at all—and they're freer, happier, and wealthier than Omnia or Djelibeybi, because they're willing to try anything and see what works.

This isn't merely a difference between religion and philosophy, because Phocian is not relying on religious dogma in his experiments. He *is*, however, guilty of excessive certainty—he *knows* Antigonus must be right about horses, and sets out to prove it, and refuses to accept the results when he instead *dis*proves it.

The Reformed Omnian Church gives up its claim to utter certainty, and Omnia becomes a healthier, happier place—but it's not all sweetness and light, as we see in *Carpe Jugulum*, where Mightily Oats struggles with his faith. Certainty can be comforting, even when it's wrong, even when it's oppressive; most people don't *like* not knowing.

So while in general Mr. Pratchett seems to be arguing that utter certainty is a dangerous thing, he acknowledges that doubt isn't especially enjoyable.

And having made that point, well, we haven't seen much more on the subject.

56

Sir Samuel Vimes and the City Watch: Who Watches the Watchmen?

THE DEDICATION TO *GUARDS! GUARDS!* reads:

> They may be called the Palace Guard, the City Guard, or the Patrol. Whatever the name, their purpose in any work of heroic fantasy is identical: it is, round about Chapter Three (or ten minutes into the film) to rush into the room, attack the hero one at a time, and be slaughtered. No-one ever asks them if they wanted to.
>
> This book is dedicated to those fine men.

That is to say that while Discworld had already moved beyond simple parody into rather deeper satire by the time this series was launched, it hadn't yet moved too far from its roots. *Guards! Guards!* has a very standard fantasy-novel plot in many regards—the long-lost heir has come incognito to the city his ancestors ruled, where he is to fight a dragon to establish his claim to the throne. The Night Watch's intended role in all this is to be useless. In any normal fantasy novel, they would either flee, or die, or stand helplessly on the sidelines. Their job is to rush in and die, or to run away. It's a long-standing tradition, dating back a couple of centuries—at least as far as Alexandre Dumas *pére*, probably to Sir Thomas Malory. These are the Saracens whose corpses Roland stacked like cordwood, the Cardinal's Guards who d'Artagnan dispatched so easily, the night watchmen young Conan kayoed or gutted or garotted in the City of Thieves. They don't usually even get names, let alone faces, families, or personalities.

And the entire premise of the Watch series is that there's one of these men who takes his job seriously, who's smart enough not to get killed, and who's stubborn enough not to run away. He refuses to fulfill his traditional role as nothing more than a minor impediment to be brushed aside by his betters; he has a job to do, and by the gods he's going to *do* it, whether anyone wants him to or not.

That man is Samuel Vimes.

There are several interesting twists on this. It's traditional that the feckless guardsmen are working for a tyrant, and Sam Vimes is indeed in the service of a tyrant—but Lord Vetinari isn't an *evil* tyrant. He's not particularly corrupt, he's not sadistic, and most of all, he's not stupid. He keeps Ankh-Morpork running more smoothly than it has in centuries. We've seen the Patrician now and then ever since the series began, but it's in the Watch stories that he really comes into his own. It was necessary for the plot of *Guards! Guards!* to work that the tyrant had to be preferable to the lost royal heir/hero; he had to be someone who *deserved* to have Sam Vimes defending him—but he still had to be a tyrant.

That's a tough role to fill, but Mr. Pratchett was up to the job, and the result makes Havelock Vetinari one of the great characters of the series, and really, one of the most entertaining characters in all of fantasy. He's a ruler so Machiavellian that he makes Niccolò Machiavelli himself look like a hot-headed fool.

Of course, Vimes himself is an even *better* character.

He, too, presented a challenge. He had to be someone who would wind up in the despised City Watch, and who would *stay* there; he couldn't be a Hero With A Destiny himself, as that would ruin the whole point of the exercise.

But he couldn't just be the standard cannon fodder, either. He couldn't be the guy who rushes into the room in Chapter Three, only to be taken out by a slash of the hero's sword. He couldn't be the guy who flings down his sword and runs when the monster appears.

There are actually several ways this could be accomplished, but the one Mr. Pratchett chose was to give us a man for whom protecting the city from itself is a vocation, a calling, not just a job—that's why he's in the Watch.

But the Watch is generally considered worthless, so he's a man sunk in despair, anger, and self-hatred, and when we first see him, he's lying in the gutter, drunk. The conspirators who want to supplant Lord Vetinari could not possibly see Vimes as a threat at that point.

They learn better.

And so does everyone else. One of the reasons Lord Vetinari deserves to rule Ankh-Morpork is that he recognizes talent when he sees it, and once Vimes comes to his attention, that talent is rewarded. Vimes is a man who can be very useful, to the Patrician and to the city, so his rise is rapid.

But Vimes is a man who was *meant* to be a copper, a man who grew up in terrible poverty and has never forgotten it, a man who sees the ruling classes as his natural enemy, a man who prefers to operate largely unnoticed, so that rise is a mixed blessing.

Which is why the Watch series is one of the longest. Rincewind and company got a healthy head-start, but the Watch has closed the gap significantly.

Once a protagonist has solved the problem at the heart of a story, that story is over and done. There's only one book about the Amazing Maurice; there's only one book about Brutha; there's only one book about Teppic; and in each case, it's because at the end, the problem that forced the character into having adventures in the first place is solved. Maurice has resolved his moral dilemmas and found himself a home, Teppic has settled matters in Djelibeybi, and Brutha has been recognized as a prophet of Om and has reformed the Omnian church. Doing anything more with those characters would feel like cheating; they're *done*.

To some extent, it seemed as if Rincewind was done at the end of *The Last Continent*; he was safely back at Unseen University, with no desire to go anywhere else. That series has only continued because Archchancellor Ridcully has no compunctions about throwing Rincewind at problems, and this sort of disruption is in keeping with the character's history.

The witches can keep going indefinitely because they're a reactive force—they respond to threats to Lancre, and threats keep turning up. There's a danger that the series might get repetitive after a while, but the witches themselves are infinitely reusable.

And Sam Vimes—well, he can keep reacting to threats to the peace of Ankh-Morpork (and he does), but on a personal level he's gone literally from the gutter to a mansion, from being ignored or despised to being internationally renowned, the second-most-powerful man in the wealthiest and most powerful city on the Disc. From a dramatic point of view, that ought to make him less interesting—but it doesn't, because he doesn't think he *belongs* in that mansion. He doesn't like playing politics. He despises war. The methods available to him as Duke of Ankh (or Ankh-Morpork, whichever it is) are not ones he's comfortable using. He wants to be back out on the streets—but at the same time he loves his wife and son, and has no intention of giving up the wealth he's attained. So even though he's ostensibly got everything he could want, he's not *done*, in the way Maurice or Brutha is. He still has his internal conflicts. He still has the Beast in his heart that he struggles to contain. He still has a city to protect from itself. There are still serious issues in his life that remain unresolved.

And that brings us to the third important character in the Watch stories, after Vetinari and Vimes—Carrot Ironfoundersson. There's one very basic issue in his life that remains unresolved, and probably always will. He's found his place in the City Watch, he's happy there, he loves the city and its people, he's made his peace with his mixed human/dwarf heritage, his relationship with Angua is gradually straightening out, but there's still the looming issue of his birthright. He is, after all, the rightful king of Ankh-Morpork—well, as much as anyone is a "rightful king." He not only has the bloodline and the sword, but all the other attributes that would make him a beloved and just ruler, a magnificent king.

The traditional thing for the lost heir in a fantasy story to do, of course, is to claim his inheritance, slaughter any dragons, villains, or guardsmen who get in his way, and bring about a Golden Age as king.

Carrot doesn't do that. He knows he *could*, but he doesn't. Instead of butchering the guards as they charge one by one into the room in Chapter Three, he's joined up with them, because when all's said and done, he thinks the city is better off with the tyrant Vetinari in the palace, and Vimes and himself on the streets. He refuses even to accept command of the Watch at the end of *Men at Arms* because "People should do things because an officer tells them. They shouldn't do it because Corporal Carrot says so. Just because Corporal Carrot is... good at being obeyed."

He's a stock fantasy character, but one who's too smart, in his peculiar way, to act out his ordained role. Just as Sam Vimes refuses to be the useless nobody his role calls for, Carrot refuses to be the straightforward hero-king he was born to be.

The other Watchmen also fail to live up to their stereotypes. Fred Colon is the bumbling old fool who really ought to die of his own stupidity in Chapter Three, stabbed in the back by someone he didn't mistrust enough, just a few weeks short of retirement.

But he doesn't.

Nobby Nobbs is the little weasel who should either abandon his post and flee out of the story entirely, or betray his compatriots for a handful of gold and then get killed in the ensuing melee.

But he doesn't.

These men are all stereotypes, and they even *know* they're stereotypes—but they're all just a little too human, a little too smart, a little too strong-hearted, to play out their demeaning parts in the standard fashion. The members of the Watch know the stories they're supposed to live out, they know (except for Carrot) that they aren't the heroes, they're just bit players—but they all rise above what's expected of them, even Carrot, who rises above claiming the throne because he sees that it's better for the city if he doesn't.

These are people who know the story they're in, whether it's the returning king in *Guards! Guards!* or the grand war for national pride in *Jingo* or the bitter race war in *Thud!*, but who insist on changing it to one they like better.

Mr. Pratchett has created something really wonderful in the Watch. I look forward to seeing more of them.

As for my title question, "Who watches the Watchmen?," the answer turns out to be obvious.

They watch themselves. That's why they survive.

57

Ankh-Morpork: Beyond the Century of the Fruitbat

RIGHT AT THE START of *The Colour of Magic*, we are informed that Ankh-Morpork is the oldest city on the Disc. It's been there for thousands of years, and the current city is mostly built atop earlier versions, so that there are mazes of tunnels and basements everywhere.

Nothing unusual about that in a fantasy novel. Where in the real world we only have maybe five thousand years of history all told, fantasy worlds regularly have tens of thousands, and often amazingly little happens in all that time. It's not particularly unusual for evil wizards to live a few centuries, for prophecies to be handed down for millennia, for royal pedigrees to matter over absurdly long times—I mean, *how* long did the Stewards rule Gondor before Aragorn showed up to reclaim the throne?[166]

In fact, fantasy worlds not only tend to have ridiculously long memories, they tend to be impossibly stagnant. Someone can get sent into magical exile for a century or two, come back, and see not much of anything changed except that everyone he knew is a lot older, or dead.

In real life, anyone who missed the twentieth century would be pretty lost.

---

[166] Nine hundred and sixty-nine years, from the year 2050 of the Third Age until the year 3019. In other words, Aragorn reclaiming the throne of Gondor was roughly equivalent to the rightful heir of Edward the Confessor showing up here and now to reclaim the English throne that William the Conqueror usurped in 1066 A.D.

Hell, anyone who missed the *fourteenth* century would be pretty lost. A Siennese nobleman who was ensorceled in 1300 and released in 1400 would have missed the Black Death and the beginnings of the Renaissance, for example, and would find that his city had gone from being a major power to little more than a village.

But we are told that Ankh-Morpork has stood there for millennia, and presumably hasn't altered all that terribly much in most of that time, but in the course of the Discworld series, that all changes. There isn't a full-blown industrial revolution or anything, but there are a few significant inventions, such as movies, newspapers, a sophisticated telegraph system, postage stamps, paper money, cameras, and personal organizers.

That's a lot to absorb.

Of course, not all of it sticks; movies turn out to be a temporary aberration caused by extradimensional entities and fade away. The rest, though, linger on.

How the people of Ankh-Morpork and their ruler, Patrician Havelock Vetinari, deal with this sudden march of progress is the subject of *Moving Pictures*,[167] *The Truth*, *Going Postal*, and *Making Money*. I include the short story "Troll Bridge" here as well, even though it isn't set in Ankh-Morpork and has no specific sociological innovations in it, simply because it's on the same general theme of dealing with changing times, and Cohen the Barbarian never quite got his own series.

There was no single protagonist for this series originally; Victor Tugbelbend is the star of *Moving Pictures*, while William de Worde brings us *The Truth*. However Moist von Lipwig, protagonist of *Going Postal*, returns in *Making Money*, so either he's a separate series, or he's taking over the series, or... well, for now, he's just a part of it.

It's not entirely clear just what's brought on these changes, and why they all happen in such a rush. Cameras, or rather iconographs, were introduced by Twoflower in *The Colour of Magic*, and may have existed for centuries in the Agatean Empire, for all we know. Moveable type had been invented before, but forbidden by the wizards of Unseen University until Archchancellor Ridcully decided it might help with his paperwork. There's no obvious reason the clacks hadn't been built sooner, nor are we ever really told much about their initial creation—they just appear.

---

[167] *Moving Pictures* is arguable, since most of it isn't actually set in the city itself and the changes aren't permanent, but I'm including it here all the same.

Of course, many of these developments are based on magic, rather than the technology we use. Iconographs don't use photosensitive chemicals, for example; they use imps with paintbrushes.[168] Commander Vimes's Dis-Organizer doesn't use electronics; it's another imp. The exact methods the Alchemists' Guild used in creating motion pictures aren't explained in detail, but also involve imps and demons. (Clearly, these imps and demons paint very fast.)

In fact, generally speaking, most of Discworld's "high tech" stuff is demonically based; imps serve the same roles that birds and small animals did on *The Flintstones*. For those of you unfamiliar with this ancient cartoon series,[169] *The Flintstones* was set in a Stone Age that greatly resembled the American suburbs of the 1950s, except that everything was made of stones, sticks, and animal hides, and critters of various sorts were substituted for machinery. Fred Flintstone was a heavy-machinery operator at a quarry, but his "machine" was a dinosaur he rode. The phonograph in the Flintstone home had a turntable driven by a small furry animal on a drive-belt, and the "needle" was a bird's beak, still attached to a live bird.[170]

Lots of cheap humor was derived from the clever substitutions of animals for machines, and the occasional snide asides these critters made—most of them spoke, a fact that the human characters generally ignored. Mr. Pratchett isn't above this sort of humor in the Discworld stories, except he uses imps rather than birds and beasts, and their comments are more likely to be dismayed or angry than merely snide. The imps in iconographs often provide a little extra commentary on events, as when one runs out of black paint in a particularly dark moment, and the imp in Vimes's Dis-Organizer is a character in its own right in its pitiful frustration with its employer's refusal to cooperate with it.

The Flintstones would sometimes rely on Rube Goldberg devices of wood, string, and hide to make up for the lack of metal and electricity, and the Disc's people also improvise when necessary, as in Otto Chriek's easily-shattered vial of blood that would restore him to life when his iconograph's flash turned him to dust. It's definitely some of the same sort of ingenuity; Mr. Pratchett just does it better.

---

[168] To Rincewind's dismay in *The Colour of Magic*; he had really hoped for a nice, sensible, technological explanation, rather than more mundane but inexplicable magic.

[169] I'm showing my age again, I suppose. Sigh.

[170] Please tell me I don't need to explain what a phonograph needle is.

And the purpose of this ingenuity, of course, is to allow the presence of familiar technological devices without the technology.

In some cases, the author doesn't bother; after all, there's no reason movable type and semaphore towers couldn't be built with ancient technology. Gutenberg's printing press didn't require steam or electricity, so there's no need for imps, either.

At any rate, in the second half of the Century of the Fruitbat (and the dawn of the Century of the Anchovy), Ankh-Morpork survived the arrival of several of these new technologies. Some of them, such as the iconograph and the Dis-Organizer, are treated as mere background details, but a few form the basis for entire novels: movies, in *Moving Pictures*; newspapers, in *The Truth*; and the clacks, or semaphore towers, along with postage stamps, in *Going Postal*.

The clacks actually appear before *Going Postal*, and both clacks and newspapers have permanent effects, as seen in *Monstrous Regiment*. That makes *Moving Pictures* the odd one out, in that movies appear and then disappear in the course of the novel, and there's no attempt to revive the movie industry in later books, no one making the odd little film.

In *Moving Pictures*, people are caught up in the story of Hollywood, out of their own control, not understanding their own actions, even while they spread their own stories of Klatchian sheiks and sword-wielding heroes to eager audiences. That's a story that has to be *stopped*.

In *The Truth* and *Going Postal*, though, the stories are unleashed and then tamed. William de Worde discovers the power of the press, the ability of the printed word to manipulate the masses, and does everything he can to direct that power in beneficial ways. The swindler and con artist Moist von Lipwig already knows how to use stories on a small scale to get what he wants, and when he's given control of the Post Office, he discovers that can scale up, that it's possible to sway not just individuals but the entire city with a good song and dance—and like de Worde, he strives to turn this power to the benefit of the entire city, rather than just himself.

De Worde does what good he can because he's determined not to be like his father; von Lipwig does so because he's determined to better *himself*, rather than his family, though admittedly he also has the bad example of Reacher Gilt to inspire him.

(Of course, we don't yet know anything at all about von Lipwig's family; it may also be motivating him.)

And one interesting feature of all of these isn't in the characters of the ostensible protagonists, but in the character of Lord Havelock Vetinari. The Patrician does not try to suppress these new technologies.

Your classic fantasy tyrant would have smashed de Worde's presses and executed de Worde when the *Times* started disrupting things. He would have sent troops to burn Holy Wood to the ground. He would have hanged Moist von Lipwig permanently, and either nationalized or destroyed the clacks.

Vetinari doesn't do any of that.

It's not that he's incapable of it, as any mime hanging in the scorpion pit could tell you; it's that he has the imagination to see that sometimes change is an improvement, sometimes a risk is worth taking, and sometimes suppressing something isn't practical. A printing press isn't a hard thing to build, really, not when you have a few dwarf artificers around; smash the *Times*, and you might find the *Tribune* appearing on the streets from somewhere deep beneath the city. The clacks change how things are done, but they do so by making people richer, and more wealth is a good thing.

Vetinari prefers to let matters play themselves out, and perhaps give them a few nudges in the right direction—or let Vimes give them a few nudges.

He *does* suppress some things, when he determines them to be too dangerous, to be a net loss to the city. He does keeps Leonard of Quirm sequestered. He's happy to see the end of the gonne in *Men at Arms*. But when something may be a net benefit, or may be more trouble to suppress than it's worth, Vetinari lets it exist.

Vetinari is a *smart* tyrant.

In a way, Vetinari is the real hero of *The Truth* and *Going Postal* and *Making Money* and several of the Watch stories. He wants what's best for Ankh-Morpork, and has mastered one of the hardest parts of governing: choosing the right man for the right job, and then letting him do it. He doesn't care whether the people he chooses like him; he doesn't care whether *anyone* likes him. He cares whether they want the same things for Ankh-Morpork that he does. He gives Vimes his head because he knows that Vimes wants peace and justice, and detests the ruling classes—and Vetinari also wants peace and justice (within reason), and knows that the ruling classes are the biggest threat to his own position.

He lets de Worde run the *Times* because he prefers the honest press that de Worde is trying to provide to the propaganda that someone else might produce.

He puts von Lipwig in charge of the Post Office because he knows he needs someone smart and unorthodox if he's ever to have a working postal service again—and at that, von Lipwig isn't his first attempt, he's just the one that works. And because it works, Vetinari moves Lipwig on to the Royal Bank.

Clearly, Lord Vetinari is the best thing that ever happened to Ankh-Morpork. It's not a coincidence that the city flourishes so spectacularly under his rule, as it did not under Lord Snapcase or Lord Winder or any of the previous Patricians, nor under any of the later kings. This is a man for whom Sun Tzu's *Art of War* is just stating the obvious, Niccolò Machiavelli's *The Prince* is a child's primer, and Peter Anspach's "Evil Overlord list"[171] is his morning reminder. He's a man who has transformed Ankh-Morpork's story from an ongoing soap opera and political intrigue with occasional episodes of war into a science fiction saga of new inventions transforming society.

In many stories, and many aspects of real life, it's taken for granted that change is a bad thing. In most fantasy novels, in particular, change is a bad thing—we start out with the happy little forest creatures and the cheerful peasants and the benevolent rulers all in harmony; then an evil wizard or a sarcastic dragon or a Dark Lord comes along and messes everything up, and Our Heroes spend a few hundred pages removing the disturbance and putting everything back the way it was, removing as many of the changes as possible and bringing back the Good Old Days. Even some of the Discworld novels follow that basic plot outline: Things are good, a problem arises, the problem is removed, things go back to being good.

But in the Ankh-Morpork series, things generally *don't* go back, and no one really expects them to. It's not just the big advances like newspapers or clacks, either; no one really expects the dwarfs and trolls and vampires to go back to Uberwald, or wherever they came from. Golems become a part of the city's every day life. Things change, and people *adapt* to the changes.

That's the science fiction model, rather than fantasy. In science fiction stories, something comes along—alien invaders, atomic war, time travel, teleportation, death rays, matter duplicators, flying cars, what-

---

[171] See www.eviloverlord.com/lists/overlord.html. Seriously, if you've never read this, check it out.

ever—and the world changes to accommodate it, and Our Heroes are the ones trying to make sure that accommodation's a good one. No one ever manages to put the genie back in the bottle; the aliens may be defeated, but that doesn't bring back the Good Old Days. The world has been changed forever.

And that's what usually happens in Ankh-Morpork. Oh, not always—Victor and his friends *did* manage to get the movie genie back in the bottle, so to speak, and the fad for Music With Rocks In passes—but usually. The city absorbs the changes, makes them its own, and goes on, not quite the same as before. It's the science fiction mindset, rather than the fantasy one, despite the wizards and dragons and trolls.

I find that fascinating.

58

Tiffany Aching: Growing Up on the Chalk

THE EXACT DIFFERENCE BETWEEN children's stories and stories for adults isn't really very clear. Some people seem to think that all fantasy is aimed at children, since after all, sensible grown-ups don't want to read about all that silly magic stuff; in fact, in Britain there are special editions of several of the Discworld novels with "serious" covers so that readers who are embarrassed to be seen with that childish fantasy stuff can look as if they're reading something important and grown-up while they enjoy that childish fantasy stuff.

And it's not as if children's books these days are written with simpler language, or with simplified morals—modern kids aren't very fond of being condescended to, and that sort of "good for you" children's book, if it gets published at all, generally sells like crap.

Nor is it a lack of sex, as plenty of adult novels (including most of the Discworld books) don't contain any significant amount of sex, nor is it a lack of violence, as children's stories have always been chock-full of beheadings, witch-burnings, man-eating ogres, and whatnot.

Nor are children's books necessarily shorter, as J.K. Rowling[172] has demonstrated more than decisively.

One wonders, then, exactly what the difference might be between an "adult" Discworld book and a "children's" Discworld book.

---

[172] Lest anyone forget, the first edition of *Harry Potter and the Order of the Phoenix* ran 766 pages. There's a quick read for a kid, right?

Mostly, it seems to be the age of the protagonist.

Some might argue, I suppose, that this would make *Equal Rites* a children's book, since Eskarina Smith is a child, but since the actual protagonist of the book is probably Granny Weatherwax, who is anything but, I reject that argument. I know childishness when I see it. So there. *Nyah-nyah.*

The other key ingredient is marketing—if it's labeled a children's book, then it is one. Some publishers have used this very cleverly, publishing the exact same book with two different covers, one labeling it as for adults, one as for children. This has often resulted in lots of additional book sales. (See what I said above about the "serious cover" Discworld books.)

At any rate, Mr. Pratchett decided some time back to get into the children's market, and he wrote *The Amazing Maurice and His Educated Rodents*, then followed it up with the Tiffany Aching series.

Maurice wasn't really all that traditional a children's book, since Maurice and the rats are adults, and it's a pretty dark story. Tiffany Aching's story, on the other hand, fits right into one of the standard children's story niches: a girl finding her path to adulthood.

In *The Wee Free Men*, she realizes she's going to be a witch, and eventually take Granny Aching's place as the witch of the Chalk. She moves from the relative carelessness of childhood to responsibility, saving her brother from the Queen.

In *A Hat Full of Sky*, she learns to be a witch, and hits adolescence and peer pressure in the process.

In *Wintersmith*, she comes of age, facing young womanhood in her relationship with the Wintersmith.

Where Discworld stories usually involve a subversion of traditional stories, though, the Tiffany Aching stories pretty much follow the old stories as they are, without parody, and with very little satire. Saving her brother from the fairies is a classic fairy-tale plot, and if this were an adult Discworld novel I'd expect to see some twist on it—a "Ransom of Red Chief"[173] story where the Queen is desperate to get rid of Wentworth, perhaps. Instead, the author plays it straight. Tiffany faces down the Queen's magic with the magic of her grandmother's stories in a fashion I find reminiscent of nineteenth-century authors like George MacDonald.[174]

---

[173] It's a short story by O. Henry. Surely you've heard of it?

[174] Author of *The Princess and the Goblin*, among other things. Well worth a read. Especially if you're one of those poor misguided people who thought modern fantasy started with J.R.R. Tolkien, rather than just being transformed by him.

These are classic coming-of-age stories, rather than satire, that just happen to be set on the Disc.

One can see how Mr. Pratchett might consider these a change of pace. One can also see why he created a new part of the Disc, the Chalk, as the setting—he presumably wanted somewhere that didn't have the accumulated satirical baggage of Lancre or Ankh-Morpork. *The Amazing Maurice and His Educated Rodents* was set in Uberwald, and at first glance it might seem as if Tiffany Aching could have been set in Lancre or the Sto Plains—in fact, Mr. Pratchett has mentioned that when he first started developing the story it *was* set in Lancre—but creating a new place avoided any concerns about continuity, any assumptions readers might have made.

Good stuff.

And that completes my list of series. But I have some more general comments about various aspects of Discworld that I'd still like to make before wrapping things up—mostly just little stuff that didn't really fit in elsewhere, about various components of the series as a whole.

PART SIX
Yet More Comments

59

The Background Characters: We're All Mad Here

AS I SAID BACK IN CHAPTER 48, if you're creating a world, you need details. If you only provide the heroes and villains, the big events and important places, you don't have a world, you have a stage set.

Terry Pratchett has very definitely created a world, not a stage set. One of the great charms of Discworld is all the eccentric little background details.

J.R.R. Tolkien created the world of Middle Earth by inventing entire languages and elaborate genealogies, and working out detailed histories and mythology. Mr. Pratchett hasn't done any of that—Discworld's history is riddled with inconsistencies, its human languages are all borrowed from Europe (though Dwarfish and Troll do appear to be inventions), and its mythology is an absurd hodge-podge.

What he *has* done, though, is to provide the sort of little details that sticks long after one has forgotten all the lists of kings and dates and explorers from history class. Your average student doesn't remember Caligula's real name,[175] but he remembers that ol' Bootsie[176] made his horse a senator.

That sort of colorful character and telling detail helps to bring history alive—even if it's invented history. Thus people like Bloody Stupid

[175] Gaius Germanicus Caesar.

[176] "Caligula" is the Latin word for an army boot, *caliga*, with a diminutive ending—in other words, Bootsie.

Johnson, Leonard of Quirm, and General Tacticus make Discworld seem more real.

They're also funny.

They're all exaggerations of real-world figures, of course. General Tacticus is every great general and military philosopher rolled into one, from Julius Caesar and Sun Tzu to George S. Patton and General Giap. Like all of them, and like Sergeant Jackrum in *Monstrous Regiment*, he's utterly pragmatic—he doesn't write about glory or conquest or martial spirit, but about how to win. His name is reminiscent of Tacitus, the Roman historian, but his reported actions and opinions are much more in the tradition of Sun Tzu, who said, "...to fight and conquer in all your battles is not supreme excellence; supreme excellence consists in breaking the enemy's resistance without fighting."

Leonard of Quirm is not just Leonardo da Vinci, but every well-meaning, easily-distracted inventor who failed to realize just how good human beings are at weaponizing things, and how willing we are to think the unthinkable.

Bloody Stupid Johnson is every artist, inventor, or architect who ever left people saying, "What was he *thinking*?" Though (this may just be me) I tend to see him as a sort of Inigo Jones gone bad.

People like these give Discworld much of its flavor. They're also handy plot devices; if a character needs a bit of strategic advice, reading Tacticus can provide it; if the Patrician needs a mechanism for some specific purpose, Leonard can devise it; and any time the plot requires some diabolical creation that no sane person would ever have built, one of Bloody Stupid Johnson's designs will turn up.

Notice, though, that they aren't *lead* characters. Tacticus and Johnson are apparently long dead; Leonard is Vetinari's captive and happy to remain so. None of them would work as a protagonist; Tacticus would be far too efficient to be entertaining, Johnson would be far too ineffective to survive a typical adventure, and Leonard far too scatterbrained to work his way unguided through a plot. The closest any of them comes to actually playing hero is Leonard's role in *The Last Hero*, where he's very much under Vetinari's supervision.

Besides these three, an entire cast of lesser characters has accumulated over time, people who are entertaining and provide humorous subplots, but who don't generally contribute much to the central storylines. Mrs. Cake, the medium verging on small, is one, as are several of her undead lodgers. Cut-Me-Own-Throat Dibbler and his numerous counterparts are another recurring pleasure.

All of these, and others, are exaggerated types; they each sum up a category the real world has in abundance. Tacticus is the Great General, Johnson is the Inept Designer, Leonard the Careless Inventor; Mrs. Cake is every busybody, Dibbler every salesman. Foul Ole Ron is not just any homeless guy, he's the quintessential street person.

They're all slightly mad. That's one reason they don't play lead roles.

They're also a stock company. When Mr. Pratchett needs a military genius he doesn't invent a new one, he just uses Tacticus. When he needs a working invention, it's Leonard's; when he needs a failed one, it's Johnson's. They've become shorthand, letting the reader know what to expect. In *Hogfather*, if the Archchancellor's bathroom had been designed by Leonard of Quirm, we would have expected it to be quirky but quite marvelous; because it was instead designed by Johnson, though, we *know* it's going to be a disaster, and part of the fun is the anticipation of just how it's all going to go wrong when Ridcully insists on using it anyway.

Likewise, we know that whatever Dibbler is selling is something we don't really want.

Of course, some of the recurring characters aren't just simple exaggerations. The Librarian, who appears in more stories than anyone but Death, isn't any mere stereotype; he's a real character, with his own personality. He does come with some running gags built in, though—if anyone calls him a monkey, for example, we know what to expect.

And part of Gaspode's charm, at least for me, is that we *don't* know what to expect. He's always true to his doggy nature, but just how that will play out can be surprising.

This accumulation of supporting characters and bit players gives Discworld a great deal of apparent depth and adds a lot to the fun, but you know, if you look at it logically, they aren't realistic at all. In the real world, people who study military strategy don't just quote Sun Tzu, they'll quote Caesar and Clausewitz and Napoleon. Great inventions weren't all thought up by da Vinci or Edison; Bell and Westinghouse and Nobel and Watt and a thousand others were responsible, as well. We don't have anyone as dominant in any field as Tacticus or Leonard or Dibbler. They're shorthand, not realistic—but they still *seem* to add to Discworld's reality.

Something funny about human perception there, I think.

At any rate, realistic or not, they add a lot of fun to Discworld. They save Mr. Pratchett the trouble of inventing dozens of new minor characters every time; he just re-uses the old ones. Which saves *us*, the readers, the trouble of learning a whole new cast every time, and is often funny, as well.

It's a win-win situation.

60

The Luggage: When Personal Furnishings Go Bad

THERE'S ONE SUPPORTING CHARACTER I didn't mention in the last chapter because I wanted to give it a chapter all its own.[177] When you ask a Discworld fan to name some of his favorite characters, you may get some of the series protagonists—Rincewind, Granny Weatherwax, Sam Vimes—and you may get some of the recurring supporting cast, such as Lord Vetinari or the Librarian.

But you'll also probably get the Luggage.

How, you might wonder (if you haven't read any Rincewind stories), does a suitcase get to be a beloved character? Obviously, this is no ordinary valise.

It is, in fact, a wooden trunk made of sapient pearwood,[178] a rare and magical material found only in the Agatean Empire. It has a body, a lid, brass fittings, and hundreds of little legs. (Artists' depictions invariably settle for mere dozens. No exact count is ever given.) It does not have

---

[177] Partly just because I liked the title I'd come up with for it.

[178] Which presumably comes from the sapient pear tree, and I find myself wondering just what the fruit of that tree is like. And what the intact tree's behavior is like—is the Luggage's surly streak inherent in the wood, or the result of being cut down and used to manufacture trunks? (There ought to be a pun on "trunk" there somewhere, but it's eluding me.) Or is it perhaps just an individual quirk, and other sapient pearwood products are friendly and easy-going?

What else is made from sapient pearwood? Surely, it doesn't all go into travel gear. Has anyone built an entire house of the stuff?

Alas, even in *Interesting Times*, set in the sapient pear's native Agatean Empire, we aren't given answers to any of these questions.

a face, yet people generally have no trouble reading its expression, or being aware that it's watching them. It cannot speak, but can generally make itself understood. It's impossibly faithful to its owner and will follow him literally anywhere, even if that means traveling unguided through space, time, or other universes. It seems to be almost indestructible; certainly, no one has ever managed to harm it in any of its appearances. It's been known to dispose of entire roomfuls of heavily-armed opponents without suffering any visible damage.

It holds whatever it's convenient for its master for it to hold—gold, clean underwear, or various other things, or even nothing at all. Enemies who fall into it (or are swallowed) are never seen again, while its master or his friends can safely shelter in it when necessary.

It's usually content to sit quietly where it's been put, but it does have a life of its own; in *Interesting Times* it went off to court a mate and sire (we presume) offspring, before faithfully returning to Rincewind's side. It follows Rincewind wherever he goes, whether that's the beginning of time, another reality entirely, or into Hell itself—but it doesn't *like* making that much of an effort; it plainly resents having to chase across the universe after its owner, and can get very cranky with anyone who gets in its way.

You wouldn't like it when it's cranky.

The Luggage is one of the great fantasy creations of the twentieth century. While the Rincewind stories are in many ways among the weakest of the tales told about Discworld, the Luggage consistently provides them with bright spots.

I didn't discuss it much in earlier chapters because it's never central to the story, it's always just a background feature, but I really didn't feel it would be right to finish up this book without devoting a little time to it. It's a vicious homicidal monster that sometimes frightens even the owner it's defending. It's killed dozens of men, it's entirely possible that it's destroyed entire civilizations, it never does anything especially new or original, yet it still somehow comes across as (a) funny, and (b) almost loveable.

How the heck does Mr. Pratchett *do* that?

61

The Villains: Elves, Auditors, and *Things*

I'VE DISCUSSED THE HEROES of the Disc in moderate detail; now it's time to consider the villains.

In the first two books there were no grand villains, just various people and monsters who wanted to kill Rincewind and Twoflower simply because they were in the wrong place at the wrong time, or had said the wrong thing, or had something the would-be killer wanted, such as money.

In several books immediately thereafter, though, the closest there were to villains were the *Things* from the Dungeon Dimensions. These were never all that well defined, which is hardly surprising, since they aren't entirely real and for the most part they're indescribably hideous. We do know they're prone to tentacles, claws, fangs, eyestalks, and that sort of thing, but unlike some authors, when Mr. Pratchett says they're indescribable, he means it.

Their motivation is fairly straightforward—they want to move to a better address, and the Disc qualifies. If this means removing the present occupants, that's not a problem.

These were a pretty good menace, and they served as a general all-purpose danger several times, but after a while they got rather dull. We'd seen them too many times, and seen them defeated too many times, to really find them a serious threat anymore. "Oh, yes," we said, "unspeakable eldritch horrors from beyond space and time. Ho, hum.

Tentacles, ichor, loathsome abominations, yadda yadda yadda. Seen it. Wonder what's for lunch?"

And it would seem that the author got bored with them, too, as we haven't seen them in quite some time now. Nary a mention in recent books.

But we've had other recurring villains. The elves introduced in *Lords and Ladies* return in more or less the same form in *The Wee Free Men*, and in *The Science of Discworld II: The Globe*. The Auditors of Reality, first seen in *Reaper Man*, return in *Hogfather*, *Thief of Time*, and *The Science of Discworld III: Darwin's Watch*. Vampires[179] are only the featured villains in *Carpe Jugulum*, where the witches of Lancre deal with them, but they cause trouble for the Watch on occasion, as well.

Stories and ideas also show up as "villains" several times, but not the *same* stories and ideas, so I don't count those as recurring villains, exactly.

There's an interesting thing about these villains: Most of them are parasites. The elves are extradimensional parasites that prey on humans. Vampires are obviously parasites—they suck blood, for heaven's sake! You can't get much more parasitic than that.

The *Things* from the Dungeon Dimensions could be considered parasites; they want to take the human world for themselves, and they sometimes take their appearance from human minds.

The shopping-mall creatures in *Reaper Man* are explicitly parasites that prey on cities. The idea of movies that gets loose in Holy Wood is a parasite. The stories Lily Weatherwax uses in *Witches Abroad* are parasitic. The hiver in *A Hat Full of Sky* is a parasite. The gonne is a parasite, of sorts. It could be argued that the gods, as seen in *Small Gods* and *Wintersmith* and elsewhere, are parasites dependent on human belief. And in every case, these are not parasites that simply kill their hosts, but beings that steal human freedom.

Surely, Granny Weatherwax's statement that sin is treating people like things reflects the author's own deep-seated beliefs. Throughout the entirety of the Discworld, throughout all the series contained in it, we find the idea that the worst thing you can do to people is to rob them of their freedom, rob them of choice, treat them like things. Elves, vampires, stories—they all deprive people of their freedom of choice, their free will, and are therefore things that must be stopped.

The Omnian Church, the ancient religion of Djelibeybi, the various

---

179 Black Ribboners generally don't count.

would-be rulers of Ankh-Morpork who seek to depose Lord Vetinari, perhaps even rock 'n' roll—they, too, are striving to control people and deprive them of their freedom.

There are, to be sure, some villains who don't care about freedom—Carcer and Teatime, for example, simply kill people. They, too, are treating people like things, but not things they want to control, merely things they want out of the way. Some of the nobles who employ assassins take a similar, if less extreme, attitude.

The non-human villains, though, the villains who exist as species rather than individuals, who reappear in multiple stories, are almost all parasites seeking control. The Auditors are refreshingly different in that all *they* want to do is wipe out all life in the universe.

Of course, they want to wipe out humanity because it's messy; they don't like free will, independence, or creativity either. It's just that rather than suppress freedom, they'd prefer to exterminate people entirely.

Clearly, this is an issue Mr. Pratchett feels strongly about—that people must have the right to go on living their own potty little lives however they please. That's most explicit in some of Sam Vimes's musings, but it's all through the series. Carrot doesn't claim his birthright because if he did, he would be intruding on that right—he knows that people *would* obey him, they *would* live out the story of the returning king instead of getting on with their own affairs, and he won't have it. *That* is what makes Carrot a *real* hero—that he wants people to be free, as far as they can be, even when they themselves would just as soon put him in charge.

All through the series, the villains are the people, ideas, stories, beings, creatures, or entities trying to tell people how to live their lives, and the heroes are the people who insist they choose for themselves.

That may seem obvious, but you know something? It's not. Plenty of authors are happy to write heroes who tell people what to do, "for their own good." Plenty of authors would agree with Lily Weatherwax that *she's* the good sister, the one making the stories come out right. Plenty of authors would have wanted our side to win the wars in *Jingo* and *Monstrous Regiment*, instead of just ending them. Plenty of authors would have put Carrot on the throne of Ankh-Morpork.

This purity of motive, this ferocious belief in the value of human freedom, is one of the things that makes Terry Pratchett as enjoyable a writer as he is. Many people pay lip service to the importance of freedom; Mr. Pratchett obviously *believes* it.

62

Überwald: Creatures of the Night (Light)

SO WE HAVE THE VILLAINS. And we have the monsters. And these two sets overlap, but they do not coincide.

Let us consider the vast land of Uberwald, home to vampires, werewolves, and other monsters. The entire place is a parody of the Hollywood conception of Transylvania, with its forests and castles and monsters and peasants.[180] There's lots of good comic material there to play with.

It's also a good source of villains—like the vampires in *Carpe Jugulum*, and the werewolves in *The Fifth Elephant*. What I find interesting, though, is that so many of the monsters are *not* villains.

Igor, for example, is never a villain. At most he's a villain's servant, and even then he may well turn on his master if he feels that said master isn't going about his role properly. In *Carpe Jugulum*, it's Igor who revives the old Count; the young Count isn't following the rules—isn't following the story. Igor (any Igor[181]) is a great believer in tradition, which is another way of saying he wants people to play out their storybook roles. He knows where he fits in the stories, and generally he *likes* it there.

As *Carpe Jugulum* explains at some length, even the traditional vampires don't need to be villains; they exist in balance with their environ-

---

[180] Yes, Hollywood, not folklore. Igor, for example, isn't from folklore; he's purely a creation of Hollywood, invented in 1931 to give Victor Frankenstein someone to talk to. The idea that vampires all wear evening clothes—Hollywood. It's all Hollywood.

[181] Except the bartender at Biers.

ment, in a situation where everyone understands the rules and abides by them.

And the *non*-traditional vampires—well, they go in two directions. There are the villainous predators of *Carpe Jugulum* who have struggled to overcome what they saw as weaknesses, so that they can dominate their surroundings rather than fit into them comfortably, but there are also the Black Ribboners, the Reformed Vampires, and the Uberwald League of Temperance. These are vampires who have sworn off drinking blood, substituting other addictions for their natural one, in order to live among humans without getting a stake through the heart. We see several of them in the course of the stories; their official motto is "Not one drop!," and their unofficial motto is "Don't be a sucker."

Black Ribboners may be villains, but they're just as likely to be heroic. Most are just people, like iconographer Otto Chriek, trying to live their own lives. They appear almost pathetic in their attempts to fit in to human society—but Sam Vimes, in *Thud!*, suspects this may be an act, a way to allay suspicion, and he's probably right. (Vimes usually is.)

Most Black Ribboners seem to wind up in Ankh-Morpork, rather than Uberwald; after all, in Uberwald traditional vampires are tolerated, so why bother? In Ankh-Morpork, though, the black ribbon may be necessary to survival.

Still, they're monsters from Uberwald who have given up monstrous behavior in order to find a place in civilized society.

Some werewolves have done the same, though they don't wear black ribbons and advertise what they are; Constable Angua is the obvious example.

Vampires, werewolves, Igors—all are outwardly monsters, but Mr. Pratchett has chosen not to settle for that. They all have the option of breaking out of their traditional roles; their physical nature does not determine their destiny. This is rather a contrast to any number of Tolkien's imitators who have given us orcs or the equivalent who are evil simply because they're orcs; the possibility of a good orc is never even considered.

But it is in the Discworld stories.

And Uberwald, a land that at first glance would appear to be nightmarish, doesn't look quite so bad as a result. The apparent horrors are not really so very horrible.

Except, of course, when they are, like the werewolves in *The Fifth Elephant*.

Black Ribboners are more funny than fearsome; likewise the traditionalists like Igor and the old Count in *Carpe Jugulum*, though they retain a little more of the old menace. But the modern vampires in *Carpe Jugulum* and the murderous werewolves of *The Fifth Elephant* manage to be genuinely scary, all the same. It's all in the attitude.

There's undoubtedly a lesson in that, but I'll let you decide for yourself what it is.

63

Reality Leakage and the Physics of Magic

ALL THROUGH THE SERIES, right from the first volume, there have been connections between the Disc and our own world. In early volumes, these were explained as the result of reality being very thin on the Disc, so that ideas could seep through from other, more real places, but that seems to have faded somewhat as an explanation, and *The Science of Discworld* instead presented us with an explicit connection between Discworld and "Roundworld."

The connection is indisputable, though, from Rincewind and Twoflower falling onto that other plane[182] in *The Colour of Magic*, to poor Hwel dreaming a mix of Shakespeare and early twentieth-century film comedy in *Wyrd Sisters*, to movies getting loose in Holy Wood in *Moving Pictures*, rock 'n' roll arriving on the Disc as Music With Rocks In in *Soul Music*, to the marching songs and Maledict's Vietnam flashbacks (flashsideways?) in *Monstrous Regiment*, and of course, to the events of the three *Science of Discworld* books.

What I find interesting about it is that the Disc started out as a collection of all the clichés and landscapes from fantasy novels, gathered together for purposes of parody, but has gradually changed, so that now it's more nearly a collection of clichés and landscapes from our world, gathered together for purposes of satire. There's no sharp break, but more and more of our reality seems to have leaked through. In *The*

[182] I know, I said I wouldn't bring it up again, but honestly, I can't help it!

Colour of Magic, Ankh-Morpork is pretty clearly medieval; by *Going Postal*, its citizens wear neckties and are more concerned with corporate finance than feudal combat.

Mr. Pratchett has said that he knows the Disc is a temporal hodge-podge, and that each element is modeled on the Roundworld era that seems most appropriate for that aspect of his creation—thus ancient, medieval, Victorian, and modern bits jostle up against each other, and Ankh-Morpork's grand nineteenth-century Opera House is next door to an Elizabethan theater, The Dysc, realism or economic logic be damned. Some things remain consistently pre-modern, so there are no internal combustion engines,[183] but that doesn't mean a crashing coach can't go up in a fiery explosion if that's what narrative necessity requires. It's all in service of the stories.

It's all built of narrativium.

Other things have changed over the course of the series, as well. It's been many a volume since we got descriptions of light, slowed by the Disc's magical field, spilling slowly across the landscape—when the subject came up in *Thief of Time*, it was only as a classroom lesson, not atmospheric narrative. Modern magic no longer tends to the coruscating light-shows described in *Sourcery*; instead the magically enhanced coach in *Thud!* is smooth and silent in operation. The number eight still has magical significance, going by the chapter numbering in *Going Postal*, but it doesn't seem to have the power it did in "The Sending of Eight"—and in *Making Money* there isn't even the altered chapter numbering. The color octarine and the metal octiron don't get the attention they used to.

In fact, magic has generally gotten less obtrusive, the better to comment on our own world and history. *Sourcery* was awash in pyrotechnics; in *Monstrous Regiment* there's nary a wizard or witch to be seen.

One reason I didn't really like the Devices introduced in *Thud!* was that they seem to be a sort of replacement for magic; they appear to be relics of an ancient lost technology. I'd prefer to see real magic remain prominent. That may just be me, though.

At any rate, the nature of the Disc's society has changed over the course of the series. It could be put down to the author's tastes and interests changing, or to the meddling of the History Monks, but I have a controversial theory of my own to propose: What if narrativium is

[183] Except perhaps in Leonard of Quirm's workshop.

unstable? What if the nature of Discworld has been changing as the narrativium that holds it together has decayed into different isotopes?

Could be an interesting thing for some over-ambitious student at Unseen University to investigate.

64

Pratchett's Place in the Pantheon

THERE ARE STILL OTHER MINOR SUBJECTS I could probably address, but really, I'd be getting into mere trivia—things like Willikins's background, the narrative function of cabbages, and so on. I'm not going to do that because, frankly, it would be silly.[184]

There are larger issues to be addressed, as well—someone could probably get a pretty good doctoral thesis out of class issues in Ankh-Morpork, especially regarding Sam Vimes, for example. I'm not going to tackle that one for three reasons:

I'm an American, Mr. Pratchett is English, and the two nationalities have drastically different attitudes regarding social class, often to the point of mutual incomprehensibility,[185] so I'm not qualified. Someone British should do it.

I'm not interested in obtaining a doctorate; hell, I'm a college dropout, never finished my bachelor's.

It'd be a whole lot of work that no one would be paying me to do.

(And a possible fourth reason is that it wouldn't be funny.)[186]

So I won't be doing anything that ambitious, and I think I've inflicted enough trivia on you fine, patient readers, so there's just one more thing I want to discuss to wrap up this book, and that's how Terry Pratchett is perceived by his readers.

---

[184] Or perhaps I should say, even sillier than the rest of this book.

[185] Most Americans don't understand their *own* attitudes regarding social class, let alone anyone else's, and get them hopelessly tangled up with money, race, and other possibly relevant complications. At least the British are aware that they *have* class issues.

[186] Insert Roger Rabbit reference here.

Terry Pratchett is the second-most-successful living fantasy author in Britain, behind J.K. Rowling. Not everyone sees him that way, though.

There are those who argue that he doesn't really write fantasy, since it's (a) funny, and (b) satire.[187] Some people have a very narrow view of fantasy, obviously; Mr. Pratchett certainly thinks he writes fantasy.

There are those who argue that he's not second to J.K. Rowling, because *she* doesn't write fantasy. Apparently she once said she didn't think of herself as writing fantasy, to which Mr. Pratchett responded, "I would have thought that the wizards, witches, trolls, unicorns, hidden worlds, jumping chocolate frogs, owl mail, magic food, ghosts, broomsticks and spells would have given her a clue?"[188]

Some people have strange ideas of what qualifies as "fantasy." So just to make sure we don't have that problem here, as far as I'm concerned, anything with wizards and dragons is fantasy, and I'm not interested in arguing about it. Trolls, flying broomsticks—fantasy. So Discworld is definitely, undeniably fantasy. So's Harry Potter, whatever his creator may think.

But neither Pratchett nor Rowling reads fantasy these days. Mr. Pratchett *used* to—he's spoken highly of *The Wind in the Willows*, J.R.R. Tolkien, Ursula K. Le Guin, and Fritz Leiber, Jr.—but no longer keeps up with the field, in part to avoid being accused of plagiarism.

There's this idea in many literary circles that literature is a sort of giant, very slow conversation among authors, that every book comments on earlier books that the author has read[189]; there's something to this in many cases, though it's nowhere near as universal as many English lit professors would have you believe. In some cases, it's fairly obvious that an author was responding to what had gone before in his genre—in science fiction, for example,[190] it's clear that Norman Spinrad's *The Iron Dream* was a comment on much of the old pulp SF he had read, and that Harry Harrison's *Bill, the Galactic Hero* was a similar reaction. Many fans believe that Joe Haldeman's *The Forever War* was written as a deliberate reply to Robert A. Heinlein's *Starship Troopers*.[191]

---

[187] No, that's not redundant. I *wish* all satire was funny! And there's certainly plenty of funny fantasy that isn't satirical. A lot of it is parody, some is farce, and some is just weird.

[188] Letter to the *Times*, July 31, 2005.

[189] Sometimes the comment amounts to, "Wow, that was cool! Can I do it, too?" Thus we get third-rate imitations of *The Lord of the Rings*. But usually it's a bit more thoughtful than that.

[190] I use science fiction only because it's the field where I happen know the best examples; they can be found in every genre.

[191] It may be true; I've never asked Mr. Haldeman, and wouldn't consider anyone else's opinion meaningful.

But if someone doesn't read in the genre he writes in, he can't very well hold up his end of this "conversation," can he?

Well, yes, he still can, after a fashion, by not limiting himself to the one genre. Or to books. The earliest Discworld books are indeed a part of the fantasy-novel conversation, responding to Leiber and McCaffrey and the *Weird Tales* gang, but later on it's obvious that while Discworld is still being used to respond to other stories, they aren't fantasy novels, but movies, fairy tales, history, Shakespeare's plays, current events, etc.

It's still fantasy, but it's not necessarily what one might call *category* fantasy.[192] It's part of the larger conversation of all popular culture, rather than just that bunch sitting in the corner talking about Tolkien and Howard. Terry Pratchett is the guy at the party with something clever to say about *everything*, whether it's music or movies or politics or whatever comes to hand, and not just his own specialty.

That may be a part of why it's so much more popular than the average fantasy novel—it's commenting on stuff *everyone* knows, not just the stuff fantasy readers are familiar with.

That doesn't make Terry Pratchett an outsider, though. He's been active in the science fiction/fantasy community since childhood, and he still is, attending conventions (and not just Discworld conventions), participating in the online fantasy community, and so on. He may not read much in the field anymore, but he certainly hasn't cut his ties to it. He's actively defended the genre in the press. Fantasy fans are proud to claim him as their own.

But there are thousands, perhaps hundreds of thousands, of Discworld readers who don't consider themselves fantasy fans, and who read no fantasy *except* Discworld.[193] His appeal is broader than that of the genre he works in—and fantasy isn't exactly an unpopular genre.

Must be nice.

There have been efforts in the press to start a feud between Pratchett and Rowling—after all, they're #2 and #1 in their field, surely they must be rivals! There have also been polls asking fans to choose between Terry Pratchett and Douglas Adams. Journalists have accused Pratchett of swiping Ponder Stibbons's appearance from Harry Potter, ignoring the detail that the first portrait of Stibbons appeared a year before *Harry Potter and the Philosopher's Stone* saw print. They have suggested that

[192] Neither is Harry Potter, for the same reasons.

[193] And maybe Harry Potter.

Rowling has stolen ideas from Pratchett, or that Pratchett has stolen things from Rowling.

This is stupid.

Writing isn't a competitive exercise, and generally speaking, names and concepts don't belong to anyone. If Rowling and Pratchett have used similar ideas, it doesn't mean either one stole from the other, only that they drew on the same sources in our shared culture. No one has to choose between Rowling and Pratchett; we can read them both. There's no need for a loser; they can both win. The pantheon of modern fantasy writers isn't monotheistic; there's plenty of room for all the gods you want to put in it. Sit J.K. Rowling on the throne of Zeus, and Mr. Pratchett can still take the role of Apollo, while Stephen King rules Hades. There's still room for nine more Olympians, and scores of titans, demigods, and the like....

That metaphor's getting a bit out of hand, isn't it? Sorry.[194]

At any rate, to sum up—Terry Pratchett's place in the fantasy pantheon is assured, in part because he's not staying securely within the usual genre boundaries. His stories have a broader appeal than most fantasy because even though they're full of wizards and dragons and trolls and witches, that's not what they're *about*.

They're about people.

And stories.

And everyone loves a good story.

---

[194] Though could I be, say, Hephaestus, do you think?

Nah, I'm not that important. More likely some obscure deity no one remembers, like the god of hangnails or something.

65

The Secret of Discworld's Success

SO, IN THE INTRODUCTION I said I was doing the research for this book because I wanted to figure out just how Terry Pratchett could take an idea as absurd as Discworld and turn it into a series of novels that sold millions of copies and became an international phenomenon. Here we are at the end, and you may well be asking, "So, did you figure it out or not?"

Very clever, but now ask yourself another question: If I *had* figured it out, would I tell you?

After all, we can't *all* write fantasy series that sell millions, and if I've figured out how it's done, I don't want *you* lot cashing in on it before I do!

But I'll take pity on you, and tell you *part* of the secret of Discworld's success—or really, four parts.

First, Mr. Pratchett writes about people, not things. I already knew that part; in fact, I'd called it the First Law of Fantasy in an article I wrote back in 1989, which you could find on my webpage[195] if you wanted to look it up. Magic spells and enchanted swords are all very well, but it's the people wielding them who hold the reader's interest.

Second, Mr. Pratchett doesn't just steal from Tolkien, the way some fantasy writers do; he steals from *everywhere*. Books, songs, TV, movies, history, news, anything and everything. If you steal from one source, it's plagiarism; if you steal from a dozen, it's research. The more sources you draw on, the better. And Discworld draws on a *lot*.

---

[195] That's at www.watt-evans.com. The Laws of Fantasy are at www.watt-evans.com/lawsoffantasy.html.

Third, Mr. Pratchett doesn't just write stories, he writes *about* stories. Too often in fiction the characters never seem to have heard any stories in their lives; the idiots in horror movies, for example, have *no idea* what's going to happen if they split up to cover more ground, or when they go down into the basement. The people of Discworld, though—they *know*. And they react accordingly. Which makes them look less stupid, and more like real people, than many writers' characters ever manage.

One could argue that that's the natural result of combining the first two, and shouldn't be listed separately, but hey, it's my book, and I'm listing it separately. So there.

And that brings us to the very last point I'm going to mention—the last part of the secret I'm going to tell you: Fourth, and finally, Terry Pratchett wears a cool hat.

I can't tell you why that's important, but I'm sure it is. So I've bought myself a cool hat, too. Bestseller lists, here I come!

PART SEVEN
References

Bibliography

NOTE: For the actual Discworld™ books, I have listed the first edition, with ISBN, in case anyone wants to track it down, and have then listed the edition(s) I actually used while writing this book. In a very few cases, these are the same and there's only one entry.

Bensen, D.R.:

The Unknown 5, New York: Pyramid Books, 1964

Brunner, John:

The Traveler in Black, New York: Ace Books, 1971

Davidson, Avram:

"Or All the Sea With Oysters," *Galaxy*, May 1958

Fforde, Jasper:

The Eyre Affair, New York: Viking Penguin, 2002

Lost in A Good Book, London: New English Library, 2002

The Well of Lost Plots, New York: Viking Penguin, 2004

Something Rotten, New York: Viking Penguin, 2004

Frazer, Sir James George:

The Golden Bough, New York: Touchstone Books, 1995

Grahame, Kenneth:

The Wind in the Willows, New York: Charles Scribner's Sons, 1933

Henry, O.:

"The Ransom of Red Chief," *Whirligigs*, New York: Doubleday, Page & Co., 1910

Howard, Robert E.:

The Coming of Conan, New York: Del Rey Books, 2005

The Bloody Crown of Conan, New York: Del Rey Books, 2004

The Conquering Sword of Conan, New York: Del Rey Books, 2005

Hughes, Thomas:

Tom Brown's School Days, Cleveland: World Syndicate Publishing, 1916?

Johnson, June:
838 Ways to Amuse A Child, New York: Gramercy Publishing Co., 1960
Langford, David:
The Unseen University Challenge: A Terry Pratchett™ Discworld™ Quizbook, London: Gollancz, 1996
The Wyrdest Link: A Terry Pratchett™ Discworld™ Quizbook, London: Gollancz, 2002
Le Guin, Ursula K.:
A Wizard of Earthsea, New York: Bantam Books, 1984
Leiber, Fritz, Jr.:
Swords and Deviltry, New York: Ace Books, 1970
Swords Against Death, New York: Ace Books, 1970
Swords in the Mist, New York: Ace Books, 1968
Swords Against Wizardry, New York: Ace Books, 1968
The Swords of Lankhmar, New York: Ace Books, 1968
Swords and Ice Magic, New York: Ace Books, 1977
Leroux, Gaston:
The Phantom of the Opera, New York: Harper Perennial, 1988
Lewis, C.S.:
The Lion, the Witch, and the Wardrobe, New York: The MacMillan Company, 1950
Prince Caspian, New York: MacMillan Publishing, 1951
The Voyage of the Dawn Treader, New York: MacMillan Publishing, 1952
The Silver Chair, New York: MacMillan Publishing, 1953
The Horse and His Boy, New York: MacMillan Publishing, 1954
The Magician's Nephew, New York: MacMillan Publishing, 1955
The Last Battle, New York: MacMillan Publishing, 1956
Lovecraft, H.P.:
The Colour Out of Space and Others, New York: Lancer Books, 1967
At the Mountains of Madness and Other Tales of Terror, New York: Ballantine Books, 1981
The Doom That Came to Sarnath and Other Stories, New York: Ballantine Books, 1971
The Lurking Fear and Other Stories, New York: Ballantine Books, 1971
MacDonald, George:
The Princess and the Goblin, Philadelphia: David McKay Co., 1920
Machiavelli, Niccolo:
The Prince, London: The Folio Society, 1972
McCaffrey, Anne:
Dragonflight, New York: Ballantine Books, 1968
Dragonquest, New York: Ballantine Books, 1971

Moore, John:
Bad Prince Charlie, New York: Ace Books, 2006
Pratchett, Terry:
The Colour of Magic, Gerrards Cross, Buckinghamshire: Colin Smythe, November 1983, ISBN 0-86140-089-5
New York: St. Martin's Press, 1983
The Light Fantastic, Gerrards Cross, Buckinghamshire: Colin Smythe, June 1986, ISBN 0-86140-203-0
Equal Rites, London: Victor Gollancz "in association with Colin Smythe," January 1987, ISBN 0-575-03950-7
New York: New American Library/Signet, Sept. 1988, ISBN 0-451-15704-4
Mort, London: Victor Gollancz "in association with Colin Smythe," November 1987, ISBN 0-575-04171-4
New York: New American Library/Signet, April 1989
Sourcery, London: Victor Gollancz "in association with Colin Smythe," May 1988, ISBN 0-575-04217-6
New York: New American Library/Signet, December 1989, ISBN 0-451-16233-1
Wyrd Sisters, London: Victor Gollancz, November 1988, ISBN 0-575-04363-6
New York: Roc Books, 1990
Pyramids, London: Victor Gollancz, May 1989, ISBN 0-575-04463-2
New York: Roc Books, 1990
Guards! Guards!, London: Victor Gollancz, November 1989, ISBN 0-575-04606-6
New York: Roc Books, 1991
Eric, London: Victor Gollancz, August 1990, ISBN 0-575-04636-8
New York: Roc Books, 1995
Moving Pictures, London: Victor Gollancz, November 1990, ISBN 0-575-04763-1
New York: Roc Books, 1992
Reaper Man, London: Victor Gollancz, May 1991, ISBN 0-575-04979-8
New York: Roc Books, 1992
Witches Abroad, London: Victor Gollancz, November 1991, ISBN 0-575-04980-4
London: Corgi, 1992
New York: HarperTorch, 2002
Small Gods, London: Victor Gollancz, May 1992, ISBN 0-575-05222-8
London: Corgi, 1993
Lords and Ladies, London: Victor Gollancz, November 1992, ISBN 0-575-05223-6
New York: HarperPrism, 1996

Men At Arms, London: Victor Gollancz, November 1993, ISBN 0-575-05503-0
New York: HarperPrism, 1997
Soul Music, London: Victor Gollancz, May 1994, ISBN 0-575-05504-9
New York: HarperPrism, 1995
Interesting Times, London: Victor Gollancz, November 1994, ISBN 0-575-05800-5
New York: Harper Torch, June 2000
Maskerade, London: Victor Gollancz, November 1995, ISBN 0-575-05808-0
New York: HarperPrism, 1997
Feet of Clay, London: Victor Gollancz, May 1996, ISBN 0-575-05900-1
New York: HarperPrism, 1996
Hogfather, London: Victor Gollancz, November 1996, ISBN 0-575-06403-X
New York: HarperPrism, 1998
Jingo, London: Victor Gollancz, November 1997, ISBN 0-575-06540-0
New York: HarperPrism, 1998
The Last Continent, London: Doubleday, May 1998, ISBN 0-385-40989-3
New York: HarperPrism, 1999
Carpe Jugulum, London: Doubleday, November 1998, ISBN 0-385-40992-3
New York: HarperPrism, 1999
The Fifth Elephant, London: Doubleday, November 1999, ISBN 0-385-40995-8
New York: HarperPrism, 2000
The Truth, London: Doubleday, November 2000, ISBN 0-385-60102-6
New York: HarperCollins, 2000
Thief of Time, London: Doubleday, April 2001, ISBN 0-385-60188-3
New York: HarperCollins, 2001
The Last Hero (profusely illustrated by Paul Kidby), London: Gollancz, October 2001, ISBN 0-575-06885-X
New York: HarperCollins, 2001
The Amazing Maurice and his Educated Rodents, London: Doubleday, October 2001, ISBN 0-385-60123-9
New York: HarperCollins, 2001
Night Watch, London: Doubleday, November 2002, ISBN 0-385-60264-2
New York: HarperCollins, 2002
The Wee Free Men™, London: Doubleday, May 2003, ISBN 0-385-60533-1
New York: HarperCollins, 2003
Monstrous Regiment, London: Doubleday, October 2003, ISBN 0-385-60340-1
New York: HarperCollins, 2003
A Hat Full of Sky, London: Doubleday, May 2004, ISBN 0-385-60736-9
New York: HarperCollins, 2004

Once More *with footnotes* [collected short works], Framingham MA: NESFA Press, September 2004, ISBN 1-886778-57-4 [Third printing]
Going Postal, London: Doubleday, October 2004, ISBN 0-385-60342-8
New York: HarperCollins, 2004
Thud!, London: Doubleday, October 2005, ISBN 0-385-60867-5
New York: HarperCollins, 2005
Wintersmith, London: Doubleday, September 2006, ISBN 978-0385609845
New York: Harper Tempest, 2006
Making Money, London: Doubleday, September 2007, ISBN 978-0385611015
New York: Harper, 2007

Pratchett, Terry & Briggs, Stephen:
The Streets of Ankh Morpork [guidebook and map], London: Corgi, 1993
The Discworld™ Mapp [guidebook and map], London: Corgi, 1995
A Tourist Guide to Lancre [guidebook and map], London: Corgi 1998
Nanny Ogg's Cookbook, London: Corgi, 1999
The New Discworld™ Companion [encyclopedia], London: Gollancz, 2003

Pratchett, Terry (text), & Grant, Melvyn (art):
Where's My Cow?, London: Doubleday, October 2005, ISBN 0-385-60937-X
New York: HarperCollins, 2005

Pratchett, Terry (text), & Kidby, Paul (art):
The Pratchett Portfolio, London: Gollancz, 1996
Death's Domain [map], London: Corgi, 1999
The Art of Discworld, London: Gollancz, 2004

Pratchett, Terry & Stewart, Ian & Cohen, Jack:
The Science of Discworld™, London: Ebury Press, 1999
Revised edition, London: Ebury Press, 2002
The Science of Discworld™ II: the Globe, London: Ebury Press, 2002
The Science of Discworld™ III: Darwin's Watch, London: Ebury Press, 2005

Pratchett, Terry & Young, Jim:
Interview: "Terry Pratchett™ on the origins of Discworld™, his Order of the British Empire and everything in between," *Science Fiction Weekly*, Issue 449

Rowling, J.K.:
Harry Potter and the Philosopher's Stone, London: Bloomsbury Publishing, 1997
Harry Potter and the Chamber of Secrets, London: Bloomsbury Publishing, 1998
Harry Potter and the Prisoner of Azkaban, London: Bloomsbury Publishing, 1999
Harry Potter and the Goblet of Fire, London: Bloomsbury Publishing, 2000
Harry Potter and the Order of the Phoenix, London: Bloomsbury Publishing, 2003

Harry Potter and the Half-Blood Prince, London: Bloomsbury Publishing, 2005

Harry Potter and the Deathly Hallows, London: Bloomsbury Publishing, 2007

Smith, Clark Ashton:

Xiccarph, New York: Ballantine Books, 1972

Sun Tzu:

The Art of War, Jackson TN: Running Press, 2003

Tolkien, J.R.R.:

The Hobbit, Boston: Houghton Mifflin 1966

The Lord of the Rings, 2nd edition, Boston: Houghton Mifflin, 1965

The Silmarillion, Boston: Houghton Mifflin, 1977

White, T.H.:

Mistress Masham's Repose, New York: Berkley Books, 1979

The Once and Future King, New York: Ace Books, 1987

Wolfe, Gene:

The Shadow of the Torturer, New York: Pocket Books, 1981

The Claw of the Conciliator, New York: Pocket Books, 1982

The Sword of the Lictor, New York: Pocket Books, 1982

The Citadel of the Autarch, New York: Pocket Books, 1983

Wouk, Herman:

The Caine Mutiny, New York: Pocket Books, 1983

APPENDIX 1

Other Discworld™ Books

(Virtually all of these are unpublished in the United States, but are or were at one time available in Britain. I don't have them, nor do I have complete bibliographic information; I merely report their existence for those who want to try to track them down. I am not listing calendars, of which there are several.)

Omnibi:

The Witches Trilogy [omnibus collecting *Equal Rites*, *Wyrd Sisters*, and *Witches Abroad*]

The Death Trilogy [omnibus collecting *Mort*, *Reaper Man*, and *Soul Music*]

The First Discworld™ Novels [omnibus collecting *The Colour of Magic* and *The Light Fantastic*]

The City Watch Trilogy [omnibus collecting *Guards! Guards!*, *Men At Arms*, and *Feet of Clay*]

The Gods Trilogy [omnibus collecting *Pyramids*, *Small Gods*, and *Hogfather*]

The Rincewind Trilogy [omnibus collecting *Sourcery*, *Eric*, and *Interesting Times*]

Rincewind the Wizzard [U.S. book club omnibus collecting *The Colour of Magic*, *The Light Fantastic*, *Sourcery*, and *Eric*]

Tales of Discworld [U.S. book club omnibus collecting *Pyramids*, *Moving Pictures*, and *Small Gods*]

Graphic novels:

Terry Pratchett's The Colour of Magic—The Graphic Novel

Terry Pratchett's The Light Fantastic—The Graphic Novel

Mort: A Discworld™ Big Comic

Guards! Guards!

The Discworld Graphic Novels [omnibus of *The Colour of Magic* and *The Light Fantastic*]

Gaming books:

Terry Pratchett's Discworld™—The Official Strategy Guide, by Glenn Edridge

Terry Pratchett's Discworld™ II—Missing Presumed…!?: The Official Strategy Guide, by Paul Kidd

GURPS Discworld™ a.k.a. *Discworld™ Role-Playing Game*, by Terry Pratchett and Phil Masters

GURPS Discworld™ Also, by Terry Pratchett and Phil Masters

Quiz books:

Unseen University Challenge, by David Langford

The Wyrdest Link, by David Langford

Miscellaneous:

Soul Music: The Illustrated Screenplay

Wyrd Sisters: The Illustrated Screenplay

Terry Pratchett's Hogfather: the Illustrated Screenplay

Terry Pratchett™: Pocket Essential Guide, by Andrew M. Butler

Terry Pratchett™: Guilty of Literature [essays]

The Wit and Wisdom of Discworld [quotes from the series]

Diaries:

Discworld™ Unseen University Diary 1998, by "C.M.O.T. Briggs," Terry Pratchett, & Paul Kidby)

Discworld™'s Ankh-Morpork City Watch Diary 1999

Discworld™'s Assassins' Guild Diary 2000

Discworld™ Fools' Guild Yearbook and Diary 2001

Discworld™ Thieves' Guild Yearbook and Diary 2002

Discworld™ (Reformed) Vampyres' Diary 2003

The Celebrated Discworld™ Almanak for the Year of the Prawn, by Terry Pratchett & Bernard Pearson

The Ankh-Morpork Post Office Handbook & Diary 2007, by Terry Pratchett, Stephen Briggs, & Paul Kidby

Lu-Tse's Yearbook of Enlightenment 2008, by Terry Pratchett, Stephen Briggs, & Paul Kidby

Dramatisations (all by Stephen Briggs except where noted):

Terry Pratchett's Wyrd Sisters—The Play

Terry Pratchett's Mort—The Play

Terry Pratchett's Guards! Guards!—The Play

Terry Pratchett's Men at Arms—The Play

Terry Pratchett's Maskerade—The Play

Terry Pratchett's Carpe Jugulum—The Play

Terry Pratchett's Lords & Ladies—The Play (adapted by Irana Brown)

Terry Pratchett's The Amazing Maurice—The Play

The Fifth Elephant—Stage Adaptation
The Truth—Stage Adaptation
Jingo—Stage Adaptation
Going Postal—Stage Adaptation
Monstrous Regiment—Stage Adaptation
Night Watch—Stage Adaptation
Interesting Times—Stage Adaptation

APPENDIX 2

Online Resources

THESE ARE LISTED IN APPROXIMATE order of usefulness, and deliberately do not include the several interviews scattered through cyberspace, which you can find by googling + interview + Pratchett.

The L-Space Web: www.lspace.org/
The most extensive Discworld fan site. Lots of annotations, bibliographic data, etc.

Terry Pratchett Books.com Discworld page: www.terrypratchettbooks.com/discworld/
An official site for the series.

Colin Smythe Ltd.'s: Terry Pratchett page: www.colinsmythe.co.uk/terrypages/tpindex.htm
Mr. Pratchett's agent provides news and information about his client.

The Turtle Moves: www.theturtlemoves.com/
This fan site first appeared while I was writing this book. Despite the coincidence of names, I have no connection with it, but it's a good site.

Discworld on Wikipedia: en.wikipedia.org/wiki/discworld_(world)
The entry point for a great deal of accumulated information about the series. It's amazingly detailed on many subjects.

Sky One's Hogfather page: www.skyone.co.uk/hogfather/
This site is primarily intended to promote the recent TV mini-series, but in the process they've provided lots and lots of nifty background material.

Sky One's Colour of Magic page: www.skyoneonline.co.uk/tcom/news.htm
Promoting the upcoming adaptation.

The Discworld Convention site: www.dwcon.org/
Home to information about the not-quite-annual Discworld fan conventions.

Stephen Briggs's website: www.cmotdibbler.com/
Some interesting (if largely tangential) information, and a source for some nifty Discworld merchandise.

The Cunning Artificer's Discworld Emporium: http://www.artificer.co.uk/
Lots of strange and wonderful merchandise.

The Home of Discworld Stamps: www.discworldstamps.co.uk/html/home.php
More merchandise.

A Mad Fan's Guide to Discworld Stamps: www.discworldstampfans.co.uk/
An obsessive fan's collection of trivia on a specific subject.

Thud! The Discworld Board Game: www.thudgame.com/
All about the Roundworld version of the famous game.